Y

NOBODY
ASKED
ME!

Jenny Sullivan

PONT

For my granddaughter,
born 15th July 2006,
Daisy Antonina Ruth
(Daisy Roo)
With all my love
Granny Jen

Published in 2006 by Pont Books, an imprint of
Gomer Press, Llandysul, Ceredigion, SA44 4JL

ISBN 1 84323 722 9

ISBN-13 9781843237228

A CIP record for this title is available from the British Library.

© Copyright: Jenny Sullivan, 2006

This book is published with the financial support of the
Welsh Books Council.

Printed and bound in Wales at
Gomer Press, Llandysul, Ceredigion

1

Merlin started it. Honestly, he's got no tact whatsoever, that man. For all he's the Merlin of Brython, he's got no commonsense, and he certainly knows nothing about women.

Imagine it: Gwydion and me, finishing breakfast. Lovely, sunny, shiny spring morning, all tweety-birdish. Me, feeling happy. All was right with the world. I was even humming while I chomped my bread and honey, and then – enter Merlin. In a Mood. When Merlin gets a mood on him, watch it, everyone.

'Bread and honey *again*?' he groused. 'What's a person have to do to get a decent breakfast here?'

Gwydion snaffled the last piece of fresh-baked, crusty bread and slathered it with salty yellow butter. 'Get up earlier, for a start. The bread's fantastic. Still hot. Well, it was . . . Shall I ask Rhiannon for another loaf?'

'No,' the wizard said, nastily, 'thank you *very* much. I'll organise my own.' He sat down, waved his hands, muttered a few words, and a Full Welsh Breakfast appeared in front of him, piping hot – and smelling wonderful.

'Oooo,' Gwydion said, speculatively, reaching out a hopeful hand for a piece of crispy bacon. And got his knuckles rapped hard with a knife for his trouble.

He clutched his throbbing fingers. 'Ow! That was uncalled for!'

'You want bacon and eggs, get your own,' Merlin growled, and glared at him over his little half-moon spectacles. Which were plain glass, not prescription lenses, but perhaps he thought they made him look intelligent or something. Why he thinks he needs pretend specs when he could vaporise every person in the castle, I haven't any idea. But he was obviously having a bad day. Best to leave him alone to get over it. Now *I* thought that, and wisely kept my mouth shut. Not Gwydion, oh no. Mouth open, foot straight in.

'Bit tetchy this morning, Merlin, me old mate!' he chortled. 'Get out of the wrong side of the bed, did we?'

Oops.

'*We,*' snarled his former tutor, 'didn't actually *get* to bed. So *we* could hardly get out the wrong side of it, could *we?*'

'Didn't get to bed? Partying all night? Ought to be ashamed of yourself, at your age, ho ho!'

Honestly, talk about trampling where angels fear to tread. What *is* wrong with him? Are all men like that? Not knowing when to shut up, I mean. Or is it just Gwydion?

'No. *We,*' (and here he looked nastily at Gwydion), 'were not. For your information, *my liege Lord Dragonking,*' Merlin stabbed his fried egg as if he hated it, and squirted yolk all down his sweatshirt, 'I was consulting my Mirror. I became somewhat perturbed, and so I referred to my Records. What my Records said entirely confirmed what the Mirror told me. Then, in the early hours of the morning, I checked my Almanac to confirm my findings. I was right. I am always right. However, I admit I occasionally misconstrue Time, which is how all this arose in the first place. By the time my research was complete, it was nearly dawn and hardly worth going to bed. And, I may add, all this effort was entirely on your behalf, you ungrateful cub.'

6

Gwydion raised an eyebrow. 'Oh, really? Well, if you get as grumpy as this doing your homework, I wish you hadn't bothered, on my behalf or not.'

At that point I contemplated crawling under the table and pretending I wasn't there. Preferably with a tin hat and full body armour on. I waited for the explosion.

The room went, suddenly, very, very quiet. The end of Merlin's nose went white, which is always a bad sign.

Then, 'Well, boy, I *did* bother. Fortunately for you.'

'Oooh, dear! Trouble?' Gwydion still wasn't getting it. He was still acting the clever-clogs, pulling funny faces at Merlin's annoyance. No wonder Merlin used to turn him into cats and stuff when he was a little kid. You'd think he'd learn, but he hasn't, not at all. There's no hope for the male of the species, is there?

Merlin smirked. It wasn't a nice smirk, but then I never saw a smirk yet I didn't want to smack off the face that wore it, and I'm not a violent person – well, not often.

'*I* might think so,' he said. 'You, in your – er – *wisdom*, Gwydion, probably won't. But regardless, I am right.' He concentrated on his bacon, eggs, mushrooms, fried bread, grilled tomatoes, laverbread, baked beans, black pudding and sauté potatoes.

Gwydion waited. And waited. When Merlin had polished off the last mushroom, and mopped his plate with the last bit of bread and butter, he rolled his eyes and said, 'And?'

'And what?'

'What are you right about?'

'What?' The wizard wiped his lips with his napkin, pushed back his chair and stood up. 'Oh, that.'

'What *that*?'

'Oh, didn't I tell you? It's time.'

'What for?' Gwydion had started off the day in a really good mood, but was starting to hunch his shoulders and Lose It.

'Marriage, dear boy. Yours. This year.' And exploding that bombshell in the middle of the breakfast table, he sailed wizardically from the room.

I closed my mouth. My jaw had dropped right down to my knees, nearly. 'What was that he said?' I mumbled.

'Oh, we have to get married this year,' Gwydion said airily. 'He must have looked at the legend, or something, and done the calculations. That's OK. *Dim problem, cariad.* Nothing to worry about, really. Oh, by the way, I'll be out with Iestyn this morning – some wolf has been upsetting the villagers and I need to have a quiet word with it.'

Nothing much to worry about? Dim problem? 'I beg your pardon?' I said, permafrost dripping from every syllable.

'I said, I'm going out with Iestyn this morning. See you lunchtime, Tanz, all right?' And off he went.

Nothing. To. Worry. About.

Dim. Problem. Cariad. Ha!

That's what *he* thought. Gwydion and bloody Merlin had just, apparently, arranged a wedding. Bingo! All done and dusted, just like that! Not just anybody's wedding, either. MY wedding! Mine and Gwydion's! And then Gwydion had toddled off with Iestyn to see about a wolf with an ASBO, and Merlin had ambled off to his tower, probably to do the *Western Mail* crossword – I knew he magicked it up every day, even though he shouldn't, by rights. And there was me, left with the wreckage of the breakfast table, the collapse of my romantic illusions and the red-hot foundations of a Really Good Temper Tantrum.

I was so furious that I wanted to pick up my side of the table, upend it on the floor, smash all the crockery and jump up and down on the pieces. Then scream at the top of my lungs, shout, bellow, stamp, kick, foam at the mouth and throw things. Then I might really lose my temper. Unfortunately the table was so big and heavy I'd probably do myself a serious injury if I tried to hurl it anywhere, and mouth-foaming was so *messy*. I angrily clattered the dishes into a pile and carried them downstairs to the kitchen.

Rhiannon and Cook were obviously having a Discussion. Rhiannon was Queen Bee in the kitchen, but Cook was King Wasp. They got on together perfectly most of the time, which is just as well when two people are sharing what often becomes a very busy, hot, frantic place when Gwydion and I have a banquet. But in between times, when they aren't so busy, they have time to snack at each other and bicker and squabble – and both thoroughly enjoy it. Rhiannon had her hands on her hips and her chin thrust forward; Cook was clutching a large wooden spoon and looking as if he might chew lumps out of it.

I had no time for this, not today. 'Stop that *riiiight nowwww!*' I yelled, slamming the dirty crockery down on the kitchen table. 'I will not have arguments in my kitchen! Grow up and get a life, the pair of you.'

Two amazed faces turned to me, jaws at half-mast.

'Sorry, Lady,' Cook muttered.

I stormed out of the kitchen, and before the door

slammed behind me, I heard Rhiannon's amazed squeak, 'What's got into her this morning?'

I stamped up to my room, fast and furious, getting dizzy with the winding spiral staircase. I slammed that door, too, and it made a satisfying crash that echoed through the entire castle. A picture fell off the wall and the tapestries shifted in the breeze. In my present mood I wouldn't have cared if the entire castle had come crashing down about my ears.

How dare they! I thought, fuming so hard, steam was probably hissing out from my ears. *How dare THAT GWYDION and THAT MAN decide it's time* I *got married! HOW DARE THEY!* I picked up a water jug and threw it at the wall. Bits of earthenware and water flew everywhere.

Now, you may be wondering what all the fuss is about. You may have thought that once Gwydion and I were back in Castell Du, after college and all that, and after I had decided that I was going to live my life here in Ynys Haf and not in the twenty-first century, my Time, I was going to meekly marry Gwydion and settle down and have babies and live happily ever after, sort of thing. All signed, sealed and settled, you soppy old romantic you.

Well, so I was. But. Big, big but. Big huge BUT.

No-one had asked me, had they?

Merlin had just announced it was Time, but then, that was Merlin, right? He didn't have a romantic bone in his entire body, although if he carried on being such a pain, he might end up with a couple of broken ones, starting with his nose, which always seemed to be poking into my business.

But Gwydion was another kettle of kippers altogether.

10

What Gwydion should have done, once Merlin had pronounced, was place his hand on his heart, throw himself down on one knee, preferably waving a bunch of red roses and a diamond ring. Then he had to tell me how terribly, awfully, passionately he adores me and ask me, beg me, plead with me to marry his unworthy self, preferably adding, in broken-hearted tones, that he couldn't possibly live without me if I said no.

And then, I'd have thought of it for all of ten seconds (well, maybe fifteen, just for the look of it), grabbed the ring and said, 'Yes, dear Gwydion, of course I will marry you. I love you too.' Then we'd have a bit of a snog, and that would be that. I could flash my engagement ring, get on the crystal ball to Mam, and we'd plan a fabulous wedding here in Ynys Haf. When she'd finished crying, that is. My mam is fond of Gwyd.

Can't think why. The rat. The insensitive rat. The horrible, beastly, insensitive, rotten rat.

But instead, what had happened?

Nothing, zilch – except 'that's OK', and 'nothing much to worry about'. Oh, and *'dim problem'*.

He hadn't even given me a kiss, not to mention actually asking! Nothing to worry about, was it? OK, was it? *Dim problem*, was it?

Just you wait, Gwydion. I'll show you OK!

2

I stamped around my room. How could I make him understand? How could I show him how much he'd hurt my feelings? I couldn't believe he'd done it!

The trouble was, I was so furious I couldn't think straight. I was steaming, and the steam was bending my brain and distorting the thinking process. I stopped pacing and decided to have a bit of a howl, instead. I threw myself on my bed and wailed and sobbed for a while. I was still furious after, but now my eyes were all red and swollen, too.

Deep down, I knew perfectly well that, when Gwydion came back from chastising the ASBO'd wolf, if I said, sensibly and calmly, 'Now look, Gwyd, that wasn't much of a proposal, you know,' he'd look at me blankly and then say something like, 'But you knew we were always going to get married anyway. Do I do romantic? I don't think so!'

Well, it might have been a foregone conclusion to him. But it wasn't to me. All right, maybe I've watched too many romantic movies and read too many mushy books. But much as I love Gwyd (and I do, I really do), a girl NEEDS a romantic proposal. Good grief, even Heledd got one. Siôn went down on one knee in the middle of a crowded restaurant and proposed to my dingbat sister – and he'd already bought the ring, too! And what do I get? 'No problem'. That's what I get. What I needed was a shoulder to cry on, an understanding ear to whinge into. But here in Ynys Haf I had no-one to turn to. My best friend T.A. was centuries away, and she was busy being a career woman, anyway. I don't expect she thinks of me and Ynys Haf much these days; she's too busy. And here was I, stuck in the Dark Ages, and no-one to moan at.

Not even Mam. Mam would understand. That's what mams do best, isn't it, understand? I sat up on the bed and swung my legs over the side. What do girls with broken hearts do?

Go home to Mother.

And mine is the best mam in the whole wide world.

I'm going home to Mam. She'll give me hugs and sympathy, and tomato soup and crusty bread.

I was going to have to do it quickly, mind, before Gwydion came back, that was for sure. In fact, I'd go right now. I wouldn't tell a soul; I'd just head for the nearest Time Door and walk through. The one at Brechfa was nice and close to home. Ha! That would show Gwydion a thing or two. No problem indeed. He'd soon learn if there was a problem or not!

I changed into a pair of leather trousers and a felt jerkin for the journey – I didn't know what the weather would be like, and I didn't want to arrive in a snowstorm and freeze to death. Besides, the wind in the Doors was nearly always freezing cold.

I didn't think there was anything else I needed. My bedroom at home would be more or less as I left it (only tidier and cleaner, I expect!) and I'd have clothes there which would still fit me.

I opened the door of my room and listened. Apart from the usual castle noises, it was quiet. The stairs to the guards' turret were on my right, and from the snores issuing from up there, they had just changed shift, which was a pain. That meant the guards on the battlements would be all alert. Best if I didn't try to sneak out, then. Anyway, aren't I the Lady of Ynys Haf? Therefore I can do anything I want, when I want.

I got as far as the main gate. Then a bossy voice said, 'Who goes there?' and a guard appeared.

'Me,' I said.

'Who is "me"?' he said, narrowing his eyes.

I drew myself up to my full five-feet-nearly and tried to look commanding. 'You know perfectly well who I am, Meirion Pugh, so don't make an idiot of yourself. And stand aside. I want to go out.'

The jaw set stubbornly. 'Ah, well. You may *look* like the Lady,' he said, 'but the Dragonking, he says we've got to be alert-at-all-times for danger from Elsewhere. We're not to let anyone pass we don't recognise. Nobody comes in without the password.'

'Meirion,' I said, my temper rapidly re-igniting, 'for one thing I am the Lady of Ynys Haf, and you've known me since you joined the Guard. For another, I'm going *out*, not coming in. And I don't need a password.' Anyway, I'd forgotten the password, if I'd ever known it in the first place. Gwydion solemnly told me every morning at breakfast, and by the time I left the table I'd usually forgotten it. I don't think he'd even mentioned it this morning. He'd been too busy worrying about some stupid wolf – oh, and *not* proposing to me.

Meirion frowned. 'Sooner or later, though, Lady, you'll want to come back in again.'

'So I will,' I said, sweetly. I patted his cheek, which made him blush, and walked past him.

'Aw, look, Lady!' he stammered, 'you can't just walk past me like that!'

14

'Watch me!' I stamped across the drawbridge, my boots echoing on the wooden planks. A duck splashed hopefully into the water, looking up at me to see if I'd brought any bread.

'You'd be lucky,' I muttered. 'The DragonPig didn't leave you so much as a crumb this morning.'

The guard ran after me. 'Lady, I didn't say, *Pass, Friend*! I've got to say *Pass, Friend*, or you can't go out.'

'Meirion,' I sighed, 'Meirion, dear Meirion, it may have escaped your notice, but I already *passed*, friend. See you again some time.' And leaving the poor worried guard chewing his gauntlet, I strode off.

As soon as I was out of sight of the castle, I shape-shifted. It's ages since I've shifted – it isn't something I do much these days, unless I have to get somewhere fast or there's an emergency. I didn't really need to hurry to a Time Door, but I had this feeling that Meirion might finish eating his gauntlet and decide to confess to the Sergeant at Arms that he'd let a strange woman out of the castle. The Sergeant might then tell him to fetch me back, even if I did look like the Lady. On the other hand, I didn't intend being brought back, and if poor Meirion was sent after me, he'd be terrified I'd turn him into something small and squishy. And in my present mood, I might.

So I shifted into a sparrow and wriggled about a bit in the feathers until they felt comfortable. Then I stretched my wings a few times, and took off. It wasn't far to the nearest Time Door, which was just as well – I was already feeling the pull of muscles I hadn't used in a long, long time.

Over-flying the village, and the small wood beyond it, I looked down and saw Gwydion and Iestyn hammering

15

along behind a very large wolf. It obviously knew it was in trouble, because it was going like merry hell, and was well ahead of them. The humans couldn't go too fast in case they rode into low branches. And since Gwydion was riding Zephaniah, his stallion, who is blessed with an evil temper, Gwyd was more in danger from Zeph than anything.

Ha! I thought. *Throw him off, Zeph!*

I was at the Time Door seconds later, and I flew down, perched on a tuft of grass, and shifted back. This particular door was one I hadn't used before – one of the bush-type Doors, and if these aren't used fairly frequently, they get overgrown. They're chiefly constructed of arches of bramble, and an overgrown one can get a bit painful.

I got out my knife to cut back the brambles across the opening. I knew that once I was inside, the magic would take over, and the tangled thorns would disappear. I shoved the knife back into my belt and pulled my collar up round my throat. I was getting ready to step into the bramble archway when I heard crashing and twigs breaking behind me.

Gwydion and Iestyn, had to be. I really didn't want to be seen going into the Door, especially not by Gwydion, so I fairly shot in, and instantly felt the mighty wind that is always there, waiting.

It howled, blocking out all other sound. I squinted my eyes against the gale, leaning forward into it, struggling onward. It's always such a temptation to turn round and walk backwards to get some relief from the wind – but that might, quite literally, be fatal – you're stuck in the Time Door until someone else happens along to use it.

So I battled on, my eyes watering, my nose running. I didn't have a hanky, and it isn't wise to use magic in a Time Door. I didn't want to try to conjure up a packet of Kleenex and end up with half a rainforest falling on top of me!

Eventually I saw a glimmer of light in the distance, and fought my way towards it. It got bigger and bigger, and at last I was there: the arched opening into daylight, and my Time, and very soon, Mam! And Sympathy, and tomato soup. Yay!

Best of all, no-one would know where I'd gone. Gwydion would really, really worry, and good job too!

What I wasn't doing, you may have noticed, was *concentrating*. I was too busy thinking cross thoughts about Gwydion, and sniffing, and looking forward to seeing Mam. Not *concentrating* . . .

At last, I was through the Door. I stepped out into bright sunshine, and was just trying to work out where I was – I certainly didn't recognise it as the Brechfa hilltop – when I was knocked flat on my face.

I smelled, first, squashed grass – it was up my nose. Then, a doggy sort of smell. Only much, much stronger. I risked a glance over my shoulder, shrieked, and buried my head in my arms again. Standing over me, a leg each side of my waist, massive jaws drooling, was the very same wolf that Gwydion and Iestyn had been so enthusiastically chasing.

I went into panic mode, absolutely certain that the huge, hairy thing would bite my head off in the next instant. I wrapped both arms round my ears, squeezed my eyes shut, and tried to roll into a ball. I squeaked, waiting for the crunch of teeth into the back of my neck . . .

3

Then I remembered. I'm the Lady of Ynys Haf, aren't I? What about some respect around here!

I concentrated hard and tried to tune into the wolf's thoughts. They were, basically, *whoopee!*

Whoopee? I thought, and cautiously rolled over. He was a very large wolf, but appeared to be very young. When he was fully grown, he'd be massive. I started to sit up, and he backed off, tail wagging, jaws grinning like an over-enthusiastic puppy. He wanted to play.

Now look here, wolf, I thought into his mind, *what do you think you're doing following me through a Time Door?*

The wolf sat on his haunches and looked worried. *The windy place was a Time Door? Oh dear. Are we lost?*

Probably, I thought back. *And you, presumably, are the wolf that the Dragonking was chasing? For frightening the villagers?*

The wolf looked a bit shamefaced, if it's possible for a face with all that shaggy hair to look that way. *I suppose so. I didn't mean to frighten anyone, Lady. I was only being friendly.*

I could see where something that big wanting to 'be friendly' might upset people a bit – especially with all those teeth. 'Can you understand me if I talk aloud?' I asked. All that thought transference was giving me a headache.

The big shaggy head nodded.

'Right. I'll talk to you normally, and you can think back at me if you've got something to say.'

Nod.

'If you go bouncing up to people and jump on them, they won't realise that you just want to play. If you lick them, they'll think you're tasting them before you eat them. Which is why Gwydion and Iestyn are looking for you. They don't want to harm you, but they were certainly going to give you a ticking-off for scaring people. And now *I'm* going to tick you off because the last thing you should have done was follow me through a Time Door. Don't you know how dangerous that can be? Didn't your mother teach you when you were a cub?'

No, Lady, he thought, and his eyes filled up with tears. *My mammy died when I was only a cub. Why can't I be friends with humanfolk?*

'Because they don't know you're only playing,' I said severely. 'I'm very sad to hear about your mother, but you really shouldn't have followed me, you know. And the worst of it is, I can't send you back alone – I have to take you back, or you could get lost in Time and then where would you be?'

He thought for a while, and then thought back at me, *Lost in time, Lady?* Now the shaggy face was puzzled – under all the hair.

'And unfortunately,' I went on, 'I can't go back right now, so you'll have to come with me.'

But what I'm going to do with you in twenty-first century Wales is going to be a bit of a problem, I thought to myself. *Wherever I am.*

I looked around. I'd thought I'd come to Brechfa, and even thinking about a place (except, of course, I hadn't, had I?) is usually enough to make sure that the Time Door delivers you there. But somehow it didn't look like Brechfa, where the Door is on top of a small, bare hill.

Not only was I not on a hill, I was surrounded by trees, and all in all, I didn't have a clue where I'd landed.

Or, it suddenly occurred to me, *When*.

I'd been so busy whingeing away in my mind at Gwydion, and feeling hard-done-by, and looking forward to getting home to Mam, I hadn't concentrated on where I was going, or when I was going to arrive there. It might be Brechfa. It might be the twenty-first century.

The best thing might be to go back through the Time Door and start again, concentrating this time. I mean, I could be anywhere, anywhen. The next living thing I saw might be a dinosaur! I stopped thinking along those lines straight away – I've seen *Jurassic Park*, and I don't want my bits nibbled on by a velociraptor, thanks very much.

'Come on, you,' I said, speaking to the wolf. 'I'll take you back now. And make sure you stay there, too,' I warned him. 'This is no place for you. Don't you ever be tempted to stray into a Time Door again!'

I promise, Lady!

I turned, patting my leg to call him to heel. We had to go through together, with me holding onto the fur of his back, or he might get lost. I was all ready to just step back into Ynys Haf momentarily, and then turn right round and do the wind tunnel again, only this time concentrating, making sure I knew exactly where I'd land up – and when.

Except the Time Door had gone. And because I'd spent the first couple of seconds face down in the grass, I didn't know what it had looked like, did I? I turned slowly on the spot.

I was in a small clearing, surrounded by tall trees – not the Forestry Commission pines that I'd expect to find at

Brechfa, but deciduous, forest-type trees that looked as if they'd been growing and seeding themselves for centuries. Between the trees were thick brambles, and a narrow path led out of the clearing. Nowhere, however, was the tell-tale shimmer of *different* air, like the illusion you get on a road on a hot day, when the heat-haze sort of vibrates above the road ahead and looks like water. As far as I could tell, there wasn't a Time Door in the immediate vicinity. Which could only mean one of two things. Either I'd wandered away from the Door, or *it* had wandered away from *me.*

I've heard of this happening, but it's a rare malfunction of the magical apparatus. Sometimes people see, say, a pair of standing stones, and wander between them just for the fun of it. And occasionally, don't wander out again, which is why the Doors occasionally shift position or disappear – but this safety feature sometimes goes awry, and then the disappearing thing happens whenever the Door feels like it.

So, two choices. Keep looking, which would appear to be pointless, because wherever the Door was, it wasn't here. Or second, go looking for the Door. With my problematic companion. I knew there was another Door a bit closer to Carmarthen – linked to Merlin's Oak. Then I thought about wandering into town with a large wolf padding at my heels . . .

I surveyed the wolf, and considered. An invisibility spell was one option. However, an invisible wolf might cause more trouble than a visible one – especially a young, playful, unpredictable one. And just imagine the havoc an invisible wolf could wreak among the cat population! Doesn't bear thinking about.

The other option, to shapeshift him, was risky. I could shift him into a doggy body – except that he would still have his wolfish instincts, and I wasn't sure how much he, being a sort of teenage wolf with lots of hormones raging about, could control them. I didn't want to end up with an attack dog that tore into anyone or anything that upset him. The safest solution was to shapeshift him into a human. I'd have to warn him, though. He might go berserk if I did, because it takes some doing, adjusting to being human, if you're not.

'Look,' I bent down a bit, so I was on a level with the beautiful amber eyes. 'I can't risk going around with a wolf, and I certainly can't either send you back, because I can't find the Time Door, or leave you here to wait for me. The only thing to do is to shape-shift you. My first thought was dog –'

He snarled. *Not dog. Not dog.*

'– don't worry, I won't.' He relaxed slightly, but was still wary. 'How about a human boy? Do you think you can manage to cope with that?'

The biggest grin I've ever seen on any creature's face appeared like magic. *Oh yes, Lady. I can be human, I know I can!* Then the smile slipped, and panic took its place. *But you'll change me back afterwards?*

'I will, I promise. Now. Just stand still, close your eyes, and concentrate. It will be quite hard at first, because your body will feel all wrong.' I remembered my first shape-shift, and how peculiar I had felt. 'You'll have to stand on your hind paws, and you'll have to sort of stretch until you have arms as well. It tingles a bit, but that's perfectly normal, so don't worry. Ready?'

The wolf nodded. He looked fairly nervous – in fact,

22

the great shaggy body was shaking. I gave him a scratch behind the ears. 'Don't be afraid. I've done this before, lots of times.'

Well, I had. But not in this direction, wolf to boy. I'd done human to animal, no problem, but not the other way about. Still, there was a first time for everything.

I put my hand on top of his head, closed my eyes and concentrated. I felt the bones of his skull begin to vibrate under my hand, and the great beast whimpered. Then the head began to push upward, and I took my hand away and opened my eyes. He was on his hind legs – measuring more than six feet tall. Much taller than me. I can barely make five feet if I'm on tiptoes. His back straightened, the shoulders broadened, and the forelegs turned into arms at the same time as the hind legs became human legs. The head was the last thing to change, and gradually the snout pulled back, the teeth shrank (thank goodness!) and the skull broadened out into a human shape. As his nose changed he began to sneeze and sneeze.

'Bless you,' I said when he had finished. 'Better?'

'Graaaowr,' he said.

'Try to speak human, wolf.'

'Graaaaaooooowr.'

He was obviously having difficulty with his new shape mouth. It was a very nice mouth. He was, in fact, a very handsome – er – wolf. He was also very bare. I averted my eyes and magicked him some jeans and a T-shirt to be going on with. He looked about fourteen or fifteen, and would certainly cut a swathe through the female population at the average Comp! Except he couldn't talk too well. Some girls go for the strong silent type, but not a type that growls, I don't think.

23

So I sat him down on the grass, and got him to sound out his vowels for a start, showing him how to make his mouth move properly, exaggerating it a bit until he got the hang of it.

'A,' I said, enunciating clearly.

'GrAAA.'

'Aaaaaay.'

'Grrr. Agh.'

'Now without the grr. Aaaay.'

'Aaaargh.'

'Nearly. Much better. Try it again. Aaaay.'

We got there in the end, much, much later.

At last he was talking, if not clearly, although quite often a growl slipped into the middle of a sentence. 'Look,' I said, 'I think if you let me do the talking, at least until you get better at it, it will be safer, all right?'

'Grrr.'

'Pardon?'

'Aaaagrhll ghrrrrright . . .'

'Try that again – hmm, we'd better give you a name.'

What did he look like? Hard to tell, really. He still looked, sort of, wolfish . . . The eyes hadn't changed, you see, and that shade of amber doesn't often happen in humans. Then I had a brainwave.

'Blaidd,' I said. 'That's Wolf in Welsh, all right?'

A grin of satisfaction appeared. To be rapidly replaced by one of consternation when he tried, and couldn't say it.

'Like this,' I said, exaggerating the individual sounds, 'BL_EYE_TH.' He still had difficulty.

'Don't worry,' I reassured him, 'I can say it, and just as long as you remember it and answer to it, we'll be fine.'

24

4

Once Blaidd was a bit steadier on his pins, we left the clearing, and set off down the rabbit path. A bunny crossed in front of us at one point, and I had to hang on to Blaidd's T-shirt to stop him taking off in pursuit.

'You aren't a wolf any more, Blaidd,' I said sternly.

'Awww!' he growled. 'I ghrungrrrry.'

So was I. 'Don't worry. Once we get out of this wood, I'll find us something to eat, all right?'

'Rrrrrrabbit grrood! Crrunchy. Wet. Warrrm blood. Delicious.'

Yuk! Too much information! 'I'm sure it is. But humans don't eat raw meat, Blaidd. You'll have to get used to cooked, I'm afraid!'

His expression would have stopped a clock.

At last we came to the edge of the wood. The countryside stretched away from us downhill towards a river. I couldn't see any houses anywhere, and there was no sign of the fat ribbon of the M4. So where the bewhatsit were we? Anyway, first things first: food.

My first instinct was Kentucky Fried Chicken – but dogs aren't supposed to have chicken bones, and maybe that was true for wolves, too – although wild wolves chomped on raw chickens (wriggly ones) bones and all, whenever they could get their jaws into them. I didn't fancy trying to explain to Blaidd that he shouldn't crunch up the bones as well as the chicken so I magicked up a couple of very large sirloin steaks. His was cooked rare, mine medium. And chips. I know all about healthy eating, I know. But steak goes with chips, and steak and chips is comfort food when I'm miserable. And I was miserable. Very miserable. So I got mushrooms and fried onion rings as well.

Blaidd got two fists onto the steak and it was gone in two bites. He ignored the chips and the trimmings. He licked his chops and then his hands. I shuddered. Wolf manners don't make pleasant company at the dinner table – even if there isn't one. Then he stared pointedly at what was left of my steak. So I magicked him another, larger steak, which disappeared just as quickly. And so did the next one, and the next. Finally, he burped loudly, dropped onto all fours, turned round three times, curled into a ball with his head nearly between his knees – and went to sleep. He might look like a human – but he was still behaving like a wolf. I was going to have my work cut out.

I finished off my meal with some sneakily magicked pistachio ice cream with chocolate-covered coffee beans and whipped cream. Periodically Blaidd twitched and whimpered – a bit like a dog having bad dreams. The sun was warm, the sky blue and hazy, and I felt fat and full and sleepy. Not content, however: I was still too angry and upset for that. But I thought that, since Blaidd was out for the count, I might as well join him. I just stretched out, pillowed my face on my arms and dropped off . . .

I woke with a sudden shock to the sounds of a struggle. Blaidd was snarling ferociously, and something was digging into my throat. I opened my eyes. I was squinting along the length of an extremely sharp sword. On my right, Blaidd was struggling frantically, pinned face down to the ground by two very large men.

Men in leather jerkins, hose and soft boots. Three

horses grazed close by, caparisoned in red with gold fringing. The three men were dressed in similar colours, their tabards bearing an embroidered insignia resembling a flying 'M'.

This wasn't, I surmised, (a) anywhere near Brechfa, and (b) the twenty-first century, either. I sat up, carefully, and pushed the sword away.

'Ye gods! It's a wench, in lads' clothing, sire!' The man with the sword looked past me.

I hadn't seen a fourth man, and turned to look behind me. He was very tall, very handsome, very dark, very just about everything a girl could possibly ask for. But there was something about him I instinctively didn't like.

He walked round me, surveying me from every angle. 'A wench in lads' clothing, as you say. And also an ill-mannered lad that snarls like a wild beast.'

'He's my – brother,' I said, hastily. 'He can't talk. He was born like it.' Which was true – if you think about it, all wild creatures are my brothers and sisters – and considering that he'd only been 'born' as a human a few hours ago, he *had* been born like it. Right now, he wasn't happy, but then having a hefty human sitting on one's back and another on one's legs does tend to spoil a person's day!

'Let him go!' I ordered. 'He won't harm you.'

The two sitters-upon sniggered at that. 'Oh, indeed he won't, wench. The lad doesn't have a sword as far as I can see,' one said. 'We, on the other hand, have one each, as well as a dagger at his throat.'

But the lad does *have teeth' and isn't afraid to use them!* I thought. I sent a further thought to Blaidd – *Calm down, Blaidd. Stop thinking like a wolf. It will get you*

27

nowhere except maybe killed. Stop snarling. Don't even think of attacking them. Relax. Let me handle this.

Gradually, the snarls stopped, and Blaidd didn't struggle any more, but I could tell by the vibes coming from him that he was uptight enough to explode.

'Right, boy,' one of the men said. 'If we let you up, will you behave?'

'Yes, he will,' I said firmly.

'No-one spoke to you, wench,' the one standing next to me said, prodding me with his sword. 'Silence.'

I opened my mouth to say, 'How dare you? Don't you realise you're speaking to the Lady of Ynys Haf?' But I didn't know where I was, did I? And I had a pretty good idea that wherever it was, it wasn't Ynys Haf. Trouble was, I didn't know *when* we were, either. It would be too much to hope for that these guys were part of the Sealed Knot. You know, the people who go around re-enacting battles and stuff at castles and museums. They looked altogether too authentic for that!

'What shall we do with them, sire?' he asked.

The leader, whoever he was, pulled on his gauntlets and shrugged carelessly. 'Two choices, Elric. Kill them now or hold them to ransom and see what we can get for them. I imagine they come as a pair – someone may be pleased enough to pay good money to get them back. Then again,' he glanced at me carelessly, 'looking at the state of them, they may not.'

I opened and shut my mouth, disbelieving what I'd heard. 'You *what*?' I managed, at last.

'Are you worth anything, wench?' he asked, gathering the reins of his horse in his right hand, preparing to mount, ride away, and leave us to his henchmen.

'I most certainly am,' I said, firmly. 'You really don't have a clue how much I'm worth.'

Which on second thoughts was probably a totally dumb thing to say, because it more or less ensured that I'd get locked up somewhere damp and dark – and probably iron-bound – until they found out by fair means, or more likely foul, who, exactly, would want to ransom me. And who could they ask? I wasn't in my own Time. I wasn't in Ynys Haf, was I?

The last thing I was going to mention was my magic. Magic wasn't a good talent to have, not in olden times. People were sort of automatically suspicious of witches – and if they got too suspicious, were likely to dangle the suspect by the neck from a piece of rope, or worse . . .

So no way on this planet, where – and whenever I was, was I going to let on that I'm a witch.

'I wouldn't normally accept the word of an itinerant wench on any matter of consequence,' the leader commented, swinging into the saddle, 'but she is not uncomely, and she has delusions of grandeur if not the actuality of it. She may be someone, she may not. Bring her.'

'And the boy?'

'Kill him.' The answer was cold and immediate.

So was mine. There was no way, on reflection, I could allow them either to take me, or to kill Blaidd, even if it meant exposing myself as a witch. Besides, if I did it right, they wouldn't know what had happened – only that something had!

The Emerald Spellorium had a page devoted entirely to this sort of situation. It involved very loud noises and very bright lightning, heavy objects falling extremely accurately onto the backs of heads, and temporary unconsciousness for the fallen upon. It took less than fifteen seconds from thunder and lightning to sleepy-byes.

Their horses, at the first inkling of magic fizzing around, took off like the proverbial bats from hell. Which was fine by me – no horses would slow our attackers down and stop them following us.

I dusted off my hands. 'That'll learn 'em!' I said, with a certain amount of satisfaction, and turned round to look for Blaidd.

Who was curled up in a ball with both arms over his head, whimpering. I went over and gave him a bit of a scratch behind the ears, and stroked his back, and gradually he calmed down. Treating him temporarily as a wolf rather than a human seemed to do the trick. He rolled on his back and waved his arms and legs in the air, realised what he was doing, and sat up – sheepishly, if that isn't the wrong term to use for a wolf-boy.

'Come on,' I urged him. 'We don't want to be anywhere about when these guys wake up, do we?'

'Grrrrro!'

We legged it. Blaidd legged it faster than me – his were longer, for a start, and he was much, much fitter.

Where are we going? he thought at me.

'As far away from here as we can get. We need a Time Door, and fast.' I was beginning to wish I'd never left home in the first place. But I had, and it was all Gwydion's fault.

But if I ended up in an ironclad dungeon for the rest of my natural, I'd certainly regret it much more than he would. And of course, since he probably hadn't even

30

realised that I'd gone yet, he couldn't come looking for me, could he? Not unless time was passing at different rates here and there, and it was the middle of the night and he was worried stiff about me, wondering where I'd got to. I hardened my heart. Let him worry! He deserved it.

I had to stop running eventually – I felt as if I was going to drop dead with a heart attack. Blaidd, however, was loping along quite happily.

I had a terrible stitch in my side, and I was gasping for breath. 'Hang on, Blaidd,' I wheezed. 'I need a rest.' Blaidd stopped and trotted back to my side.

Are you tired already, Lady? he thought at me.

'Exhausted,' I gasped.

When I had my breath back, I took stock of where we were. We'd run fairly blindly away from the four men – just downhill, fortunately. We were close to the river, and there was a small bridge spanning it. I knew that the bridge itself was unlikely to be the Time Door, but quite often the Doors are near running water.

We crossed the bridge, which was small and humpy-backed – absolutely ancient, in twenty-first century terms, but obviously fairly newly built, which was weird. But when castles and stuff were first built, they were all new and intact and modern, weren't they? They didn't have tumbledown walls and wrecked towers, and pigeons roosting on the windowsills and stuff. Castell Du is a good example: after six hundred years or so, it will probably be a real wreck, but right now it is brand new, and shining – I made sure of that. It's my home, after all. Well, it was. Right now I wasn't sure of anything, except I didn't intend to creep back and apologise. *I* didn't have anything to apologise for, did I? With just that thought, suddenly, I was right back where I started, mad as a bee in a beer-bottle.

On the other side of the river there was a high outcrop of rock – almost a cliff – with a path going up the side of it, winding between huge boulders. Time Doors are often on top of hills, and that seemed like a good place to begin. Halfway up, I looked around me. I could see for miles in all directions!

When I got my breath back, and we started off up the hill, I suddenly felt weird. A sort of edgy feeling, as if I was being watched. Then, suddenly, I knew. Gwydion – or someone, possibly Merlin – had missed me already, and was scrying to see where I'd gone.

Ha! Thought they could follow me that way, did they? Well, they had another think coming. I knew how to turn off my aura, didn't I?

And so I did. I could always turn it on again when – and if – I *wanted* to be found. But I wasn't ready for that, yet, so there.

It didn't occur to me that I might be altogether safer if they could scry me – they couldn't get at me, after all, could they? But no. Off the aura went and *Ha!* I thought. *That'll teach you!*

And then all thought was driven from my head, because we were at the top of the hill.

And down in the valley on the other side was the most beautiful castle I'd ever seen in my life.

5

Sun bounced off battlements and pennants flapped frantic in the breeze. The castle glowed in light mellow as runny honey, and the grass near the drawbridge was as short as if ride-on mowers had been invented. There was what looked like a jousting arena, with a long pole to separate the contestants, and brightly-coloured pavilions were scattered like huge blossoms on the green. Men sat outside them, lolled on the grass, sharpened saws on whetstones and wheel-sharpeners, fletched arrows and jogged up and down in a keep-fit sort of way. It looked like a film set for *Robin Hood*.

No, I suddenly realised, this wasn't Nottingham. It was Camelot. Somehow I knew that it had to be Camelot. Pure instinct, if you like – somewhere I'd never been, ever, but there was a sort of *deja-vu* about it, an 'I've been here before sometime' sort of feeling. Besides, Merlin was forever popping back and forth between Our Time and this one – he was perpetually sorting out – or trying to – Arthur and Gwenhwyfar. And if Merlin was a regular comer and goer, there was a Time Door here.

I turned to Blaidd with a great grin on my face – he was backing away, his wild instincts nervous of the colour, motion and human life below.

I grabbed his hand and hauled him back. 'It's all right, Blaidd. I'll take care of you, don't worry. But look, we need to stay close, because if you get lost and I can't find you, you'll be stuck here in human form for goodness knows how long – then you'd really be in all kinds of trouble.'

He looked utterly miserable. *Do we have to go down to the human lair, Lady?*

'I don't want to,' I said, 'but I think that's Camelot, and if I'm right, then there's a Time Door in there somewhere, so I can take you back and change you into a wolf again.'

He thought again, *We've really got to go down there?*

'Yes, Blaidd,' I said, as gently as I could. 'We really, really have to. But if you stick close to me and pretend you can't talk at all, you'll be OK. I'll pretend I'm someone posh, and you can be my servant.'

Posh?

'Sorry. I mean noble. I shall be –'

You are noble. You are the Lady.

'Well, yes. I suppose I am. But I don't look it dressed like this –' I indicated my sensible leather pants and jerkin. 'I'm going to have to look like a Lady if I want to convince anyone. And act like one, too.'

Which might be a bit harder. The royal occupants of Camelot wouldn't think much of a Lady arriving with just one servant, would they? So I needed a cover story. I chewed my chewing nail – and then an idea came.

First things first. I surveyed Blaidd. Jeans and T-shirt wouldn't do at all. He needed a livery. Blue and silver, that sounded good. I concentrated hard, and instantly Blaidd was dressed in a blue velvet jerkin and hose, with a tabard over the lot. I needed a wossname – an escutcheon – to emblazon on the front of the tabard. I thought for a while. The letters 'Y' and 'H' in fiddly, elaborate lettering appeared intertwined on the front and back of the tabard. I gave him a shield, with the same insignia on it, and lastly gave him a sword and scabbard buckled onto blue leather harness.

Buckled knees, too. He puffed out his cheeks and sagged. *Heavy, Lady!* he complained.

They probably were, for someone predominantly wolf, not too used to walking on two legs. I relented and made the sword of aluminium instead of steel – it hadn't been invented yet, and I'd have to disappear it before I left here, so that some future archaeologist wouldn't get totally confused when he or she found an aluminium sword in an Arthurian dig! Not, of course, that it would be an Arthurian dig. The historical imbeciles of the future had decided that Arthur was nothing more than a legend based on an uncouth, illiterate Celtic Dark Age warlord. Ha! That's all they knew. They didn't believe in dragons, either, despite the evidence! They were so dumb, they labelled dragon skeletons as dinosaurs! I mean, where's their imagination – like: 'Hey, guys! It looks like a dragon, flies like a dragon, eats like a dragon – obviously, guys, it's a dinosaur!' Duh.

Anyway, back to Camelot. Blaidd sorted, me next. I needed to look rich, and well-dressed and haughty. I could do the first two, no problem, but the third might be a bit more difficult. I don't do haughty – bad-tempered, yes, spoiled brat sometimes, complete pain occasionally, yes, but haughty, no. Still, it wouldn't be for long. Once I found Merlin's Door, I'd be through it like a mole down a hole. I'd deliver Blaidd back to Ynys Haf, shapeshift him back to wolf, turn him loose, find another Door and head for home and Mam. And a bit of mother-love and lots of sympathy and some Heinz tomato soup and crusty bread and Welsh salty butter. And definitely no Gwydion telling me that getting married was *'dim problem'*. Grr! Do you know, whenever I even thought of it, I started to simmer again. Ha! I'd show him. Ooh, did he ever owe me an apology! *And* a proper proposal.

Mustn't waste time getting mad again, when what I had to do was get changed. I concentrated hard and magicked up a form-fitting, lowish-necked (no point in having a plunging neckline if it's not plunging anywhere in particular) amber velvet dress, a few shades lighter than my hair. I got pretty amber satin slippers, magicked my hair (which is NOT RED, thank you VERY much) into an elaborate style and added a pointy headdress with an amber veil flowing out behind me.

Blaidd blinked. *You* – he thought, and then stopped.

'Yes?' I asked, knowing perfectly well how good I looked.

You look different, Lady!

Well, thanks. I think. Safer not to ask what he meant!

'Right, Blaidd. When we get down there, just let me do the talking. Try to look protective and fierce –'

He snarled, loudly, and dropped into a crouch.

'– but DON'T snarl, Blaidd, and try to remember to stand on your hind legs. That's not protective; it's more *come-outside-and-say-that, chum*! Try to forget you're a wolf. Just try to look – well, strong and silent, all right? I'll do the talking. You just stay close and concentrate on being strong and stern. Can you do that?'

He scowled, ducked his head and looked at me under his eyebrows – and his ears moved! 'And please don't do that wolf-thing with your ears. Humans don't. But the fierce look is fine. Just don't try to talk – or crouch for a spring – or waggle your ears. All right?' Good thing he didn't have a tail, I suppose.

The more I thought about it, the more I realised there were an awful lot of other don'ts I'd have to tackle, but there wasn't time for that now.

'Right.' I started walking down to Camelot – then realised that a posh female wouldn't arrive at the castle on foot, would she? But we didn't have horses available. I sighed. I could have magicked a couple up, but I was pretty sure that they'd take one look at Blaidd, magic or not, and think 'wolf!' and 'aaargh!' and promptly scarper.

'Blaidd,' I said. 'We have to get inside Camelot without anyone seeing us arrive, understand? I'm going to shift you into a bird, and we'll fly in, all right?'

I'm not a bird! he thought indignantly. *I am wolf!*

'I know you are, Blaidd, I know. But if you go down there as a wolf, you're going to make lovely target practice for every bloke on the battlements with a bow and arrow. You'll be a hairy pincushion in no time.'

Ah.

'So. I'm going to change you – just for a little while – into a bird. We'll fly into Camelot and then I'll find a quiet corner and shapeshift you back. Not back to wolf, mind, back to Blaidd. All right?'

He nodded. And growled.

'And try not to growl, please!' Maybe I should smack him with a rolled up newspaper every time he did it, the way you train puppies. Except that newspapers were in short supply in Camelot.

I shifted the two of us into sparrows, gave him a brief flying lesson – he had a tendency to try and run in the air, using his wings *and* his legs – and then we took off for Camelot.

It was the weirdest feeling, sailing over those battlements. Nobody took a blind bit of notice of two sparrows fluttering overhead, of course. The inner courtyard was busy with people coming and going. It was clean and tidy – no piles of rubbish in corners or empty barrels and sacks lying about. A couple of small boys were practising archery, and a couple more were mounted on small ponies, taking clouts at a hideously-painted wooden head set on a swinging device. If they hit it in the right place, they got away unscathed. If they didn't, the arm of the swing whizzed round and clouted them one!

Blaidd and I soared over them, past a tall tower. Through the arrowslits, I could see people inside the rooms – the castle appeared to be full to bursting, with almost every chamber in use. I found us a quiet corner of the battlements.

We landed, and I shifted myself first, the easier to shift Blaidd back. I let him sit on the flagstones, a tiny, fluffy bundle of untidy feathers, while I straightened my wimple, shook out my dress and looked down to shuffle into my slippers properly, willing away the sensation of talons rather than toes.

The cat was on him before I even saw it. It snatched him up and shot down a spiral staircase at the speed of – well, a determined, hungry cat. There was only one thing to do – I shot down after them, screaming the shifting spell as I stumbled down the stairs. Blaidd changed in the nick of time. The cat, realising that its prey was swelling in its jaws, dropped him and stared. Blaidd shot up to his full height, and with a lightning-quick movement, grabbed the cat by the scruff of its neck . . . And was about to rip its throat out.

'*No*, Blaidd!' I yelled, just in time.

The cat dangled in the air with an expression of utter panic. Blaidd put his face very close to the cat's, slitted his amber eyes, flattened his ears back against his head and growled, deep and low in his throat.

I've never seen a cat faint before.

Blaidd laid the limp body on the staircase and grinned.

'Sorry, Blaidd. I didn't even see the cat until it had you.'

No matter, Lady. I was going to teach it a lesson – maybe break its teeth. But you changed me too fast.

He probably would have left the poor cat toothless, sparrow or not. I suppose if you think like a wolf, you act like a wolf! The cat wouldn't have known what hit it, a tiny bird socking it in the chops!

'Right, Blaidd, straighten yourself up – oh, good grief. I forgot about your hair, didn't I?'

His hair, of course, was as wild and rough and shaggy as it had been when he'd been a wolf. I magicked a comb and tried to smooth it down. It stayed flat for about two seconds.

'Ah well,' I sighed. 'I suppose we're stuck with it. Makes you look fierce, anyway. Ready?'

He nodded.

'Right then. Let's go and find that Time Door. I don't want to run into anyone if I can help it – the less explaining we have to do the better. If we meet anyone, I'll just nod as if I'm supposed to be here and we'll keep on going, all right?'

We set off down the spiral stairs, which were even and new, without the deep indentations you find in castles in the twenty-first century, grooves that have been worn into the stone by thousands of feet and hundreds of years. Whenever we came to a door, I listened at it. If there was silence, I opened it and peeked. If I saw anything that looked remotely like it might be a Time Door, I was ready to shoot in and give it a whirl.

We were almost at the bottom of the stairs, now. Light filtered in through an open door. I'd have to be very careful crossing the inner courtyard. I wanted to avoid conversation at all costs. What I wanted was to find the Time Door, get the pair of us through it and away from here. Camelot was far too complicated for me – I knew all the Arthurian stories; I'd loved them since I was a little girl, all that about Lancelot and Galahad and Medrawd and Gwenhwyfar and Morgan le Fay. Dad used to tell them to me. I also knew quite a lot about Camelot, of course, from the tidbits that Merlin let slip after he'd been here on one of his jaunts. From what he said, it wasn't quite like the stories, all shiny and virtuous. In fact it was a really good place to stay away from. There was so much intrigue, Merlin said, so much backbiting, so much magic flying around, both black, white and in-between, that a person needed to be alert the whole time.

I opened the last door – a guardroom from the shields and stuff hanging on the walls and lying around on wooden benches and racks. Nothing remotely resembling a Time Door, however, so I shut it again. I put up a hand to caution Blaidd to stay behind me and not go rushing out, and stopped him just in time. I poked my nose round the open door into the courtyard.

And found myself eyeball to eyeball with a pair of startled brown eyes.

6

'Aaargh!' I squawked, and stepped back before I cannoned into the body attached to the eyes.

'Sorry!' I blurted, before I could help it. Never apologise, that's my motto, it's a sign of weakness. Or at least, only if it's absolutely necessary.

'So you should be,' spat the owner of the eyes. 'Don't you know better than to hurtle round corners like that? Where are your manners, girl?'

I got my dignity back. And a distinct sense of rattiness. Girl? Who did she think she was talking to? 'As a matter of fact,' I said, coldly, '*I* wasn't hurtling anywhere. I was going very carefully. I looked before I even stepped out of the doorway. It's you that was going too fast. Girl.'

'Urghrrl,' Blaidd agreed softly behind me, and I dug an elbow sharply into his ribs to shut him up.

The owner of the eyes straightened her back and glared at me. 'How dare you speak to me like that? I should lock you in a dungeon and throw away the key! Who are you, anyway? I've never seen you before. What are you doing here? Where have you come from? Answer me immediately, do you hear?'

'If it's any of your business,' I said, pushing past her, 'I am the Lady – um –' *oh, blow it, tell the truth. No-one will have heard of me here, and anyway I've got 'YH' on Blaidd's livery*, '– Tanith of Ynys Haf.'

'Never heard of you,' the girl snapped. 'Or the place. Ynys Haf? Island of Summer? No such place. You're lying, aren't you! Has someone sent you to spy on me? Medrawd? It was Medrawd, wasn't it?'

She was about my height, with dark, thick hair flowing in a single plait down her back. She was thinner than me, and looked about fifteen, and there was no way that I, Tanith, Lady of Ynys Haf, with an honours degree from the University of Wales, Aberystwyth, was going to be put down by some snotty little madam with attitude.

'I'm not a spy for Medrawd – or anybody else for that matter. And the fact that you've never heard of Ynys Haf is your problem, not mine,' I said. 'I don't tell lies,' (except when I have to). 'Come, Blaidd!' I stuck my nose in the air and was marching towards an open door into another tower to get away from her when she grabbed my arm.

'Have you no respect for your betters at all, girl? You dare to turn your back on your Queen?' she snapped.

I stopped marching. An 'oops' sort of feeling crept up my spine. 'My *Queen*?' I gulped. Surely not. This arrogant little brat couldn't be Gwenhwyfar, could it? One of the Three Gentle, Gold-Collared Ladies of Brython? 'What?' I mumbled. 'You? Queen?'

'I am Gwenhwyfar, wife to Arthur and High Queen of Brython,' she said, snootily. 'And I will ask you once more, girl. Who are you?'

Girl? There it was again. I hate that. Who did she think she was? Well, she was Queen, but so what? No call to be rude. I decided not to curtsy. *So sue me*, I thought. 'As I said, My Lady. I am Tanith of Ynys Haf.' No way was I going to call her Highness or Majesty.

'And where is this Ynys Haf? I have never heard of it, so it can't be an important place.'

More important than you'll ever know, you pompous little twonk. 'A small kingdom in the west of Wales, My

Lady.' Best to stick fairly close to the truth. I tried an insincere grin which probably appeared as a sickly smirk. 'But then, one as obviously exalted,' *(at least in your own opinion)* 'as you would hardly have heard of my insignificant land.'

'As you say, I am far too important to have heard of it,' she agreed. 'It must be very small and insignificant. What are you doing here in Camelot?'

What on earth could I tell her? I frantically considered and discarded half a dozen options.

'Well?' The royal foot was tapping impatiently.

Brainwave. 'My – er – lord,' (no need to be specific!) 'has sent me to find the Merlin of Brython.'

'Merlin?' Her face turned thunderous. 'Boring, interfering old –' She didn't finish that sentence, perhaps luckily for my innocent lugholes – although we obviously had one thing in common, our opinion of Merlin! 'The Merlin is my husband's chief counsellor.'

'I know.'

Gwenhwyfar lifted a dark eyebrow. 'But for once he is not here, and very pleasant it is without him, I can tell you. What do you want with him?'

Enough was enough. 'That, My Lady, is my concern,' I snapped. Oops. Nearly forgot. 'Or rather, my lord's.'

She brought the eyebrows together in a scowl that would have made it rain in Dale in a heatwave. And that's the sunniest spot in Wales! 'I demand that you tell me.'

'Demand on,' I said, coldly. 'That is my business, and mine alone, Queen Gwenhwyfar. Blaidd?'

My wolf-boy tucked himself in at my heels and trotted after me. I was half-expecting Gwenhwyfar to shriek for the guards to arrest me and bung me in the nearest dungeon. But she didn't. Perhaps she wasn't used to people standing up to her.

I got inside the door of the next tower along – a bigger structure than the last one, with wider stairs and an altogether grander appearance than the last, which looked sort of more hopeful – Merlin didn't stint himself when it came to comfort. Though his working area at Castell Du was tatty and untidy, his personal apartments were quite something – I suspected he even had satellite TV!

Inside the entrance, I turned round to see if a squadron of men-at-arms was chasing me. No, only the Queen, trotting like a determined puppy in Blaidd's wake. I folded my arms and glared at her. Persistent little madam, wasn't she?

'What?' I demanded.

'I'm sorry,' she said, meekly, her eyes filling up with tears. 'I didn't mean to be so horrible. You startled me, that's all, and when I'm afraid I get defensive.' She sniffled pathetically.

Oh, I hate to see people cry! 'You startled me, too,' I admitted.

'Look,' she said. 'I'm sorry I was such a cross-patch. My name is Gwenhwyfar. I'm married to Arthur, the King, but I'm not really a queenly sort of person at all, really I'm not. I'm just ordinary, like you.'

That's all you know, I thought.

'I'm sorry. You scared me, jumping out at me like that. I thought you were Medrawd. I don't like Medrawd. He's a horrible bully. My husband treats me like a child, not like a grown woman, and I don't have any friends, not really. Oh, there're lots of important court ladies who fuss around me, but I don't think they like me much. All they

44

do is sit and sew. There's lots of knights and courtiers that flatter me and pretend they like me, when I'm sure they don't, not really. They're all "Highness this", and "Highness that", and bowing and stuff, and it's boring. Sometimes I imagine they are laughing at me behind my back. They are only nice because they want something from Arthur and think I can get it for them. You're –'

'Bad-tempered?' I asked, gently.

She giggled, and slapped her hand across her mouth to hide it. 'I'm sorry. I was going to say *different*.'

You don't know the half of it, young Gwen! I thought. 'Why? Because I was rude and impatient with you?'

'Partly that. I just want someone to treat me like an ordinary, real person for a change and not go pretending to like me. Will you be my friend?'

A Major Complication. But what could I say? 'I will try, My Lady,' I began, 'b –' I never got the 'but' out.

'Call me Gwen, please?' she begged. 'Come for a walk in the garden with me, and tell me all about yourself. Tell me what it's like where you come from – Ynys Haf, is that right? Tell me about your lord. Have you got a nice new castle? Is it as grand as Camelot? Oh, please come; if I go back to my chamber, they'll make me sit and sew. I'm so tired of listening to whose grandchild learned to walk first.'

Now that I could relate to. But tell her about myself? No way if I could help it. I hadn't forgotten the high-handed attitude to witches in the past, even if the King's half-sister Morgan le Fay was one. The thing was, she had friends (or at least family) in high places. She was too powerful to risk offending, so she was OK, wasn't she? I was pretty powerful too, and had friends in high

45

places. But not here. They'd try to get rid of me before you could say Lancelot's Legwarmers. Especially if they knew about witches and iron, they'd have no problem at all, would they? They'd have me helpless in a minute if they knew what I really am. I'd have to be really, really careful – and now it looked like I was going to have to be Gwenhwyfar's Best Buddy. Difficult, to say the least.

Queen Gwenhwyfar led me and Blaidd – who was beginning to look slightly more relaxed – away from the stone buildings into a walled area filled with low beds of sweet-smelling herbs and flowers.

Gwenhwyfar glanced over her shoulder. 'Does your man *have* to follow us everywhere?' she frowned.

'Blaidd? Well, he's my bodyguard –'

'Blaidd? Wolf? How strange! Is that because he is as fierce as a wolf when he is protecting you? Is it?' she rattled on. Real chatterbox, this one.

'More or less,' I admitted.

'Is he completely, utterly loyal? Would he die for you? Oh, how romantic that would be! Have you had him long? Oh, I would love to have someone completely loyal to me. I don't have anyone, really, except Arthur, who doesn't count because he's married to me and he has to be loyal.'

'Blaidd isn't a possession, Gwenhwyfar. He's a – person.' Well, right now he was. Sort of.

'Oh, pooh. I don't care. Send him away, please. Or make him wait somewhere. I don't want him listening while we talk. Talk between *really good* friends is secret, isn't it? I have such a lot to tell you.'

Since we'd met all of ten minutes ago, and five of them had been spent bickering, I wasn't about to spill too many of my secrets, thank you very much! She worried

46

me – she was a real danger to herself, and other people too – if she went around confiding her secrets to complete strangers. All the same, I said, 'Blaidd, will you stand guard at the gate, please?'

'You say *please* to him?' she asked, wide-eyed.

'Of course. My mam taught me to be polite. *Be polite to others and they'll be polite to you.*'

She sniggered. 'Try telling that to Merlin! He's polite and he's horrible at the same time, because you know that what he says is the opposite to what he's thinking. Do you know, I really think Merlin hates me.'

'No he doesn't. That's just Merlin being Merlin. He's like that with everyone.'

'So you do know him?'

Rats. Open my mouth and put my foot slap bang into it, right? 'Sort of,' I admitted, fingers crossed in the folds of my gown. 'He is a friend of my – um – family.' Well, he was. Mam knew him and so did all the Aunts. 'I've – er – met him once or twice,' I admitted.

'You know what he's like, then.'

'Oh, yes. I certainly do.'

'But you still came to Camelot to find him?'

'Sort of.'

'Why?'

That was a good one. 'I – um – have a message for him.' Too true I did. And briefly, it was, 'Stop meddling between me and Gwydion and butt out. And don't you interfere in our lives ever again! And now show me the way out of here.' However, perhaps this conversation was getting too personal. 'You don't like Merlin?'

'Merlin,' she said, the distaste obvious, 'is just like Arthur. He treats me as if I'm a half-witted child.'

Really? I thought, *I wonder why that could be?*

'He talks to me as if I don't have any sort of a brain in my head at all. I'm a married woman, and Queen of Brython; he ought to respect me! And Arthur is just as bad! When he's here,' she added bitterly.

That was better – she was off and running on her own troubles, so I was safe for a while.

'Often away, is he?' Of course he was, I'd read the stories, hadn't I? He was a busy man!

'Do you know, we've hardly had a single decent conversation since we got married? He sort of pats me and sends me off to bed because there's always something important he's got to do. I'm important too, aren't I? I hardly ever see him! He's always away talking to wicked barons and rescuing people from dragons and stuff like that,' she complained.

'Have you thought of taking up a hobby?' I asked. Then I remembered. She did, didn't she. She took up – or would, in the future – Sir Lancelot. He was her hobby while Arthur was away . . . Oops.

'A hobby? No. I have a tiercel, and a sparrowhawk, and my husband has promised me a dear little merlin. My birds are my pets. I talk to them lots, because there's no-one else I can talk to, is there?'

She had misunderstood my question, perhaps luckily, thinking that the sort of hobby I meant was a miniature peregrine falcon. After all, what sort of a hobby could a bored olde-tyme lady take up? Women's rugby?

'Right,' I said. Then, trying to get a handle on where we were in Arthurian times, 'Have you been married long?'

She stopped walking and screwed up her face. 'One

year, two months and –' she counted on her fingers, '– five days, if today is Wednesday. Is it?'

I didn't have a clue what year it was, let alone what day. 'Not long, then.'

'No. And I might as well not have bothered. It was lovely at first. I'd heard all about Arthur from the bards, of course, and my father. He was full of Arthur's grand ideas for new laws and justice and all that. Arthur was lovely and kind then. He used to bring me presents and everything. Then we got married, and my father gave him this stupid round table as a wedding present, and we had to take the thing apart and lug it across country in slices, like a giant cake. And once Arthur had it put together again here at Camelot –' She shrugged and pulled a face. 'He had this idea for this band of special knights who would sit at the table and talk about law and order, and go off and rescue maidens and stuff like that. Since then, I've hardly seen him. If it isn't some maiden tied to a rock for a dragon to eat, it's some Black Knight that needs killing. He never talks to me any more, and I'm bored. Oh, you will stay and be my friend, won't you?'

I was saved from answering that one by a very loud growling. Not one growl, but what sounded like a whole dogpack of growls, snarls, yips, yikes and yelps.

And Blaidd's unmistakeable deep snarl loudest of all. Even though he was in human form, his wolf nature was still there – and was being extremely vocal!

'Quick,' I said, picked up my elegant amber skirts, and ran like the clappers for the gate.

7

The growling and snarling got louder – and angrier – as I got closer to the gate.

Outside it, a cluster of men was shouting and waving fists, laughing and jeering at something on the floor. One weaselly-looking individual appeared to be collecting bets.

I elbowed my way into the circle, to find Blaidd rolling on the ground with a very large wolfhound. They obviously didn't like each other much, because Blaidd was trying desperately to get his teeth socked into the wolfhound's hairy throat, and the wolfhound was trying to do the pretty much the same to Blaidd.

'Whose dog is that?' I demanded. 'Call it off at once!'

Nobody took a blind bit of notice. Up to me, then. 'Blaidd! Stop it. Get up.'

Can't, Lady. This apology for a wolf will kill me if I do. If I let go he'll rip out my throat.

'That's not a wolf, Blaidd, only a wolfhound. It's tame. It's a dog. And you haven't got your usual teeth!'

If I had my own teeth, this stupid creature would be dead already! These short fangs are useless!

It was a sort of Mexican stand-off. Neither of them dared let go – they both knew it would be the last thing they did. There was only one thing for it. I threw a quick enchantment, split it in mid-air (and that's not easy to do, I can tell you!) and zapped the two of them simultaneously. Wolf-boy and dog sighed and fell peacefully asleep, relaxing into a tangle of arms, legs and paws.

'They can't stop yet!' somebody complained. 'Which of them won? I had a bet on that! Wake them! Make them fight until one wins!'

'You ought to be ashamed of yourself,' I snapped, hauling the comatose wolfhound off the gently snoring Blaidd. 'Betting on a boy fighting a dog!'

'The boy was doing pretty well,' another man said, grinning. 'I was about to lose my gold, so thank you, Lady, for preventing that. 'Oi!' he yelled, shooting out an arm and grabbing the bet-taker, who was trying to fade into the background with all the stake money. 'Money back if you don't mind, squire!'

'The boy could have been killed!' I said, furiously.

'He most certainly would have been, if he had harmed Brenin in any way,' said a languid voice. 'Brenin is an extremely valuable hound. I would have slit the boy's throat in an instant if he had damaged my beast.'

I swung round. The speaker was a slim, dark-skinned, slightly lopsided-looking little man who managed to look both marginally handsome and thoroughly unpleasant, simultaneously.

'Oh, you would, would you?' I said, sarcastically. 'Your dog attacks a boy, and you –'

'But you see, you are jumping to conclusions, my dear girl. And your conclusions are wrong. The dog didn't attack the boy. The dog growled at him, true. But the boy attacked the dog. One of them would certainly have been killed if –' he looked at me suspiciously, '– if they had not almost miraculously and simultaneously fallen asleep. Now I wonder how that happened?' He looked at me, one dark eyebrow raised questioningly.

'The boy is my servant,' I said, swiftly. 'He has terrible

51

fits and falls unconscious quite often. The dog must simply be exhausted.'

'You think so?' The weaselly man prodded the dog with his boot. 'Brenin?'

The huge body moved with the pressure of the foot, but didn't otherwise stir. It would, given an hour or so, be quite happy, without even a headache, although it might be a little confused after such a long nap. Long enough for me to get Blaidd safely away, anyway.

Gwenhwyfar came trotting up, her skirts held daintily in both hands. 'Oh, Lady Tanith,' she squeaked, 'is that your serving man? Is he dead?'

'No. Just had a bit of a fit, that's all. I'm sure he'll be fine.' I suddenly had a brainwave – maybe I could get us out of this circle of staring men – and away from the sinister character who was looking at me altogether too curiously. 'Highness, where can I take him until he recovers?'

Gwenhwyfar was immediately all efficiency, delighted to take a leading role and issue orders. 'You, Peredur, and you, Gwyn, carry him to my chambers. *Don't* put him in my bed, mind,' she added hastily. 'He's probably got lice. Common people do, don't they?' She shuddered. 'Put him on the couch.'

Great – although I didn't particularly want Blaidd ending up a permanent fixture in Gwenhwyfar's quarters. She was daft enough, capricious enough, to decide to nurse him back to health – common, lousy and flea-bitten or not.

'You're right, he probably does have lice, Your Highness. He'll have his own, as well as picking up more from the wolfhound. Perhaps it would be best to take him somewhere else?'

'The stables, perhaps?' Peredur suggested. The stables,

52

of course, weren't up several flights of spiral stairs, and he was probably thinking of his poor back!

The stables, however, were not too brilliant an idea. If the horses got a whiff of wolf . . .

Fortunately, Gwenhwyfar's Florence Nightingale complex was stronger than her distaste for lice. 'Oh, pooh. What are a few lice? Take him to my chamber,' she commanded. 'This poor boy needs attention.'

Peredur, somewhat gingerly, picked up Blaidd's arms and Gwyn his feet, and between them they lugged him towards the gatehouse tower. I gathered up my long, clinging skirts (which are a real pain when you're used to trousers, I can tell you) and made to follow them. A hand seized my arm.

'Let me go,' I snapped. I hate people grabbing me like that, especially people I don't know.

'Only when you tell me who you are and where you have come from,' the dark, weaselly man said, his fingers digging viciously into the soft flesh above my elbow. 'I haven't seen you here before – and yet something about you is very familiar.'

I shook myself free. 'I've never been here before,' I snapped, 'and who I am is none of your business.'

He grabbed me again. 'How dare you speak to me like that? Don't you know who I am, girl?'

I was getting SO fed up with people asking me that! First Gwenhwyfar, now this bloke, whoever he was. They really should know better, because it only damages their egos even more when you say, 'No, should I?'

'You would be wise to learn manners if you know what's good for you. The Queen called you – what was it? – Tanith? An unusual name, My Lady.'

'And your point is?' I asked, icicles on every syllable.

'My point, Lady Tanith, is that young women who try to worm their way into the Queen's household need to take great care. There is frequently unforeseen danger in high places. Climb too far too fast, and you may fall. And hurt yourself . . .'

'Is that a threat?' My temper was rising so quickly I could feel the magic tingling in my blood, which was always dangerous – high magic pressure is much worse than high blood pressure.

'No. I'd say it was more of a promise, Lady Tanith.'

He released my arm and stood back. His smile was the most unpleasant I've ever seen.

Gwenhwyfar reappeared in the tower doorway. 'Tanith, the boy is waking. You should come.'

Oops. Had to get there fast. I'd thought the spell would last longer than it had. I brushed the man aside and headed for the tower door, scrambling up the stairway in Gwenhwyfar's wake.

At the top, she stopped and turned towards me. 'Why were you talking to him? I thought you were my friend. Do you know him?'

'No, I don't. I don't think I want to, particularly. He seems like a nasty piece of work, whoever he is.'

'You don't know? That's Medrawd. Arthur's nephew. He's a horrible, horrible man. He frightens me.'

We were at the door of her chamber now, and I staggered through it, my heart pounding from galloping up the stairs. Half-dead with exhaustion, I still felt my nerves twitch at discovering that the man I'd just faced down was Medrawd, who has gone down in history as A Nasty Piece of Work.

Blaidd was stirring and moaning in the middle of a circle of twittering women.

'There. The fit is over,' Gwenhwyfar said, nodding in satisfaction.

'Just placing him upon your couch has revived him,' one of the men said, and she brightened instantly.

'Ooh, do you think so?' she asked. 'Just putting him on my couch made him better?'

Yeah. Right. What planet was this girl from?

Shunting her gently to one side, I knelt down beside Blaidd, grabbed a handful of shaggy hair and tugged it, hard.

'GrrrrowOw!'

'Pay attention, Blaidd,' I hissed. 'You've been unconscious because I zapped you. It was the only way to get you out of the predicament you landed yourself – and me – in. Now just lie still and shut up. Don't you dare even think of growling!'

Sorry, Lady.

'Later. Right now, just leave it to me to get you safely out of here, all right?'

I turned to Gwenhwyfar. 'Highness, when we met –'

'Gwenhwyfar,' she burbled. 'We are friends, Tanith – to you I am Gwenhwyfar.'

'All right. Gwenhwyfar. Fine,' I muttered absently. 'As I was saying, am I allowed to stay at Camelot? If I am, where can I sleep and have my poor, sick servant close by –' I added hastily, 'until Merlin comes?'

'The castle is crowded, because Arthur has arranged a tournament to celebrate Medrawd's birthday tomorrow. But there will be somewhere, I'm sure.' She glanced around, a little frown appearing between her eyes. 'Ah.

Lady Angharad. You can move in with Lady Alys. Tanith, my new friend,' (and here she patted my arm affectionately) 'can have your room.'

From the look Lady Angharad gave me, she wasn't too ecstatic. And from her expression, Lady Alys wasn't overjoyed at the prospect of a roomie, either. Two more people who probably wouldn't like me much. Ah well. You can't cook a kipper without breaking eggs.

'Peredur,' Gwenhwyfar commanded, 'take the boy to Lady Angharad's room.'

Peredur bent down and hauled Blaidd to his feet.

I gave Blaidd a look that stifled the snarl at birth.

He stumbled along, half-carried, one arm draped around Peredur's shoulder, while I followed. We went up another flight of stairs to a small chamber with tapestried walls, a low bed and a chest with a candle on it. An opening in the wall led to a very pongy garderobe, and a small door on the right side of the room proved to be another, smaller chamber. Peredur dragged Blaidd through and laid him on the floor.

'Thank you,' I said to Peredur. 'You're very kind.'

He shrugged, and blew out his breath. 'The lad is brave, if foolish. But – I should warn you, My Lady. He would do well to learn control of his temper.'

'He will,' I assured him. 'He's young, and doesn't understand life at court yet.' *And he's not too sure about walking upright and wearing clothes, either!*

Lady Angharad came in then, her face, as my mam would have said, like a slapped backside. 'I'll take my things now,' she snapped, opening a chest and scooping up armfuls of linen. 'I'll come back for my gowns.'

She swept out of the door with her nose in the air, and

56

went stamping up the stairs. Lady Alys's chamber must be up almost in the attics – no wonder she wasn't pleased with me!

I turned my attention to Blaidd. 'Right. What happened?' I snapped. I was so not happy with him. He'd put both of us in terrible danger, and all because he couldn't control his temper. Or so I believed.

He thought back at me, *I waited, as you instructed, Lady. The man came –'*

'Medrawd?'

If you mean the dark, crooked man, yes, Medrawd. He had his dog leashed. It insulted me. I don't take insults from low dogs, Lady. I am Wolf.

'I know, Blaidd. But you're going to have to learn to keep your temper, not go around attacking dogs.'

I kept my temper, Lady. But Medrawd unleashed his hound and set it at my throat. I defended myself.

This was different. If Medrawd had ordered his wolfhound to attack what looked like – but wasn't, of course, though he didn't know that – a defenceless young boy, he really did live up to his reputation.

Oh, Lady, if only I'd had my sharp, long teeth I'd have torn his throat open and snapped his sinews and ripped into his veins and drunk his hot, red blood and –

'Yes, thanks, Blaidd. Too much information there, mate. In future you'd better stay close to me just in case Medrawd has another go at you.'

Medrawd knows you, Lady?

'No. I don't think so. But –'

But I was sure Merlin had mentioned that Medrawd had some magic. I would have to be mega-careful.

8

Once I was left alone in the little chamber, I magicked myself some decent clothes, and some sensible, comfortable plain ones for Blaidd. If I was going to be at court for any length of time, I had to at least try to look like a lady. I felt like magicking up a wardrobe, too – hanging my new stuff in the garderobe didn't appeal at all – I didn't fancy ponging like a public loo. However, an MFI wall unit might be a bit suspicious . . . I chucked a cleansing spell down the hole in the wall, which helped a bit, but nothing short of a disinfectant depth charge would clean it properly.

Gwenhwyfar doodled in shortly after to check on 'her' patient. She patted his back, and Blaidd stood patiently while she twittered at him. Then, duty done to the lower classes, she turned her attention to me.

'At supper tonight, you will sit at table with Arthur and me. I expect you will like Arthur. Everybody does.'

I'm sure they did – but all the same, top table with posh people didn't suit me at all – it was a safe bet the enchanting Medrawd would also be on it, and the further I stayed from Medrawd, the happier I'd be. Not a lot I could do about it, however – I needed Gwenhwyfar's friendship as well as whatever protective cover she could give, while I searched Camelot for Merlin's Time Door.

I used Blaidd being poorly to get him a tray of food from the kitchens. Otherwise, he'd have had to eat with the servants, who would be full of questions Blaidd couldn't answer. In fact, I didn't want him going anywhere without me if I could help it. A young serving girl staggered into the room, dumped a tray of cold meat, bread and ale and batted her eyelashes at Blaidd.

'Thank you,' I said, 'that will be all.'

She left with a flirtatious glance over her shoulder. Luckily, Blaidd didn't notice. He was a handsome lad and I certainly didn't want romantic stuff messing things up even worse than they were already.

'Blaidd, you stay here, eat, and then get some sleep. I'll be back as soon as I can. You should be safe enough until then. All right?'

Yes, Lady. I shall stay on guard for you.

'Great,' I said, absentmindedly, struggling to do up the back of my green brocade gown. In the end I gave up and magicked the fastenings closed. I decided not to bother with putting my hair up – all that fiddling with pins and stuff was a pain, and if I magicked it up it just felt stiff and uncomfortable and not a bit like me. So I just brushed it and let it hang loose over my shoulders, jammed a headdress on top and peered into the sheet of polished metal that served as a mirror. I seemed to look OK.

I closed the chamber door behind me and followed the crowd to the Great Hall. It was huge, echoing with laughter and voices. The air was full of smoke from two great fireplaces, and burning braziers dotted here and there. The lower end of the table, below the large silver salt-pots, looked like being much more fun than the top end, where all the posh people sat. I lurked around the middle, hoping I could get away with being a bit anonymous, but then Gwenhwyfar arrived with Arthur, and peered about, looking for me. When she spotted me, she sent a servant to fetch me to the raised platform – in full view of everyone, just where I didn't want to be.

I climbed up the two wooden stairs, feeling curious eyes on me. Gwenhwyfar grabbed my hand and towed me to a seat beside her. I almost sat – but then realised that Arthur hadn't, yet, and I knew enough to realise protocol dictated that nobody sat until the King did.

'Arthur!' she said. 'This is Lady Tanith. She came to Camelot only today, and she's going to be my best friend.'

'Is that a fact, now?' Arthur said, putting an arm around his little wife. He was tall, and his eyes were kind, but he was so *old!* Compared to Gwenhwyfar, he looked almost old enough to be her father. His hair was greying, his face lined, and he looked as if all the troubles of the world were weighing on him. He looked like what my mam called 'A Bit of a Worrier'.

'My Lady,' he said, politely, and took my hand. He smiled down into my face, a lovely, gentle, sweet-natured smile, and I had to smile back. I liked him instantly. I bobbed a little curtsey. 'Gwenny, dear – your new friend is unmarried,' he said. 'My knights will be tumbling over themselves to pay court!'

How did he know that? Then I realised: I'd left my hair down, hadn't I? Married women in those days always wore theirs pinned up.

'You're very kind, Your Majesty,' I muttered, wishing I'd used my brain. Arthur let go my hand, still smiling his gentle, pleased smile.

'Tanith, sit here, beside me,' Gwenhwyfar insisted, like a child at a birthday party.

That was fine by me. Medrawd had just entered, and was making his way up towards the dais. 'What about Medrawd?' I whispered. 'Where does he sit?'

60

'Beside Arthur,' she whispered back. 'On his right side, because it's his birthday tomorrow.'

Thank goodness – both Arthur and Gwenhwyfar were between Medrawd and me. The less I saw of that character, the happier I'd be. And probably safer, too.

'Medrawd's mother will be sitting next to you,' Gwenhwyfar muttered. 'I don't like her, she frightens me, but I think she's a bit nicer than Medrawd.'

Was she nuts? Medrawd's mother? Morgan le Fay, as powerful a witch as ever there was. At least as powerful as me, maybe even more so. And to make matters worse, there was no way she could ever be described as a Goodwitch. I didn't want to mess with Morgan. If she found out I was a witch, I'd be in deep, deep fertiliser.

And I was going to be sitting next to her at supper – which is one sure way to ruin an appetite!

I looked round the Great Hall, trying to find the lady in question, but couldn't see anyone who looked remotely evil enough. And then a soft voice spoke behind me.

'Gwenhywfar? My dear, you are looking quite beautiful tonight.'

The words positively *dripped* insincerity! The speaker was most definitely Morgan le Fay. If she was Medrawd's mother, she had to be forty at least – but looked no more than twenty. Her hair was glossy black, her skin unwrinkled and white, and her figure young and slender. I glanced at her hands, usually a dead giveaway when it comes to age – but they were hidden by the long, pointed sleeves of her gorgeous crimson velvet dress. Beside her I felt dowdy.

And then she glanced at me, smiling, showing perfect, even teeth – and our eyes met. The eyes gave her away:

they were older than the dark hills of Wales, and filled with the sort of chilling knowledge that nice people don't ever acquire, or want to.

'Why, a new face to grace our company!' she murmured, those dark, terrifyingly cold eyes giving me a sort of instant X-ray. 'And you are . . .?'

'Tanith, Your Grace,' I muttered, and bobbed a curtsey. She was Arthur's sister; I had to be polite and respectful. And very, very careful.

'Taaaniiith,' she drawled. 'And your estates, Lady Tanith? Where are they?' The smile was white and even, but didn't get anywhere near her eyes.

Rats. I had to tell her. Because I'd already told Gwenhwyfar where I'd come from, I had to tell Morgan le Fay – and she'd probably know, unlike Gwenhwyfar, exactly where Ynys Haf was – because of Merlin. And could probably guess who I was, and what!

Then Arthur clapped his hands. The room fell silent, all eyes on the King.

'My Lords, my Ladies, friends, please welcome our guest of honour – my dear nephew Medrawd, on this his birthday!'

Medrawd made his entrance, glittering in black velvet and pearls, and knelt before Arthur. 'Dear, dear Uncle,' he murmured. 'You do me such honour. I am unworthy of it,' he added, although he didn't sound as if he believed he was unworthy of anything very much.

We were all standing behind our chairs, waiting for King Arthur and Queen Gwenhwyfar to sit. Although I'd escaped answering Morgan le Fay, the question would be asked again sooner or later – and I was stuck with sitting next to her for the whole evening. I'd probably not be able to eat a thing; I'd be too busy concentrating on not saying anything that could give me away. My stomach roiled unpleasantly. I felt sick now, not hungry.

Gwenhwyfar stood on tiptoe, and tugged her husband's sleeve. He bent down, his expression affectionate. She whispered into his ear and he glanced along the table at me and nodded.

'What – two such beautiful ladies sitting together?' he said, beaming benevolently. I looked around for the two beautiful ladies, and then realised he was talking about me and Morgan le Fay.

'We can't have that – such a waste.' And King Arthur, bless his cotton socks, summoned two of his knights to sit between Morgan and me, which put us far enough away from each other that I shouldn't have to talk to her at all if I played my cards right. My whole brain felt light with relief, but Morgan wasn't pleased at all. She'd been looking forward to a nice, relaxing inquisition, I think.

'My' knight was probably about twenty-five, and judging by the raw scar that bisected his face from his right eyebrow to the jaw-line, a battle-hardened soldier. He leapt athletically onto the dais, took my hand and bowed over it, all very courtly. He introduced himself as Gareth of Ynys Môn, which didn't ring any bells, so obviously he was one of the less famous Knights of the Round Table. I mean, everyone's heard of Lancelot and Galahad and Pellinore and that lot, but I didn't remember any tales about any Gareth of Ynys Môn. Morgan le Fay's knight, on the other hand, looked worried stiff having to sit next to the scary lady. He went as yellow as custard when Arthur called him, and tripped over the edge of the dais climbing up, poor chap.

'Your name, My Lady?' Gareth asked, still hanging on to my hand.

'Tanith,' I said sweetly, and yanked it back.

Then Arthur and Gwenhwyfar sat, and at last we could all relax and eat. Well, eat, anyway. Now I didn't have to worry about verbal jousting with Morgan le Fay, I was starving again!

Small boys with large, steaming platters and jugs scattered throughout the Great Hall, and people helped themselves to meat, using their knives and fingers to eat with. I noticed that some of the men wiped their fingers on their clothes, or on the hairy backs of lurking hounds (yuk). The ladies seemed to favour a delicate lick from time to time to keep their fingers clean – but one man on a table at right angles to the dais offered his fingers to be licked by a large hound puppy under the table, before sticking them in the communal dish. Most people tossed their chewed bones over their shoulders to the dogs – but some people tossed them back in the bowl!

The food was spicy and flavoursome. The roast pork smelled gorgeous, the crackling golden and crisp. I ate chicken in a fruity sauce, beef and a couple of other meat dishes I couldn't quite identify. There was a huge pike, stuffed with smaller fish, and a roasted swan with its feathers stuck back into it, poor thing. I just ate (but not swan) and hoped for the best. There were big, creamy syllabubs for pudding, and various pies and stuff, and candied fruits, and cheese and nuts, and by the time I'd waded through that lot, I was feeling fairly comfortable inside. So comfortable I was beginning to wish I hadn't magicked the laces of my dress quite so tight!

The small boys cleared the platters away, the tables set

up on trestles on the hall floor were stripped and taken away and the benches were pushed back against the tapestried walls. It was time for entertainment.

I glanced down the table in Medrawd's direction. He was whispering behind his hand to a manservant, who was bending over him in order to hear. Then the man slipped through the curtains at the side of the Hall and disappeared. I wondered what that was about – Medrawd probably up to no good, I thought, but then the entertainment got under way and I forgot about it.

There were some pretty good jugglers – they chucked blazing torches to each other, which was spectacular, then some tumblers did some fairly standard flip-flops and cartwheels and stuff, and finished off with a pyramid of people with a nervous and wobbly small boy on top. A bard warbled a couple of tunes from the Camelot Top Ten, and then the highlight of the evening – a travelling Mage.

I felt sorry for the poor man immediately. He was good – but not good enough, unfortunately, when, unknown to him, his audience included Morgan le Fay! He did some simple conjuring – coins out of people's ears, flash-bangs in the fire, long trails of coloured ribbon from his mouth, and a kicking rabbit out of a hat. Halfway through his performance I risked a sideways glance at Morgan le Fay. Her eyes were half-closed, and her expression was extreme boredom. Boredom, that is, with a good dollop of malice . . .

Suddenly, she looked up and caught my eye. She smiled, mockingly, and raised an eyebrow, then pointedly shifted her gaze to the unfortunate Mage. Unfortunate because I knew, even if he didn't, that something unpleasant was about to happen to him. The poor man was in the middle of some complicated and rather amateurish business with a piece of string and a silvery hoop, his wide sleeves flapping, the tawdry spangled stars on his food-stained black robe glinting in the torchlight.

Morgan showed him magic. Suddenly, the hem of his spangly robe began to smoulder at the back. He didn't notice, although a lot of people in the body of the Hall did, and nudged each other, grinning. The cloth caught and flared, flames shot up and he began running in circles, beating frantically at his blazing robe. All his audience collapsed in shrieks of laughter, until someone fetched a bucket of water to chuck over him to put him out. He was bedraggled and embarrassed and unhappy, and I felt very sorry for him. He just stood and dripped, opening and shutting his mouth helplessly.

I felt so sorry for him that I almost took pity, and was about to magic up an easy spell which would allow him to escape with some shreds of dignity left. I almost did – but I felt Morgan's eyes on me and suddenly realised that this was a trap: she'd set fire to him deliberately to see if I'd react.

And I so very nearly had. She suspected.

So the poor Mage's dignity had to suffer, I'm afraid.

I sat back, angry with myself for almost being so careless. Gareth, beside me, was hysterical with laughter, and I was on the verge of saying something sharp to him to shut him up when, faintly at the back of my mind, I heard *Help me, Lady! Help!*

9

I shoved back my heavy chair and leapt to my feet. Gareth got up too, wiping tears of laughter from his eyes.

'*Beth sy'n bod,* My Lady?'

'Nothing, Sir Gareth. There's nothing the matter. I mean, yes, there is. Something's wrong – oh, please excuse me. I feel –' I deliberately didn't say *what* I was feeling. All I knew was Blaidd was in trouble.

It was terribly bad manners to leave the Great Hall before Arthur and Gwenhwyfar did, but it couldn't be helped. I clapped my napkin over my mouth as if I was going to throw up, galloped through the Hall, feeling hundreds of eyes on me, and took the stairs to my chamber two at a time, pounding round and round and up and up until I was dizzy and breathless.

The door was wide open, and I paused on the threshhold, horrified. Everywhere were signs of a desperate struggle, furniture overturned, the coverings ripped off the bed and the bed-hangings dragged from their hooks. The tray of food the serving girl had brought was scattered on the floor, the meat gone, the bread left, the pieces soaking up the liquid from the smashed pottery beaker. But no Blaidd. I shot through into the small ante-room. He wasn't there, either.

I stood in the middle of the room, clamped down hard on my fear, closed my eyes and sent out thought-waves: *Blaidd? Where are you, Blaidd?*

The silence in my head was almost deafening. I tried again. *Blaidd? Answer me, Blaidd. Can you hear me? Blaidd?*

But there was no reply. I sat on the edge of the ruined bed, tried to think. Tried not to panic. Where could he be? From the state of the room he hadn't gone anywhere voluntarily. He'd fought like a terrified wild thing. But who would want to kidnap a harmless boy? No-one knew what he really was except me. So why would anyone take him away? Could it be someone trying to get at me? To force me to reveal myself as a witch?

After what happened to the Mage, I had a feeling that Morgan le Fay at least suspected, even if she didn't know – and if Morgan le Fay knew, presumably Medrawd would, too. Which brought me back to my original question: who would want to kidnap a harmless boy? And why? The answer had to be in Blaidd himself. And yet – Blaidd was only a shapeshifted half-grown wolf, and in his current shape, more or less harmless.

I was the only person aware that he wasn't what he seemed to be. Blaidd might look like a normal teenage boy – but he wasn't. And anyone who had seen him attack the Irish wolfhound that afternoon knew he was totally unafraid. He'd thrown himself into the fight – but who would kidnap him just because of that? Then, into my mind flashed a memory of a serving man, his hand on the dagger at his belt, bending over Medrawd at the supper table.

Medrawd had seen Blaidd lose his temper: in fact, Medrawd had provoked the outburst in the first place. The wolfhound may have snarled at Blaidd, but Medrawd had unleashed the hound; Medrawd had encouraged dog and boy to fight to the death.

Medrawd. But why? I couldn't begin to guess. Why would he want Blaidd? Did Medrawd think he was a threat or something? Or was it me? But he couldn't know who I was, surely? No. Some other reason. But what? I put my head in my hands and tried again. *Blaidd? Answer me, Blaidd, if you can hear me!*

Nothing.

Someone rapped at the door: Gareth of Ynys Môn hovered in the doorway.

'Are you ill, Lady Tanith? Gwenhwyfar sent me to find you: she's worried about you.'

I shook my head, and tried to smile. 'No. I'm fine, thank you. I just felt –' I left the sentence unfinished because I didn't want to lie.

Then Gareth noticed the state the room was in. 'What happened?' he asked.

'Ask me another, Gareth, I don't know. When I came upstairs I found my chamber like this.'

'Who did it? Has anything been stolen?'

'Nothing – except Blaidd.'

'*Blaidd*?' he looked mystified. 'There was a wolf in here?'

'No. Blaidd's a boy. He's my – um, manservant. He wasn't feeling well, so I had some food brought up for him. I left him here to rest while I came down to supper. When I got upstairs, he was gone.' I gestured around the wrecked room. 'And this is the result.'

I started to sniffle instead. I just felt a big fat failure. I'd let poor Blaidd get captured, and all because I –

Go on, Tanith. Admit it, my mind said sternly. *Because you ran out on Gwydion like a spoiled brat.*

I wasn't taking that from anyone's conscience, let alone my own. *Well, he didn't ask me, did he? He took me for granted, didn't he? Who does he think he is?*

69

Dragonking of Ynys Haf, that's who. And just because he didn't do the mushy bit, you go storming off in a huff and that poor wolf followed you through the door and now look what you've done, you idiot!

OK, maybe I'd let my conscience win this time. Now I had guilt. The sniffles got wetter.

Gareth came and sat beside me on the bed, took my hand and patted it.

'Don't cry, Tanith. Dry your eyes and think. Does the boy have any enemies?' he asked, gently.

He was right, of course. Snivelling and feeling sorry for myself wouldn't help Blaidd one bit. I wiped my nose on my sleeve. 'Only one.'

'Who?'

'I can't be sure, but I think – Medrawd?'

'That wouldn't surprise me – I find him hard to love, Arthur's nephew or not. But why would he go to the trouble of abducting your manservant?'

I shrugged. 'I don't know, except – well, this afternoon, I was with Gwenhwyfar in the garden, and I left Blaidd by the gate because she wanted to talk, and Medrawd came along with his wolfhound, and the hound insulted Blaidd –'

Gareth stared. 'I beg your pardon? Say that again – the *wolfhound* insulted your manservant?'

Oh, jam and butter it. Me and my big mouth. Well, it was said, now. 'Yes.' I didn't go into explanations, despite the baffled look I got. 'And then Blaidd lost his temper and insulted the hound right back. Medrawd let the hound go and the first I knew of it was when I heard them snarling at each other. I ran back to the gate and they were trying to rip each other's throats out. I managed to stop it, luckily before either of them was badly hurt.'

Gareth gave me a long, assessing look. It said, *Mustn't mock the afflicted*. And then I saw his expression change as his brain supplied the alternative. *But if you aren't an apple short of a pie, then you must be a –*

A wi –. Gareth put my hand carefully back into my own lap, as if it might possibly turn into a live snake.

I sighed. I had to trust somebody. 'I know what you're thinking, Gareth, so I'd rather you didn't actually say it, all right? Let's let it lie. Just content yourself that you're probably right.'

He swallowed, and his Adam's apple bobbed nervously. 'I know what you are, Lady, and I swear that none shall know of it but me.'

He gave me his word, in English and in Welsh, as a Knight of the Round Table. 'Well, Lady, if you're a – a –'

'A one of them?'

'Yes. A one-of-them.'

'Mmhm?'

'Then *Blaidd* is –?'

'Blaidd is – or was – a wolf. A young one, and a not very bright one. If Medrawd's got him, I don't know what I can do to get him back. I can't even hear him any more.'

Wherever he was, I should have been able to 'hear' his thoughts if he directed them at me.

Unless, of course, he wasn't in a fit state to hear anything. No. He couldn't possibly be dead. Why would anyone kidnap him and then kill him? If he were unconscious, though, I couldn't hear him, and he couldn't hear me, could he? 'Perhaps,' I said slowly, 'I can't hear him because he's unconscious.'

'If that's so, Lady, then sooner or later he will be

conscious again, and then you will hear him, won't you? And then –'

'Then I can go and get him.'

'*We* can go and get him, Lady.' Gareth smiled. Despite the angry scar bisecting his face, he was handsome, and he did have such a kind look. Maybe I had a friend here besides the Queen. I suspected that she, if push came to shove, wouldn't be much help in a crisis, mainly because the centre of Gwenhwyfar's world was Gwenhwyfar, and everyone else merely a minor satellite orbiting around Planet Gwen.

'Thank you, Gareth.' I meant it, too.

He stood up. 'I doubt we can do much more tonight, Lady, especially if Medrawd has the boy. I mean the wolf. There is no love lost between Medrawd and me.' He stroked the scar that marred his face.

'But,' he continued, 'on the morrow, perhaps . . .'

On the morrow! What had Gwenhwyfar said about tomorrow? A tournament in Medrawd's honour. Well, if Medrawd was busy at the tournament, then Medrawd shouldn't be too bothered with Blaidd, should he? Assuming that it definitely was Medrawd who had him. The more I thought about it, the more I thought it must have been. I mean, who else?

I said goodnight to Gareth, closed and barred the chamber door, and set about picking up the overturned chairs and stools, and remaking the bed. I gave up on rehanging the bed curtains – that was a job for an expert. They were full of dust and made me sneeze anyway. Eventually, tired, lonely and unhappy, I climbed into bed. I needed to get a good night's sleep, but the chances of that were fairly low. My conscience was nagging away like toothache. It was all my fault, after all. I'd started it all, hadn't I, by walking out on Gwydion in a huff. It hadn't been my fault that Blaidd had followed me, and it hadn't been my fault that the Time Door had misfunctioned and vanished. But if I'd been concentrating on Where and When I was going, instead of whingeing away in my head about nobody understanding me, and not being asked and feeling hurt and all that, none of this would have happened, would it?

A guilty conscience is a lousy sleeping pill!

10

I fell asleep at last, but not for hours, and waking up the next morning was not a lot of fun. I hadn't drunk much of the mead that had been passed round the tables, but all the same my head ached. A loud rapping on the door finally got my eyes open, and I struggled to sit up.

A serving girl came in with a loaded tray of food, followed by another bearing a large bowl and a ewer of hot water for washing. The girl with the food gave me a beaming, gap-toothed smile as she dumped the tray on my bed, but the other kept her head lowered as she placed the dark metal bowl on a nearby table and poured the steaming water into it. She scuttled out of the room, clutching the empty ewer without even glancing in my direction.

When I looked at the food on the tray, my stomach lurched – fatty cold roast pork was not what I needed right then! So, since I was alone, I did a tiny bit of magic and served myself some buttered toast and marmalade. I'd just finished the last slice when the door flew open and Gwenhwyfar trotted excitedly in.

'Aren't you up yet, Tanith? Come on, hurry up, won't you? It's a lovely day outside, even though it's only May. Oh, it's going to be so exciting! I can't wait to put my new dress on!' She was bouncing with delight. 'Do you think anyone will be killed?'

Yes, I thought, grumpily, *you, if you don't shut up and let me wake up in my own time.* I'm not a morning person, especially when I've got a Class A hangover and I haven't even been drinking to earn it.

She rattled on regardless. 'There will be knights from all over the Kingdom: Arthur said there are even some from the Out Isles – and one has come all the way from France, too! Of course, it would be better if they were coming here to honour me, and not Medrawd, but I suppose it is *his* birthday. I know it's an awful thing to say about Arthur's nephew, but Medrawd isn't a nice person, and he's really, really horrible to me.'

There were times when she reminded me of my big sister, Heledd, in her teens, loudly rebelling against Mam and Dad for all she was worth. 'I expect he's just as horrible to everyone, Gwenhwyfar,' I said, clambering out of bed. 'I wouldn't take it personally. He's a horrible sort of person.'

'No, he's *extra specially* horrible to me. He's sarcastic, and he says things that I think are compliments until I think about what he's said, and then I realise he's really insulting me. Don't you think that's unkind?'

'Yes,' I said, taking the line of least resistance.

'You have to hurry,' she prattled on. 'The tourney begins in an hour and you aren't even dressed yet. Goodness, you aren't even out of bed, are you? I have to hurry back and put on my gown. It's special: Arthur had it made for me from cloth of silver, and I shall shine like the stars and dazzle everyone. I shall look more beautiful than anyone else,' she babbled smugly. 'I'll certainly look better than Morgan. She always wears red, anyway, with that silly insignia of hers, that silly jumbly-M mark. Mind you,' she giggled, suddenly. 'That always really puts old Merlin's back up – it's so like the insignia he makes his servants wear, when he's here.'

Something clicked into place in my brain, but it was

too early in the morning to follow the click and make it a conscious thought. 'Look, Gwenhwyfar,' I muttered. 'If I'm going to be ready for the tournament, I'd better start getting dressed. I'll see you there, shall I?'

'No! I'll wait for you. I'll help you dress. You're my best friend, aren't you? It will be fun.'

Not for me it wouldn't. I do not like to talk in the mornings, all right? In fact, I don't *do* mornings. That clear? No. Unfortunately it wasn't.

'What shall you wear?' She darted into the garderobe and rummaged through the gowns hanging on the pegs hammered into the wall. I was glad I'd had the forethought to conjure up some clothes the night before: suppose she hadn't found anything there? That would have made even a complete airhead like Gwenhwyfar wonder.

'I like the white silk brocade one best,' she called, 'but I think it needs a touch of colour. It will set off my beautiful silver one nicely, but it won't look better than mine, of course. I have a headdress that will go perfectly with it. I'll go and fetch it.'

I could have magicked up any headdress I wanted, but I didn't. I just made the most of her absence and climbed out of bed.

The water the girl had poured into the bowl was cooling rapidly. Best I washed before it got completely cold. I took off my nightgown, dropped it on the floor, and bent over the bowl. The water was still, and the darkness of the bowl gave it the appearance of a mirror. I raised my hands to plunge them into the water, and then stopped. There was an image reflected in the still water – but it wasn't mine!

76

Somebody was scrying me. Or trying to. Someone had arranged for that water to be sent, and for the special dark bowl to contain it. I had, fortunately for me, switched off my aura, which meant that I could see out, but they couldn't see in. Except I'd already used a bit of magic that morning, hadn't I, to magic up my toast. I hoped that hadn't made a chink in my magical armour. I peered hard into the bowl, but the face was hidden by hair that had fallen forward. Dark hair. She drew back, frustrated, and shoved the hair from her face.

Morgan le Fay.

I was right. Morgan was suspicious about me, and so she was checking up on me. But thank goodness, it appeared she couldn't see me! The switched-off aura was holding. Otherwise, she'd have been able to see exactly what I was doing, whenever she wanted. I hastily increased the aura-blocking force field around me, to make up for the illicit toast, and glared at the woman's reflected, angry face. How dared she?

Ha! I thought. *You think you're so smart! Well, I'm a match for you anyday, you, you* – I was having trouble thinking of something bad enough to call her. I plunged my hands into the water, destroying the image, and washed myself. Then I slung the water down the garderobe, and put the bowl outside the door. I didn't want *that* around any longer, that was for sure! The bowl's outer surface was decorated with what looked like small, evil-looking imps, and the ornamental border depicted deadly nightshade in bas relief!

Gwenhwyfar scampered back in, bearing two tall, pointy headdresses with trails of light fabric sprouting from the top like filmy yacht sails.

'There's a lovely red one,' she said, waving it at me, 'or there's this pretty blue one. Which do you want? I like the red one, but Morgan will be wearing red, she always does, and besides, well, with your hair –'

– which ISN'T red, it's auburn. 'The blue one,' I snapped, 'will do fine.' I clambered into the white silk, and struggled to do up the fastenings at the back.

'Oh, for goodness sake turn round,' Gwenhwyfar said, darting round behind me to do up the laces. 'Breathe in, will you! More than that! Really suck in your breath! Your waist is huge, isn't it! I must ask the seamstress to make you a stronger corset!'

'No you blooming well won't!' I retorted. 'I'm only a size ten! I'm not big, I'm normal. You're just a lot smaller and skinnier than me.' *And very, very young,* my mind said. She was, she really was, too young to be married, especially to a man of Arthur's age, even if he was a nice, kind, good, thoughtful man. And with what I knew about his and Gwenhwyfar's future, he was going to need all the goodness and thoughtfulness he could call upon. Poor Arthur. Poor little Gwenhwyfar. It's a definite drawback, having a sort of hindsight about the future! I wondered how Merlin stood it, sometimes, but then remembered that Merlin isn't human: he's elemental, and has about as much sensitivity as –

As someone who could come down to breakfast and say, 'It's time you got married,' just like that, and expect everyone to be delighted and just carry on and rush to the altar. Ha!

I shook myself. No time to brood on that right now. I had to find Blaidd. I blanked out Gwenhywfar's chatter, and sent out a thought: *Blaidd? Can you hear me? Blaidd?*

Nothing.

Blaidd? Blaidd?

And then there it was. A tiny, almost inaudible sound, half-whimper, half-groan. *Lady?*

Blaidd? I sent again, *Blaidd? Where are you?* But this time there was no reply.

'Tanith? I said, are you all right?' Gwenhwyfar's voice broke in. 'I was so worried when you rushed away from the table last night. I hope you aren't going to be ill today. That would spoil everything. Well, it would for you. I expect I should enjoy myself anyway.'

Thanks a bunch, Gwenny, for your concern. Obviously the Florence Nightingale mood had worn off. 'I'm fine, thank you. I just felt strange for a moment. I'll be all right, don't worry.'

'But I dooo! That was why I sent Sir Gareth after you last night. He's very handsome, isn't he? Although that scar is rather ugly.' She opened her eyes wide and shuddered. 'Medrawd did that to him, you know. They were practising in the tiltyard, and Gareth was using a blunted weapon, the way they always should, but Medrawd cheated and used a sharp one. Gareth was so handsome before he got that awful scar. Arthur was really furious with Medrawd. He sent him away from court until he was prepared to apologise to Sir Gareth.' She sighed. 'I don't think he ever did, though. He just came back after a week or two, and I expect by then Arthur had forgotten about it. He seems to forgive Medrawd just about anything, and he has so much on his mind, poor dear.'

Of course. But that explained a lot about why Gareth was prepared to help me. If truth be known, it was Morgan le Fay who really worried me. Medrawd was a pain, but as far as I could tell, if he had any magic, it wasn't particularly effective. But Mam Morgan was another cauldron of cocopops altogether.

'There! You look quite pretty,' Gwenhwyfar said, satisfied. 'What are you going to do with your hair?'

'Oh, just brush it,' I said, absentmindedly, and she seized a bone comb and began dragging it painfully through my hair. 'Ow! Thanks, Gwenhwyfar, but I'll do it – you're yanking it out by the roots!'

I combed the sleep-snarls out of my hair – gently – and rammed the headdress on top of it.

'Oh, for goodness sake!' Gwenhwyfar tutted, and adjusted it so that it sat tilted back slightly, the gauzy, trailing fabric flowing over my back. I peered into the murky metal mirror – and caught another quick flash of Morgan. She couldn't see me, anyway. I stuck my tongue out at her, and surveyed my reflection. Not bad.

Once I was dressed to her satisfaction, Gwenhwyfar and I drifted down the stairs, across the inner ward, and out through the castle gates onto the green. It was a gorgeous day. The sun was hot, and I was glad that the wooden grandstand thing had a cloth canopy over it, because the sun would have been shining straight into my eyes, otherwise, and even in a light silk dress I'd probably have roasted.

The field looked like the Millennium Stadium on an International Saturday, only brighter. Instead of the solid phalanx of red jerseys, plus the opposition colours, there were solid blocks of black and silver, red and gold, green and gold, blue and silver, amber and gold, every colour imaginable like an ambulant rainbow. Dotted about were gaily-coloured stripy tents with pennants floating from their centre poles, the gleam of armour, the glint of sunlight on steel, the lush emerald grass, and the brightly caparisoned horses. The air smelled of crushed greenery, horses, perfume, sweat, and the smoke from campfires and outdoor cooking stoves roasting meat on spits, dripping fat into spitting yellow flames. There were tumblers, jugglers, fire-eaters and side-shows. Everyone was busy, especially Ye Olde Pickepocketes, I imagine.

'Isn't it wonderful?' Gwenhywfar sighed. 'Medrawd is so lucky to have a tourney in his honour!'

'Shall we sit down?' I suggested. I wanted to concentrate on trying to raise Blaidd.

'Oh, goodness, Tanith! Where are your manners? You know perfectly well we can't sit down yet!' she said, scandalised. 'We have to wait for Arthur and Medrawd, first! Don't you know anything? Haven't you ever been to court before?'

I shook my head. I hadn't. Only Gwydion's, and that was so laid-back he'd be horrified at the thought of anyone having to stand around waiting for him to sit down or start eating before they could begin. Come to think of it, I couldn't imagine Arthur and Gwenhwyfar squabbling at breakfast over the last bit of toast, or taking a picnic out to the riverbank on a hot afternoon, just the two of them, either. And swimming in the cool, clear water, and drying off in the sun after, and – my eyes prickled. I *missed* my Gwydion.

Suddenly there was a blatt of noise that made my eyes cross. 'Good grief!' I shrieked. 'What *is* that?'

'Oh, Tanith,' she chortled. 'You are funny! That's the court heralds, of course. It means Arthur and Medrawd are coming.'

The terrible squawking continued. If I'd been Arthur, I'd have sacked the lot of them and got a nice harpist in – there wasn't one of them in tune with another out of the twelve of them standing there, red in the face and puffing their cheeks out like bullfrogs. Arthur appeared, tidily dressed in purple velvet (he was going to swelter), leading Medrawd by the hand.

Behind Arthur and Medrawd came Morgan le Fay, and behind Morgan was a familiar face. Who? I knew him from somewhere.

It was the red tabard with the squiggly 'M' on it that placed him for me. It was the leader of the four men who had ambushed Blaidd and me. The ones I'd zapped with thunder and lightning, and left snoring happily in a heap on the grass.

With any luck, he wouldn't remember me. Would he? His eyes drifted towards me, past me – hooray!

And snapped back.

Rats. He remembered.

11

The eyes narrowed in concentration in the dark, handsome face, and he bent forward towards Morgan le Fay, whispering into her ear. Her eyes flicked towards me. Oh, rude words. *Very* rude words. The quicker I got out of here, the happier I'd be. And safer. Gwenhwyfar skipped up the steps to sit beside Arthur, and Morgan and the dark man settled in the row behind the King, Gwenhwyfar and Medrawd. The man hadn't taken his eyes off me.

Morgan stared at me, too. What could he have told her? That he'd been on the point of capturing me and dragging me back to Camelot for their Mistress, I suppose, which was all he actually *knew,* right? But then, of course, there'd been a convenient thunderstorm, hadn't there, and they'd all abruptly gone to sleep for no apparent reason. Then, they woke up, probably with nasty headaches and without prisoners. Nothing out of the ordinary there, then. I wish. How should I know I'd run into him again? I glanced nervously back at the dark man. Although I knew perfectly well that the best thing to do was completely ignore him, pretend he wasn't there – I just had to go and look at him, didn't I? Our eyes collided, and he levelled a gloved forefinger at me, sighting along it.

I gulped and wished I were someWhen else. Got to get out of here, fast as I can. While I still can. 'Blaidd?'

Silence.

'Blaidd. Can you hear me?'

Silence.

'Blaidd. Little wolf. If you can hear, answer me.'

Ladyyy? It was more of a groan than anything.

Suddenly, Gareth was beside me, taking my hand and conducting me to a seat in the grandstand.

'Lady, are you well today?'

'Shhh!' I hissed. 'I'm listening.' I tried again. 'Blaidd?'

Here, Lady.

'Where?'

It's dark, Lady. I can't move. They have blindfolded me, and it is so dark. I have no voice. Help me, Lady!

This was awful: his panic and terror were almost tangible. 'Blaidd, do you know who captured you?'

No, Lady. I tried to fight, but they hurt me. Too many of them, too few of me.

'Was there anything about them that you recognised?' I needed a clue, however small.

He fell suddenly silent in my head, as if thinking.

'What, Blaidd?'

They smelled of dogs, Lady.

'Ah. Can you still smell them, Blaidd?'

On the thing that covers my jaws. It stinks of dog.

'Hang on, Blaidd. I'll try to find you as soon as I can – but first I have to get away from here.'

Which would be goodness knows when, because the tourney was about to start. How could I possibly get out of the wooden stand to look for my lost wolf-boy with so many people around?

'I must leave you soon, Lady,' Gareth whispered, as the arena filled up with tumbling figures – the warm-up act before the home team and the visiting knights started beating up on each other.

'Oh, really? Why?' Not that I cared much – except I

84

might need him to run interference on Morgan and/or Medrawd if they decided to have a go at me.

'I am to take part in the tourney. I have been drawn against a strange knight from the Out Isles. Everyone is talking about him.' He grinned proudly. 'And I am to have the honour of fighting him! Swords, on foot.'

'Swords?' I stared at him. 'Isn't that dangerous?'

He shrugged. 'Not as dangerous as meeting him in battle would be, Lady. At least our swords will be blunted, and the worst either of us can expect from the other is a ding on the helm and a cracking headache tonight.'

'Hmm. Well, be careful, all right?' I didn't want my only ally to get damaged.

'I shall. Lady –' He went bright pink and looked at his knees, fetchingly clad in tights with one purple and one green leg.

'What, Gareth?'

'May I wear your favour pinned upon my sleeve?'

You what? Then I cottoned on – oh, crumbs. He was trying to make me his Lady Fair. Just what I didn't need, a complication like that. But if I turned him down he'd get upset, and I didn't want that, either. I decided the safest course was to simply agree, which meant I had to give him something of mine to wear. 'Oh, all right. If you really insist.'

'I do not insist, Lady Tanith – but I would be honoured.'

'So what do you want?'

'A glove is customary. But you aren't wearing any. Or a kerchief?'

'Sorry. My mam says I've never got a hanky when I need one.' I shrugged. 'What else do you suggest?'

He unpinned the pale blue, flowing veil from the top of my pointy hat. 'May I have this, My Lady?'

'Feel free.'

He handed it to me, and I pinned it onto his sleeve with a sort of brooch he handed me. 'There.' To my twenty-first century eyes it looked right stupid, that drift of pale blue against his leather jerkin, but there you go. This was Camelot.

'I must go and get ready. Shout for me, Lady?'

'Oh, you can count on it,' I assured him, and getting pinker by the minute, he excused himself past half a dozen sets of knees.

I checked up on Gwenhwyfar and Arthur. Neither of them was watching me: they were busy enjoying the performance of a team of acrobats tumbling and leaping around the arena. Medrawd was leaning slightly back next to Arthur, and Morgan le Fay was whispering into her son's ear, her face concealed by his.

This was my chance. I shuffled past the indignant knees again, and got muttered at, but I didn't care.

I scurried down the grandstand steps as fast and as unobtrusively as I could, and slipped behind it into the cool gloom and the smell of crushed grass. 'Blaidd?' I called. 'Blaidd. Can you hear me?'

Yes, Lady. Can you help me now?

'I'm trying to, Blaidd, but I don't know where to begin to look for you. Can you help me? Give me any clue where to find you? Are you in a building, do you think?'

There was silence. Then, *The ground doesn't smell of good earth. Not of stone, either.*

'Is it wood, Blaidd?'

Don't know. Not a tree smell.

'Keep thinking, Blaidd. Keep listening and sniffing. If there's anything you notice, tell me. I'm coming for you. I'm looking. Don't be afraid.'

I'm not afraid, Lady.

But he was. I could tell by the bravado with which he said he wasn't.

It would have been easier if Blaidd's voice in my head had got louder the closer I got to him, but it didn't work like that. I either heard him or I didn't. There was no volume control there or clue towards distance. So, what might have a wooden floor and yet not be in a building? I scratched my head under the pointy hat.

'Blaidd?'

Lady?

'Can you thump your feet on the floor?'

Silence. Then, *Yes, Lady.*

'Did it sound hollow or solid?'

Pause for thought, and possibly another thump. *Solid, Lady.*

Rats. Unlikely to be in the castle, then. The ground floors, as far as I was aware, all had stone flagged floors, and the upper ones would have rung hollow when thumped. So, maybe wooden floors laid on something solid. What? Where?

I stopped behind a purple and orange pavilion and munched my chewing fingernail, trying to think. Wooden floors on something solid. Didn't make sense.

Yes it did. The curtain covering the door of the pavilion swished aside, and I got a glimpse of the interior. Temporary wooden floors: rough planking laid on solid earth. That had to be it! Blaidd was being held captive in a pavilion somewhere. It surely had to be somewhere on the field, had to be. All I had to do was –

– search about fifty thousand pavilions until I came to the right one. Start looking, Tanz! If only I could use my magic to scry him, but I didn't dare. I'd have to drop my guard, and also the shield protecting my magical aura. Morgan le Fay would be on it like a terrier on a rat, and that would be the end for me. I doubted that, even with all my experience, I could win a magical battle against Morgan le Fay, who had centuries of evil and magic behind her. I only had good magic. She had all the dark powers behind her, and she wasn't afraid to use them. She'd swat me the way I'd swat a mozzie. Splat. And to be honest, half of the witch thing is about what's going on in a person's head. I didn't believe I could beat Morgan, and therefore it was unlikely I could. It was a scary feeling, that.

Big sigh. Ah well. Start looking. I plodded to the first stripy tent and peered through the flap. No-one but a skinny squire fast asleep on a sheepskin. On to the next. This one I backed out of in a hurry when a large gentleman wearing only a pair of baggy drawers threw a boot at me for interrupting his armouring process. Nothing daunted, I kept looking. Tent after tent after tent. I was dimly aware of crashing and bashing from the arena, of cheers and shouts and the odd bellow of pain. Occasionally two squires would rush past lugging a stretcher bearing a moaning, swearing, battered knight, but whatever was going on in the way of entertainment didn't concern me at all.

Lady!

'Blaidd?'

Lady, the men have come back! My hind legs are free, Lady! They are making me go with them. I can't see! What will happen! Will they kill me? Fearfearfearfear!

I could almost taste his panic. 'Keep calm, Blaidd. Try to concentrate on what you can hear. What you can feel. What you can smell.'

He calmed slightly. *Yes Lady. I hear you. I'll try. There are shouts, Lady. Grass underfoot. My legs are free. I could run, but I am held too tightly. I can't see!*

'Don't try to run, Blaidd. They will probably hurt you if you do. Go where they are leading you. I'm looking for you. I must be close.'

At least, I hoped I was. But I didn't honestly have a clue. He could have been anywhere on the entire vast field, thronged with busy people. Then, almost without realising it, for some reason I tuned in the voice of the bloke who was doing the introductions on the field. He was bellowing through a megaphone, which gadget I strongly suspected might be down to Merlin on one of his past visits.

'H'AAND NAOW, YOUR RRROYAL HIIIIIGHNESS, QUEEEN GWENHWYFAR, LADEEEZ AN' GENNELMEN! FOR YOURRR H'ENJOYMENT! H'ORGANISED BY LORD MEDRAAAWD HIMSELF, A H'EPIC BATTLE BETWEEEEN MAAAAN AND BEEEEAST!'

Man and beast? What on earth –

'H'AY WIY-ULD WOOOOLF, LADEEZ AN' GENTS, H'UP H'AGAINST A WIY-ULD H'AND SAVAAAAAGE BHOOY!'

Oh, no. One of them had to be Blaidd. The question was, which one?

12

I started shoving my way towards the barriers holding people back from the arena. I had no time to do the ladylike polite bit – I had to get there fast. 'I'm coming, Blaidd, I'm coming!'

Hurry, Lady. It is so loud here . . .

It was loud, it was. It was even hurting my ears. There was a babble of shouts and yells, and loud rattles and clanks from the arena, and shrieks of excitement from the little kids getting under everyone's feet. I shoved and pushed and got sworn at and shouted at, and shoved (and occasionally swore) back, but I persevered and got to the edge of the arena at last. By this time I was across the other side of the field from where I'd begun, by the grandstand, immediately opposite where I was standing now.

Gareth appeared at my elbow, suddenly. 'Did you see me, Lady? I hammered that knight into the ground. He'll have a headache when he wakes up. He'll creep back home to the Out Isles knowing I bested him. Ha!' Gareth had a purple bruise over his right eye, and was grinning from ear to ear with triumph.

'No, Gareth, sorry, I didn't. I was busy looking for Blaidd. I missed it.' I turned my back on him and stared into the arena, where a team of men was erecting something alongside a large square-shaped object, covered with a cloth, with a set of four wooden wheels sticking out of the bottom of it. What was going on?

And then I saw Blaidd, struggling frantically, being dragged along between two men, big, burly blokes that could have shifted King Kong, no problem, without expending too much energy. Blaidd didn't stand a chance.

Circumstances didn't improve. I suddenly realised what the team of men had been organising.

Square in the centre of the field they had erected a huge iron cage. The men dragged Blaidd into it, cut his bonds with a knife and whipped off the cloth covering his face. Then they got out of the cage in a hurry. Blaidd in a cage: he'd be mad with terror – and fury. And then, from the edge of the field, a second cage was pushed towards the larger one containing Blaidd. When the two cages were side by side, the cover was whipped off. Furiously pacing inside, claws clicking on the wooden floor, snarling at the men surrounding it (who were careful to keep out of reach of the scimitar teeth) was an exceptionally large full-grown wolf.

Blaidd would have had difficulty defeating it even if he'd been in his own shape. This was, without doubt, a wild alpha male, probably a pack leader, that would have Blaidd for breakfast without any problem at all. Blaidd's young wolf instinct wouldn't have been to attempt to fight. He would have instantly submitted, no questions asked. He would have rolled on his back with his four paws in the air, tongue lolling, fast-talking in Wolf to save his life.

But thanks to me, stupid, thoughtless me, he was in human form, although he would still be thinking like a wolf. He might still roll on his back, instinctively, but it wouldn't save him this time. And rolling on his back with his paws in the air wouldn't impress this wolf. It would see defenceless human, not wolf in human shape.

My own immediate instinct was to shapeshift him back to wolf, quick, regardless of the consequences – except that Medrawd had carefully organised an iron cage, hadn't he? Because, being magical, I couldn't get past the iron bars, could I? Any spell I threw would fall harmlessly to the ground outside the cage. I was, in short, totally scuppered. And Blaidd was on his own.

The smaller cage was shoved close to the larger one, and a grille was lifted on the big cage. And then a second grille, on the smaller cage clanked upward. The huge beast paused, considering, reluctant to go forward – but a spear jabbed into the shaggy hindquarters produced a ferocious snarl. The wolf swung round and there was a loud clashing noise as his teeth collided with iron bars. I felt so sorry for them both – one way or another, both creatures would surely die.

And then the alpha male was being forced through into the other cage, his eyes fixed unblinkingly on Blaidd, who was standing in the middle, squinting in the brightness, half-blind after being kept in the dark with his eyes covered. The wolf lowered his head, stopped, sniffed the air. Advanced a step towards Blaidd.

I couldn't bear to look. Arthur and Gwenhwyfar were both on their feet, and Arthur was waving his arms, and apparently shouting, although at this distance I couldn't hear him. Medrawd, beside him, shrugged, and gestured towards the cage. I couldn't hear what was being said, but it looked as if Arthur wasn't happy with the entertainment his nephew had provided. Dear Medrawd was probably reminding his uncle that it was *his* birthday after all, and Birthday Boys get what they want.

Arthur was my only chance – Blaidd's only chance. I couldn't shapeshift him, which is the only thing that would have given Blaidd even the slightest chance. The wolf lowered his head more, growling, edging closer.

I took the quickest way – straight across the field to the

grandstand. As I hurtled past the cage, my skirts clutched high above my knees, my stupid pointy hat falling off my stupid pointy head, I caused shouts of laughter, and didn't care. I'm not big and strong – but I can run when I have to, and cowardice is one thing that gets my legs going like an Olympic athlete's. I shot across the field like an arrow out of a bow, sending out to Blaidd on the way. 'Try and stay away from the wolf if you can! Remember you can climb, and he can't . . .'

But wolves could jump, couldn't they? And this one would probably be very, very tall if it reared up on its hind legs. It would have no trouble reaching Blaidd anywhere within the cage.

It's all –

'It isn't all over, Blaidd! Not until the fat lady sings.'

I – fat lady? What –

Red-faced and sweaty, I reached the foot of the stand. I snatched the megaphone from the surprised announcer and bellowed into it.

'Your Grace!' I screamed at Arthur. 'This is not a contest for men of honour to witness. It is a disgrace to the Knights of the Round Table. I beg you, Your Grace, stop it before the boy is killed.'

Arthur looked down at me, and shrugged, as if to say, *well, it's Medrawd's treat, what can I do?*

Good King Arthur, behaving like a wimpish jobsworth? Well, I wasn't having any of that. I shoved people aside and hammered up the steps to the royal box – or at least, the posh seats they were sitting in. Gwenhwyfar was watching me with her mouth open.

'Your Grace,' I gasped, my heart bashing against my ribs. 'Please, Your Grace – the boy is my manservant, and he is, he is – half-witted, that's what he is. It's a horrible, unjust, cruel thing Medrawd is doing.'

'The boy is being punished,' Medrawd drawled, still seated, his arms laid casually along the back-rest of the bench.

'What for?' I snapped. 'Upsetting you? Big deal.'

'The boy damaged my wolfhound. The brute cost me a small fortune a month ago, and your boy attacked him. It will be weeks before he can hunt again.'

'And because a boy bit your dog, you've shoved him in a cage with a wild animal? Your Grace, this isn't fair!' I protested.

'It does seem a little excessive,' Arthur said.

'A little excessive, Your Grace? It's murder!'

'It's my birthday,' Medrawd said, like a petulant child. 'You said I could have a tourney in my honour, Uncle. Well, this is what I want to finish it off. It's been boring until now. This will be amusing. And it's what I want.' I swear, he even stuck his bottom lip out.

'*Amusing*? Killing an innocent boy? And it was you that set your wolfhound on him, anyway. Blaidd just defended himself. I hope you can live with yourself, Medrawd!' I snapped.

Medrawd spread his hands in a 'who, me?' gesture. He sneered. 'There's no blood on my hands, *My Lady*.'

I didn't like the way he said that.

'Oh,' Arthur murmured suddenly, looking past me. 'I wouldn't worry too much, Lady Tanith.'

'What?' I shrieked. 'Not worry? Are you nuts? I'm responsible for that boy! Any minute now he's going to be ripped to shreds by a wolf, and you say I shouldn't worry? What kind of king are you anyway, Arthur?'

That got his attention. 'I am *your* King, My Lady, and you would do well to remember it.'

I was past caring. 'Don't you threaten me! You're not my King! My King is – well, never mind. But if you let Medrawd get away with this –'

'Get away with what?' Arthur said mildly. He was grinning. 'If you turn and look, Lady, you will see that your fears are –'

I turned, expecting to see Blaidd in small pieces and the wolf licking his chops. But the fight wasn't over yet. The two of them were rolling on the floor of the cage. Blaidd had his arms and legs locked round the big wolf's body; they were face to muzzle, and Blaidd was – licking the wolf's hairy face. Licking it.

And simultaneously getting his own face comprehensively washed by a large wet tongue. They were rolling together like puppies.

I closed my mouth, turned my back on the royal bods, tottered down the stairs and back to the field. I plodded across to the cage and peered through the bars – from a safe distance – I keep as far away from iron as I can, let alone ravening wolves.

'Blaidd?'

He removed his nose from the attentions of the wolf's slobbery tongue and turned his head towards me. Blaidd had a grin from ear to ear, and the wolf was whining in delight, his tail going like a metronome.

Lady?

'What's going on, Blaidd?'

It's my brother, Lady! My lair-brother. We have not met since he left the lair when I was born.

That accounted for the difference in sizes then – Blaidd

was half-grown when he was in his natural shape – this wolf was fully grown, magnificent.

'How did he know –'

That I am Wolf and not human? You changed my shape, Lady, but you cannot change my smell. And I still speak Wolf. He knew me as soon as he got my scent. As soon as he set eyes on me, and I talked to him, he knew me.

Phew. Now all I had to do was get Blaidd – and his big brother – out of the cage and away from here. That wouldn't be quite so easy, since I seemed to recall I'd just been extremely rude to Arthur, High King of Brython. Maybe a teensy weensy apology might be called for. I needed to get on Arthur's good side, if only to prevent Medrawd thinking up some other way to get at me through Blaidd. I didn't think for a minute that it was Blaidd he was after – or that he'd give up easily.

'I'll get you both out if I can, Blaidd,' I reassured him, but he was back licking his brother's nose. The crowd was going wild at the sight of the wolf and boy bonding! They didn't seem at all upset by the lack of bloodshed, which said rather more for the pleasant peasants than it did for Medrawd and his lot.

I plodded back across the field, trying to look dignified despite my crimson face, the rivulets of perspiration trickling down my back and my pointy hat dangling from its string. I grabbed the hat, broke the string and carried it the rest of the way tucked under my arm. If all else failed, maybe I could use it as a weapon and poke Medrawd in the eye with it.

Conscious of every single eye in the stand fixed on me as I climbed the steps for the second time, I got pinker and hotter and more uncomfortable with every step. I finally reached Arthur and Gwenhwyfar, and pasted a sheepish grin on my face. 'I –'

'That boy has such a way with animals!' Arthur said excitedly. 'I would have him in my service, Lady Tanith, if you will release him from your own. I have in my menagerie beasts that will not eat, whatever we give them, and pine and die – wildcats, bears, wolves – and if the boy cares for them, bonds with them as he has with the wild wolf, they will surely settle. Their sad condition makes me unhappy.'

Not as unhappy as it made the poor beasts. The best thing for the inhabitants of Arthur's menagerie was a swift return to the wild, but this wasn't the time or the place to suggest it. Arthur had given me a chance to get Blaidd out of the cage and into safety, so I grabbed it with both hands.

'Your Grace, if you want Blaidd in your service, I shall be honoured.' I had my fingers crossed inside the pointy hat at this point. I'd leave him for a while. A very short while. In the long run, Blaidd wasn't going anywhere except safely back to Ynys Haf.

'Good. You may choose a manservant from my retinue in his place.'

'Thanks, but I don't want a manservant,' I said. 'There's something else I'd like instead, though.'

The King raised an eyebrow. OK, so I was being a bit cheeky, considering I'd just insulted him.

'And that is?' he asked.

I glanced at Medrawd, who was sulking fit to bust. Good, Medrawd. Go boil your nasty little head. 'I would like the wolf set free.'

Medrawd shot to his feet in protest. 'Uncle –'

'No. That I can't allow, I'm afraid. It is a wild animal, and dangerous. I should have it killed for safety's sake, but if you don't wish it to be slaughtered, I shall keep it in my menagerie instead.'

OK. I'd settle for that for the time being. I'd get them both out – and back to Ynys Haf as soon as I could. It was a mystery how the wolf had got here in the first place – if he was Blaidd's brother, then he should be safely in Ynys Haf, too.

I bobbed a polite little curtsey. 'Thanks, Your Grace.'

Arthur issued orders. 'Drive the wolf back into the small cage and take it to the menagerie. Release the boy and send him with the wolf to settle him down.'

'Can I speak to the boy, Your Grace?' I asked quickly. 'He won't know what's happening. He might panic – and pass his fear on to the wolf.' I didn't want either of them harmed, accidentally or otherwise. I wanted to be there when they were moved.

Arthur gave a dismissive sort of wave and I took that as a cue to scuttle down the steps and back out onto the field again. Gareth fell into step beside me.

'Lady, you took a risk that many knights would not dare. Medrawd is not a man to cross. I beg you, take care. He will certainly have his revenge.'

'Oh, I shall, don't worry,' I muttered. *And,* I thought, *I'll find some way of getting my own back on that weaselly little rodent if it's the last thing I do.*

I reached the cage just in time. The two brawny men who had held Blaidd captive were about to jab the wolf with the business end of their spears to drive him back into the smaller cage.

'Stop that at once!' I commanded, and rather to my surprise, they did. 'The boy is now the King's servant. The wolf is the King's, too, for his menagerie. His Grace will not want either of them harmed. Let the boy persuade the wolf back into the cage.'

Reluctantly, they stood back.

'Blaidd, listen to me.'

Blaidd stood fearfully in the middle of the cage, one hand clutching the thick fur on the back of his brother's neck. The wolf was above waist high on him, and its tilted amber eyes were watchful.

I hear you, Lady.

'Blaidd, the King wants you to work for him, with his animals. I have persuaded him to take your brother, too. He will be put in a cage, but I promise you I'll get him – and you – out of there as quickly as I can. You can take care of him. And you might be able to help some of the other poor creatures in the menagerie.'

Blaidd's eyes were on me. *I hear you, Lady. I trust you. I shall do as you say.*

The wolf at his side tensed, rose to his feet and let out a low snarl. Blaidd made a rumbling noise in his throat, and the wolf subsided.

He knows that we can trust you, Lady.

I looked straight into the amber eyes and thought, *You are a creature of Ynys Haf. I shall not fail you.* Unblinking, the massive beast stared back.

I am yours, Lady.

And then the massive shape of the wolf slunk into the cage, and Blaidd went with him, to be trundled across the field towards Camelot, and the menagerie.

13

Back in my chamber, Gwenhwyfar was poking into presses and cupboards, having a good old snoop. Cheek! Luckily I didn't have anything much in there – just underwear and stuff I'd magicked up to keep me going while I was here. Fortunately, I'd taken the safe route and opted for olden-days-type underpinnings – can you imagine what Gwenhwyfar would have made of an underwired bra and lacy knickers? A serving girl – the same quiet one that had brought the water in the dark scrying-bowl that morning – was up on a stool rehanging the torn down bed-curtains.

'Tanith, what on earth possessed you to cross Medrawd like that?' she squeaked. 'Don't you know how dangerous he is? He has more power than you can begin to imagine.' She whispered, conspiratorially. 'Some people say he's a wizard. But I don't think so. I think he's just horrible. But his mother – well, she's definitely a witch, although no-one ever says so. One at a time they are bad enough, but together . . .' She shuddered.

'I know exactly how powerful they are,' I said, sourly. 'And believe me, I shall get my own back on Medrawd for what he did to poor Blaidd. I'm not afraid of him.' I wasn't, either. But Morgan le Fay . . .

'Oh, yes. Poor Blaidd. But he's only a manservant, and well, yes, I suppose it was a *bit* naughty, but –'

'A *bit naughty?*' I exploded. 'He had Blaidd kidnapped, dragged from my room, tied up for a whole night all by himself so that he was terrified, and then he tried to feed him to a wolf! *A bit naughty*?' What planet was this girl on?

'Well, if you put it like that.' She pulled a face and hugged herself. 'But it was ever so exciting, wasn't it? The wolf could have torn the boy limb from limb. It would have been ever so exciting!'

She had sort of a weird outlook on life, this girl. But then, I suppose this was the Dark Ages – and I couldn't expect her to be terrifically enlightened towards what she saw as unimportant people like Blaidd and her servants. She was a product of her Time, the same way that I am, I suppose. I kept trying to feel sympathetic towards Gwenhwyfar – when you know what's going to happen to a person in the future, it tends to colour the way you treat them – but there were times when it was hard.

'I don't think Blaidd found it ever so exciting,' I said sourly.

She pouted. 'Well, I did. And he wasn't eaten in the end, was he? So no harm done.'

'No thanks to Medrawd.'

'He's still really furious, you know,' she added, giving a twirl in front of my metal mirror and simpering at her reflection.

'I can cope with that,' I muttered.

'Good. Because I wouldn't like anything to happen to you. Since you came, I've stopped being bored, so that's really excellent, isn't it?'

Oh, ever-so-jolly-good.

The serving girl who was re-hanging the bed curtains jumped off her stool, picked it up, and scuttled out of the room without even glancing in our direction – or making a curtsey towards her Queen, who luckily didn't notice.

Gwenhwyfar stopped pirouetting and started primping her hair. 'Anyway, what are you going to wear to supper?'

'Not a clue,' I said, barely hearing her. Something had registered as not right, but I wasn't quite sure what. Something out of place? I needed to have a bit of a think and a look round. But first I had to get rid of Gwenhwyfar. 'Why don't you check out my gowns in the garderobe?' I suggested. 'Then you can pick one out for me to wear.' I gave her my full attention and a big, insincere smile. 'You always know what's right.'

'I do, don't I?' she said. 'It's called style, you know.'

Oh, good grief!

She toddled into the garderobe, and toddled out again straight away. 'You haven't got any gowns left,' she said. 'What happened to them? There were three or four in there yesterday. Where have they gone?'

There certainly had been. I'd magicked them there myself, and very stylish and tasteful they were too. I went to look, and sure enough, the pegs were empty. I was gobsmacked. Who would take my clothes? And more to the point, why?

'You could wear something of mine, I suppose,' Gwenhwyfar said, dubiously, 'but you're so hu- – um – I mean, you're a bit bigger than me.'

I didn't give two owl hoots in a barnyard about not having anything to wear: what I wanted to know was who had taken my stuff. I stood in the empty garderobe (which at least didn't pong quite so much any more), and stared at the empty pegs, completely at a loss.

'I'll go and see Lady Angharad,' Gwenhwyfar decided. 'She's big, too. She'll have something that will fit you. I expect she'll let you borrow something.'

Since Lady Angharad (a) did not regard me as her favourite person because thanks to Gwenhwyfar I was occupying her bedroom, (b) was the size of the back end of a large house, and (c) was on the shady side of fifty if she was a day, I certainly didn't fancy borrowing one of her dresses. I'd magic something up as soon as I could get rid of Gwenhwyfar.

'Thanks,' I said. 'That would be great.'

She scuttled off to annoy Lady Angharad and I sat on the edge of the bed, trying to suss out what was wrong with the room – besides the missing clobber. Something, definitely, but what?

Suddenly, the door opened again, and a pile of fabric entered with a pair of feet underneath. My dresses were back; I recognised the colours.

I got up and took the bundle of silk, velvet and brocade from the owner of the feet. Underneath was the bed-hangings girl, who seemed to be twice as busy as any other chambermaid at Camelot. She was everywhere.

'Thank you,' I said, and dumped the dresses on the bed. She turned to scuttle away, but I grabbed her arm and hauled her back. 'Why did you take them?'

'I – oh, I – to brush them, Lady,' she stammered. 'They get terrible dusty, hanging in the garderobe like that. A good going-over with a stiff brush brings them up lovely. I was told they must be back in your chamber before you returned, but the Mistress said I had to do the bed-hangings, first, and never mind the dresses. So she made me leave them and come up to do the hangings.' She looked as if she was going to burst into tears. 'I can't be everywhere at once, Lady!'

'That's all right. But who told you to do it?'

She looked shifty. 'Mistress O'Leary, Lady.'

Well, what did I know? Maybe it was the house-

103

keeper's job to look after guests that didn't bring their own lady's maid with them. At least I had the gowns back. But all the same, the excuse of brushing dust out of them didn't ring true, somehow. The dresses were all brand new, never even worn, and there wasn't a speck of dust on them. Good thing I'd gone for authenticity, mind – just think if I'd whacked in a concealed zip! Well, mainly gone for authenticity: there was one thing that wasn't authentically old, but that was hidden.

'I'll hang them up again, shall I?' she offered.

I nodded, and watched her trundle from bed to garderobe and back again, four times, once for each dress. She was almost running in her haste to get away. Then she stood in front of me, twisting her hands in her pinny nervously, looking at her feet.

'Can I go now, Lady, please?'

I nodded, and she scuttled thankfully away, closing the door softly behind her.

As soon as she was gone, I went to inspect the dresses. There they were, as if they'd never been away.

I gathered up the pale blue velvet folds of one, and felt it with my fingers. It felt the same. I felt around the hem, felt nothing but fabric. I ran my hands down the bodice – which should have been stiffened in the traditional way, with whalebone, but I wasn't a twenty-first century member of Greenpeace for nothing. That was the one thing I'd cheated on: I had introduced the Dark Ages, all unknowing, to the wonders of plastic strips. They looked enough like whale-bone to fool the naked eye.

I felt my way down the bodice, feeling the hard strips underneath. Suddenly, my fingers tingled and then went numb. I felt dizzy, sick, and almost collapsed.

What was the matter with me? Was it all the sprinting about I'd been doing? Stress? I couldn't be ill! Oh, crumbs! I remembered *when* I was, suddenly, and hoped it wasn't time for a bout of Black Death. That would really put the spanner in the magical works, the Lady of Ynys Haf catching the plague and popping her clogs, wouldn't it?

I felt sick, horribly sick, and horribly scared, too. I tottered out of the garderobe, certain I was about to throw up. But as soon as I was away from the dresses, I began to feel slightly better. How weird! First I feel sick, and dizzy, and weak, and then, almost instantly, I feel better.

OK, stop and think, Tanz. What was I doing when I came over all peculiar? Checking the dresses out, that's what. I went back to the blue velvet and touched it again. The skirt, the sleeves, the bodice. Instantly my hands tingled, and the sickness hit. I staggered back.

I magicked a pair of sharp scissors and, fighting back an almost overwhelming urge to upchuck my breakfast all over everywhere, I picked carefully at the bodice seams, my head spinning, swaying on my feet. Then I thought – why am I being so careful? These are magical clothes – I can reproduce them perfectly any time I want.   And unmake them just as easily. I disappeared the scissors and stepped back from the blue fabric. The dress instantly fell to the floor in its component parts.

It wasn't whalebone stiffening the bodice. Wasn't any carefully crafted-to-look-like-whalebone plastic, either. There were thin strips of *iron* encased in the fabric.

No wonder I'd been feeling so utterly awful. Whoever had taken the dresses hadn't brushed them. They'd carefully replaced the bodice stiffening with iron, knowing that if I were a witch, it would affect me. And, of course, if I were taken ill because of the iron's effects, I'd be instantly betrayed for what I am.

Unless I found the iron first, of course. It was a sort of 'Catch 22' situation. If I didn't find the iron, and I was a witch, I wouldn't be able to wear any of my dresses without being horribly ill. If I did find it, and took it away, I'd be fine. And then whoever had done it would only have to check my wardrobe, find the iron boning gone, and would know I was a witch. They knew a witch couldn't bear to have iron in the same room. If I was close to it for long enough, I should die, simple as that. Whoever it was – and who else but Morgan le Fay – would have proof. When she had that, she had the perfect weapon to get rid of me. Like I said, a witch in these times ain't exactly Little Miss Popular.

So. What to do? I had to find some way to keep her guessing. I couldn't just knuckle under, could I? Couldn't wear the dresses, couldn't not wear them. Couldn't take the iron out, couldn't leave it in. Couldn't go around starkers, had to have clothes. Couldn't magic more clothes: Gwenhwyfar would wonder where I'd got them. Everything I'd 'brought with me' she'd already inspected, and she'd notice something that suddenly appeared. So, what?

Then I had a brainwave. I stood just outside the garderobe and from a safe distance I transported (magically) the contaminated clothes to the top of the open shaft and dropped them down. They plummeted instantly and presumably ended up floating in the moat. Wherever they were, they'd be utterly ruined, and the iron in them would ensure they sank.

I got back into the chamber just as Gwenhwyfar trotted through the door, with a chambermaid staggering under the weight of a pile of gowns.

'I've got one from each of my Ladies, Tanith,' she announced. 'There must be one that's as bi- – the same size as you. Come on, let's try them.'

The Ladies, not being particularly well-disposed towards me, had not been particularly generous. They had without exception chosen their dullest, drabbest, oldest, tattiest and most hideously-coloured clothes to donate to Gwenhwyfar's charitable collection. Dresses that, had this been the twenty-first century, would have been the ones that they bought in the New Year Sales and hated as soon as they got them home. No matter. Now, at least, I had a way out.

'Take off your gown, Tanith,' Gwenhwyfar ordered. 'We'll try them on now.'

'No,' I murmured, holding my hand across my brow. I didn't want her there while I was trying on. 'I don't feel well, Gwenhwyfar. Do you mind if I rest now, and try the gowns on later? I'm sure there will be something I can wear. You're so very good to me.'

'Yes, I am, rather, aren't I?' Gwenhwyfar agreed, looking pleased with herself. 'Very well. When I'm all ready for supper, I'll send my girl to help you dress. Have a good rest. I'll see you later.'

The girl unloaded the dresses onto the bed, and the pair of them departed, closing the door behind them.

As soon as they were gone, I sifted through the ghastly collection. They were even more hideous than at first glance, and most showed distinct signs of either being crumpled up in a chest or having been hung in garderobes

– smelly ones – for far too long. No matter. I chose one that looked near enough my size, that was an almost pretty chestnut brown, a colour I knew would suit me. I dumped all the others out of sight, and did some magical fiddling with the chosen one.

The first thing I did was disappear it, and magic a new one that didn't pong something awful, fitted me perfectly, was the same colour and fabric – only cleaner and brighter – and most important, didn't have any whalebone, plastic or iron in it anywhere. Ha! Nobble that one, Morgan, if you can! I magicked the prettiest pair of matching slippers, a dear little headdress that draped rather than stuck up like the stupid inverted ice cream cones everyone else was wearing, and a gorgeous amber necklace to wear with it.

And then, because it really had been a very, very stressful day, I decided a nap would be a brilliant idea.

I carefully hung up my new dress, took off my bedraggled white silk, draped it over a chair, and climbed into bed in my shift.

It's probably really, really lucky that I'm sick easily. When I was a little kid, whenever Mam and Dad wanted to take me anywhere, we always had to take a plastic ice cream box in the car with us, because as soon as we went more than half a mile out of town, I was throwing up. So I was used to it, sort of, and knew what it felt like.

And lying there on this comfortable bed, I knew, without any doubt at all, that I was about to be very, very sick. And yet I hadn't eaten anything since the toast at breakfast, and that was so long ago I didn't think it could possibly be that. It couldn't be the iron – I'd got rid of that. But one thing was certain, as soon as I was horizontal, I knew I was going to be sick.

I rolled off the bed and staggered to the garderobe. And wasn't sick. Once again, I felt instantly better. Weirder and weirder.

Thoughtfully, I came back into the room. The closer I got to the bed, the worse I felt.

So what? And where?

14

It had to be something to do with the bed. But how could anyone nobble a wooden bed? Put a spell on it perhaps? Then, suddenly, I remembered that the girl who had taken the dresses for 'brushing' was the same girl who had been up on a stool fixing the bedhangings.

She'd taken the stool away with her, but I dragged the little table from the corner over to the bed and climbed on it. The closer I got to the bed the worse I felt, and when I was up on the table on a level with the top of the canopy, I felt so sick and dizzy I had to hang on to the bed-frame to stop myself falling off.

And there was Morgan le Fay's second-string insurance, in full view. Not only were four thick rods of iron laid across the bed top to bottom and side to side, but there were also several other horribly sinister things up there that could only have been left by someone wishing me the worst possible kind of ill. Morgan le Fay must have been working all night to create some of them, and several small rodents and a lot of wax had been sacrificed to the cause. No wonder I was feeling ill! If I'd fallen asleep there, I'd probably have been dead by morning. No-one would ever have been any the wiser. Except, of course, Morgan le Fay – and the servant who had done her bidding. Who, had she known it, was probably in great danger herself. If anything had happened to me, Morgan wouldn't want a witness around.

But what could I do? I needed the iron and oher disgusting debris taken away. I certainly couldn't move it myself – that would reveal that I'd found it, and knew enough about magic to get rid of it – just being in the same room as it would make me a very poorly girl indeed. So there was no way I could possibly sleep in that room and still remain safe. No. I had to get out of there, and get out fast.

I could have left Camelot altogether, slipped away and taken my chances on finding another Time Door. Except that there was still Blaidd – and now his brother wolf, too. I couldn't possibly leave them in the menagerie.

But the immediate and most important thing to do was get out of this room. I hopped off the table and shoved it back where it had been, stood as far away from the deadly bed as I possibly could, and chewed my fingernails. All of them, not just the one I keep for nibbling on in times of crisis. This was a ten-nail problem.

I got even crosser with Merlin – and, by extension, with Gwydion, too. This was all their fault, every bit of it.

And if you'd had the sense you were born with, you'd have stayed in Ynys Haf and talked it through with Gwydion rather than going off in a huff . . .

Shut up, conscience. I don't want to hear that right now, OK? Let's have a bit of sympathy here. Whose side are you on anyway? I admit, it did occur to me – in passing – that it would be dead easy just to switch on my magical aura again, and let Gwydion find me – but pride wouldn't let me. I'd got myself into this; I'd get myself – and Blaidd and his lair-brother – out.

OK, Tanz. Think sneaky. You are in a room you don't want to – can't possibly – be in any longer.

The seventh fingernail worked. Inspiration came. Dear, kind, non-magical Lady Angharad, whose chamber this was. Who needed thanking for donating one of the hideous dresses. I climbed back into the dirty white silk, and used magic to do up the laces at the back.

I shut the door firmly behind me, feeling better all the time, and went looking for Lady Angharad. The chamber she had been relegated to was upstairs, nearly in the attics. I went up to the next floor and rapped on a door. It was opened by one of Gwenhwyfar's Ladies.

'Oh, it's you, is it. What do you want?'

Not what you might call friendly. But then, I'd pitched up and Gwenhwyfar had made me her favourite, hadn't she? Lots of badly out-of-joint noses, I expect. Royal courts were like that in those days – probably still are. 'I'm looking for Lady Angharad.' I pasted on an anxious smile.

'You will find *poor* Lady Angharad,' the woman said, stiffly, 'in the chamber above. Sharing a *very small* chamber with Lady Alys.' And the door was slammed firmly in my face.

Oh, dear. Ah well, I couldn't help it if I was unpopular, even though it wasn't my fault but Gwenhwyfar's, for making me her 'best friend'. I plodded up another flight of stairs, and bashed on another door. Lady Angharad opened it. If Lady Number One was chilly, Angharad was positively gelid.

I turned on the charm. 'Lady Angharad,' I began, 'I –'

'You belong downstairs, Lady Tanith,' she hissed. 'The Queen's favourites get the *best rooms.*'

Oooh, deeear. 'The Queen has taken a liking to me, it's true,' I admitted. 'But I confess that something troubles me.'

'Oh, really?'

'Yes. And I don't think it's at all fair that you should have been evicted from your beautiful chamber just for

112

me. I really think you should have it back again, Lady Angharad.' I decided to lay it on with a trowel. 'I'm not worthy of Gwenhwyfar's favour: I've hardly been here five minutes, and you must be one of her oldest, dearest and most faithful friends. Please – shall we change places? I can sleep up here, if Lady Alys doesn't mind.'

The door was whipped out of Angharad's hand, and her rather younger roomie, Lady Alys, appeared.

'Yes!' she said.

'Yes, what?' Angharad turned to look at her.

'Yes, Lady Angharad should have her room back. It's only fair that the Queen's senior ladies should have the finest chambers.'

I hid a grin. Lady Alys had obviously had enough of sharing her small space with the elderly Angharad. 'Lady Alys is quite right. Please say you'll take it back? I felt quite dreadful seeing you evicted from your rightful place yesterday. I'm nobody, after all,' I said, creepy as a worm on holiday. 'Please, Lady Angharad – I shan't sleep a wink if I know you are suffering up here.'

Behind Angharad's back, Lady Alys wore a broad grin.

Lady Angharad sniffed. 'Well. This chamber is extremely small. It is cramped and stuffy. And I admit I felt a little put out by the Queen's high-handedness.'

A little put out? She was chewing rugs over it!

'I'm sure you did, and quite rightly, too.' (Make that two worms on holiday, liberally coated in sun-tan oil.) 'Now. If only Lady Alys can bear to share her chamber with someone as unimportant as me . . .'

When Lady Angharad turned to look at Lady Alys, she'd wiped the smile off her face. 'I suppose you can,' she said, 'if it means –' She shrugged, eloquently.

If it means you get rid of the bad-tempered, nagging old biddy! I thought.

They didn't need asking twice. 'You may carry my gowns.' Lady Angharad shot back inside the chamber. I followed her in, and allowed myself to be loaded up with her stuff, Alys picked up an armful and the three of us staggered down the stairs and delivered Lady Angharad to her own chamber.

I collected my gown for the evening, popped into the now empty garderobe and, out of sight, magicked up a few more in drab browns and greens that would just about resemble the donated ones. Alys collected the rest of my stuff, and we went back upstairs.

It wasn't a luxurious chamber; it was right under the sloping attic roof, and because it was in a tower, the only place we could stand upright was in the middle of the room. But there was a window, and best of all, there wasn't any iron in there at all.

'You can sleep over there, if you want,' Alys said. She was a bit older than me, probably around twenty-five, and very pretty.

'Thanks,' I said. 'Where can I hang my clothes?'

'There's some pegs on the wall behind that curtain,' she said, waving at it. 'I hope you don't snore.'

'I don't know if I do or not,' I admitted. 'I'm usually asleep at the time.'

'Lady Angharad snores,' she said, darkly. 'She snores like a whole sty full of prize pigs. And she nags. She made me tidy up all the time, and complained about how long I took getting to bed, and about just about everything I said or did.'

'I'll try not to get in the way,' I said. 'I'm probably just as untidy as you, so if you don't nag me, I won't nag you. I won't be here very long, I hope.'

'You aren't staying? The Queen won't like that. She likes you. Where are you going?'

'Home,' I said. 'I want to take Blaidd – my servant – back. He's had a bad time of it here, thanks to Medrawd, and I think he deserves a break.'

Alys shivered. 'I don't like Medrawd. I hate him. The trouble is, he seems to like me. Every time I turn round, he's there. He caught me in the Queen's ante-room last week, and tried to kiss me. It was horrible!'

'I can believe it,' I said. Medrawd getting amorous must have been like snogging a snake. Yuk.

'Actually, I'm quite glad to have somebody sharing a room with me – for protection,' she went on. Then she grinned. 'But not Lady Angharad.' Then she looked worried. 'But the Queen said you should have Angharad's chamber, didn't she? Will she be angry?'

'Why should she be? It's my fault, after all, isn't it? I'll have a word with her, don't worry.' I thought I could handle Gwenhwyfar. 'Look,' I said, 'I'm going to leave you in peace for a bit. I need to go and get something sorted out, all right?'

'Whatever,' she said, airily.

I still had Blaidd to worry about, and I'd left him alone far too long. I headed off down the stairs and out into the courtyard. I grabbed a passing small boy and got directions to the menagerie, which was inside the castle walls, but tidily hidden away near the mews.

I smelled it before I found it – it had the throat-tearing stench of wild animals kept in cages too small for them, in dark and unhappy conditions, without exercise or the freedom that was their birthright. It was a hellish place.

Inside the dark, stinking, squalid building I found Blaidd, huddled against the bars of his brother's cage, weeping bitterly. I propped the menagerie door open with a lump of wood, to let in some air, knelt beside him in the smelly straw and put my arms round him.

'Sssh,' I whispered. 'Don't, Blaidd! I'll get you out of here, I promise.'

He lifted swollen eyes to my face. *When, Lady, when? This is a terrible place. My brother will die in here, Lady, and so shall I!*

'As soon as I can, Blaidd. I'll try to get both of you out tonight. We'll go right away from here, I promise.'

Then, the menagerie darkened. A grossly fat man was blocking the light, a hunk of cheese in one hand, picking his teeth with the little finger of the other.

'Hey!' he said loudly when he saw me. 'What you doin' in by yer? Yew got no right in yer, you 'aven't.'

'I'm checking on my servant,' I snapped back. 'And I'll go where I please. How dare you speak to me like that?' There are times when 'coming the Lady' is the only way to go!

Bullied right back, he looked uncomfortable. 'I'm the h'animal keeper, I am. You got no business down yer, not if the King or Lord Medrawd ain't wiv yer.'

'I have the King's permission,' I said – and I did, more or less. 'So listen, and listen well.' I got up and glared at him. 'You horrible little man. Call yourself a keeper? With wild creatures in dreadful conditions like this? No wonder they're dying! It's all your fault!'

He shrugged. 'Don't matter. We can always trap

116

another 'un when they dies. Wolf'll die soon, so you can take the boy away. Useless, 'e is, anyway. Won't do nothin' I tells 'im. Won't muck out the cages nor nothin'.'

'Nor should he!' I said. 'He isn't here to do your work for you. Now. Either you clean this place up, or you'll be sorry.'

'Oh, yeah?' he sneered. 'And oo's goin' ter make me sorry, missy? You and oo's army?'

'Oh, I don't need any army, thank you,' I said, sweetly. 'I'll take that as a no, shall I?'

He bent and picked up a pebble, threw it deliberately past me, close to my head. It rattled off the bars of a cage behind me. I turned.

And saw a bedraggled little bundle of fur, in a tiny cage fastened high up on the walls. The creature inside staggered to its feet and let out a pathetic whimper. It was a fox cub, not even old enough to leave its mother. I felt my blood pressure begin to rise. And my magic pressure . . .

'What's that poor little thing doing in here?' I hissed, so angry I could hardly breathe.

'Dug it up yes'day. T'other one died s'mornin'. This 'un survives, I'll turn it loose for Lord Medrawd. 'E'll set 'is dogs on – give 'em a bit of fun.'

That did it. It was one almighty instance of temper-loss. One moment of blind fury. Basically, I totally lost it, chucked one very rapid spell, and the bloke was history.

Well, not so much history. Ratstory, actually.

15

The former menagerie keeper took one look at all the creatures he had so mistreated, and decided to disappear – well, like a rat up a drainpipe! He scuttled into the wolf's cage (stupid), just missed getting snapped in two by a vengeful set of large choppers, then legged it through the bars towards the nearest hole in the wall. I hoped there was a very much larger rat inside that hole, a rat with Serious Attitude to beat up on him until his eyes crossed and his teeth dropped out.

That showed him, Lady! Blaidd said, swiping tears from his eyes. *Can we go now?*

And then it sort of dawned on me what I'd just done. I could have kicked myself for being so stupid. I'd gone and used magic, hadn't I? Why hadn't I just gone and stood on Camelot's battlements, waving a big flag, and screamed through a megaphone, 'Hey, look at me, Morgan le Fay! I'm a witch, just like you! Wanna come and get me?'

By now, Morgan probably had her ears pricked up so high they'd poke her hat off. There she'd been, trying to discover if I was a witch by using iron dress-boning and wax dolls and worse stuff, and here was I, giving her a free demonstration. Dumb, or what? I sighed. I might as well have simply ridden in on a broomstick with a black cat riding pillion, right?

'We're going now, Blaidd, don't worry. First, let's get your brother out of the cage.' The great grey wolf sat back on his haunches, watching as I peered at the padlock securing the cage. Made of iron, of course, and there was no way I was going to touch it. Even being near the iron in the cage was giving me the willies.

I've tried to break the bars with my hands, and my brother has bitten them, but they are too hard.

'Too hard for me, too, Blaidd,' I muttered. Ah well, in for a penny, in for a pound. What difference would it make now if I used more magic? 'Stand back, Blaidd – and you get to the back of the cage, too, please,' I said in wolfspeak to his big brother. Obediently the wolf got up and moved as far away as he could get. I knew I couldn't magic the iron – couldn't open the lock, couldn't bend the bars, couldn't disappear them.

What I could do, however, was disappear the wooden floor of the cage, because underneath that was nothing but hard-packed earth. I magicked up a couple of spades, handed one to Blaidd, and started digging. He dug for a couple of strokes, then threw the tool away in disgust, got down on his knees and started scrabbling away with his hands. As soon as the floor was exposed, I was able to zap the wood, send it back where it had come from, which must have surprised a forester or two!

With Blaidd digging into the earth floor from outside, and the grey wolf from inside, we soon had a hole big enough for Big Brother to wriggle out of. He slurped Blaidd's face, and mine too, in thanks.

I'd intended to rescue Blaidd and his brother, then just leg it, get away, scraping the dust of Camelot off our feet forever. But I'd seen that fox cub, and in the darkness of the menagerie I could hear the shuffles, grunts and moans of other wild creatures imprisoned in tiny, hideous cages. How could I leave them behind when there were people like Medrawd in the world?

I shut the menagerie door and barred the inside, then magicked up a battery torch – which I should have to magic away again before we left – and went to see what else was there, caged in the stinking darkness. A huge brown bear, chained to a wall. Luckily, the collar the iron chain was fixed to was leather, which wouldn't present a problem. Smaller animals were in wooden cages, which made it easier. Wildcats, pine martens, stoats, weasels, wild boar, foxes, just about every species of wild life in Brython. One by one I freed them, and they milled around in the torchlight. I left the tiny foxcub until last. I stood on a box, reached up and opened the cage. It mewed at me like a kitten, too young even to snarl. I lifted it out, cradled it, soothing it as best I could.

I still had to get us all out of here. I could hardly unbar the door and march out, followed by a procession of wild animals. I stroked the mewing cub to calm it, and thought, hard. The trouble was, it was possible that Morgan and Medrawd might possibly have picked up on the magical vibes from the spell I'd used, and might already be looking for me. I'd shielded my aura again, straight away, as soon as I realised what I'd done, but I had a horrid feeling it would have been too late anyway.

Most of the castle traffic went in and out of the main gate, across the drawbridge, which was manned night and day. But there was also a small gate hidden away at the back of the castle that opened on to the fishponds outside the walls. I'd seen servants going in and out of that door. It was probably always kept bolted on the inside, and there were usually a couple of guards stationed next to it. We could perhaps get out that way – but first I'd need to get the guards away from the door somehow. So. What I needed was a diversion. But what?

I chewed on one of my remaining nails, thinking hard. I'd have to use magic – I couldn't think of any other way of distracting the guards without me being there to do it. A good explosion would be just the thing – except that explosions were always likely to damage people.

Besides, what did I know about explosions? The closest I'd ever got was a particularly loud banger one Bonfire Night.

Bonfire Night. Fireworks. Bangers. No. Not bangers. Rockets! I could fire a rocket from a hidden place, aim it to burst over the main gate, and while all the guards were running to head off an attack at the front of the castle, we could leg it out the back, couldn't we!

I magicked up a couple of giant rockets, and made all the animals get as far back against the walls as they could. I told each one in mind-language to close its eyes when I gave the signal. I just hoped the tiny spell I used wasn't enough to allow Morgan le Fay to pinpoint where I was in the castle. Using more magic would be like putting a big, fat blip on her magical radar screen. I gave the fox cub to Blaidd to hold, which was something new for both of them!

I dug the rockets' sticks into the earth of the menagerie floor, aiming them at the outside, at an angle that I hoped would take them sailing over the wall and into the sky over the main gate.

I put my ear to the menagerie door and listened. I couldn't hear any footsteps, or voices. I opened the door a crack and put my eye to the gap. It was almost dark. No-one seemed to be about. I opened the door wider, and checked the rockets' angle for aim. Looked OK. I shut the door again, magicked up a box of matches, found a muttonfat rushlight and lit it. Then I signalled all the animals to close their eyes and, as fast as I could, lit the blue touchpapers on the rockets and opened the door wide.

I stood well back, closed my eyes against the glare and hoped for the best. For a few seconds nothing happened, and then, one after the other, six huge rockets zipped from the earth floor, snaked into the sky and began to explode in wonderful showers of multi-coloured stars and sparkles.

That got everyone's attention! People ran towards the drawbridge from all over Camelot. I took the fox cub from Blaidd, and with the animal escapees nose to tail behind me, slithered round the outside of the menagerie building, across to the deep shadows of the great curtain wall, and round to the little fishpond gate. We froze, breaths held, as a pair of guards pounded past, heading for the main gate and the excitement, and then we scuttled off again.

The gate was in deepest shadow, of which we took full advantage, huddling out of sight while Blaidd tried to slide the iron bolts across. They were stiff, and the door creaked as he swung it open, but at last, freedom lay ahead. I shooed the motley collection of animals outside. Bear, wolf, wildcats, stoats, weasels, pine-martens, beavers, wild boar, they slipped one by one out to freedom until only Blaidd and his brother, and me, with the fox cub in my arms, were left. I pulled the door closed behind me. No point in advertising that we'd gone, was there? The rocket bursts were dying away now – someone was screaming hysterically about a dragon attack, and the sound of heavy boots on the drawbridge echoed in the darkness.

Where shall we go, Lady?

'Anywhere, Blaidd, away from here. Somewhere there must be a Time Door that we can use, and then we can all go back to Ynys Haf.'

What about the cub, Lady? He belongs here.

'You're right, he does – but without a mother he'll die.'

The great grey wolf padded silently away, keeping to the shadows as much as possible, the rest of us following. I glanced over my shoulder to make sure we weren't being followed. The other animals had all disappeared, and even though I had betrayed my witchhood and given Morgan le Fay all the ammunition she needed, I'd got away. With luck I'd find a Time Door and I need never go back to Camelot, ever. I'd really learned my lesson about Time Doors and concentration. Going through one while thinking of something else is a recipe for disaster. The other thing I'd learned was that Camelot isn't all it's cracked up to be.

Soon we reached the foot of the hill above the castle. There should be a Time Door up there somewhere – I knew there was, because I'd used it, hadn't I?

The fox cub was whimpering in my arms, and I stroked the hard, warm little head comfortingly, but it didn't stop.

The cub needs food, Lady, Blaidd suggested.

He was almost certainly right, but I had nothing about my person that would be suitable to feed a fox cub this young – he needed milk – and if I used my magic to get some, it would be like texting Morgan le Fay – *hey, Mrgn, ovr hre, can't w8 2 c u XX.* Not a good plan at all, right?

So I stroked the baby and tried to hush him.

But small creatures, when they are hungry or miserable or frightened or confused, don't keep their voices down. The whimper became a whine, the whine a yelp, and the yelp a high, panicky 'yip-yip-yip' that would be heard a mile off if anyone was looking for us. It must be suppertime by now, back at Camelot, and chances were that once the excitement was over, Gwenhwyfar would come to find me and then there would be alarums and excursions all over the place. And if they were already looking, they might follow any noise in the hope it would lead them to us.

I sighed. Only one thing for it. I called a halt, magicked up a bottle of warm milk, and sat down to feed the baby while Blaidd and his brother kept watch.

16

Goodness, the poor little feller was hungry! He downed that bottle, and then another, and then half of another before he hiccuped a bubble of milk, closed his eyes with a contented sigh, and fell asleep.

We must go, Lady, Blaidd said, into my head. *My brother's ears are sharper than mine – he says there are people coming up the hill, and they will be here soon. Besides, the moon will not stay hidden for ever – now it is behind clouds, but they are drifting away, and then –*

'Right. Point taken. Better get moving, then.' I struggled to my feet, the cub cradled in my arms. 'Look, Blaidd – I think it would be best if I shifted you back to wolf again. You'd have a better chance of survival in your natural shape . . .'

But what about you, Lady? Won't using your magic betray you even more? Shouldn't you shift, too? At least that way you will be harder to recognise if Medrawd catches us.

I sighed. 'I'll stay my natural shape, I think. I wish I could shapeshift and get away from here.' I glanced down at the cub. 'But I can't leave the cub behind, and he's really too young to shapeshift.'

I concentrated on Blaidd, and watched his outline shimmer and change shape. He dropped swiftly from two legs to four, his face pushed out into a muzzle, his feet and hands shrank into paws, and hair sprouted thickly. When he was all wolf again, he shook himself all over, like a dog coming out of water, getting comfortable in his skin, and his brother nudged him with his nose.

OK, you guys, I mind-talked, *let's get out of here as fast as we can. You two run for it.*

Blaidd turned his shaggy head and looked at me, the amber eyes knowing. *We will not leave you, Lady. Not until we are all safely through the Time Door.*

'That's kind, but if I get caught, you two get lost, quick. No point in Medrawd getting us all, is there? You'll survive just fine without me – but I need to get back to Ynys Haf. Or, if not Ynys Haf, somewhere well away from Camelot. Let's get up the hill and find that Time Door.'

The two wolves loped ahead, while I scrambled up behind them, stumbling and tripping over the stupid white silk dress, my arms full of fat, comatose fox cub. I glanced down at it. *I just wish we could find your mam for you.* The moon came out, suddenly, and I took the opportunity to glance behind me. At first I couldn't see anyone following – but then light glinted on steel, and sound drifted to my ears. Scary sound for someone running away – dogs, barking. No. Barking was wrong. They weren't barking – they were 'belling'. Which is the sound that hounds make when they are on the trail of something . . .

And the something was me. Blaidd and his brother would be fine now – they could get away, even with hounds in pursuit – but Medrawd and Morgan le Fay wouldn't give up on me that easily. If I couldn't find that Time Door, I'd really be in trouble.

The next minute, something screamed, loud and eerie, too close for comfort. My heart did a double back flip, a triple salchow, three cartwheels and a bellyflop. It was the weirdest sound I'd ever heard, and my first thought was that it was something supernatural. At least a ghost, and possibly even a werewolf . . . Then reason reasserted itself, and I began to giggle at my stupidity as I realised what it was. I gave the cub a kiss on top of his fuzzy little head.

'I think,' I whispered to him, 'your mammy is looking for you. Well, babe, luckily for you, she's found you.' I bent down, laid the tiny, sleeping creature on the ground, and stepped back. *Come and get him,* I sent out. *It's all right. He's safe. No-one's going to harm him – or you.*

A dark shape slipped silently out of the bushes, and went straight to the cub. The vixen sniffed at him, and then looked at me fearlessly. Her teeth closed on the loose fur at the scruff of her cub's neck, she lifted him, and then she disappeared into the bushes.

When she'd gone, I felt all sniffy and sentimental. Baby creatures affect me like that.

A cold nose nudged my wrist. *Lady, we should move faster if we want to get away.*

I wiped my eyes surreptitiously. *I know, Blaidd, I know. But first* – I swiftly magicked myself a rather more practical outfit than the one I was wearing. Leather trousers and boots were what was called for, and I felt instantly more comfortable, capable – and warmer, too. OK, so I had to use magic. But since Morgan le Fay had probably already picked up on the traces of the magic I'd already used, a bit more wouldn't matter one way or another. And if I could get us to a Time Door before the pursuers caught up with us –

Wherever the Time Door was.

I knew roughly the direction it had *been*. I crossed my fingers and hoped it had had the common decency to come back. Time Doors shouldn't behave like that. Maybe it was on the fritz, malfunctioning.

The belling of the hounds seemed to be getting louder, and now I could hear shouting. They were getting too close for comfort. Time we weren't here.

The two grey shapes loping ahead of me, I scrambled up the hill to the small wood at the top. Blaidd and Brother disappeared into the trees, and I was seconds behind them. I glanced up at the full moon, wishing it was my moon, and not Camelot-time moon. *Please, Lady, I thought, desperately, please let the Door be there!* I wasn't sure if the Goddess of the Moon was still looking after me – if so, now was the time to show it!

I peered around me, staring through the trees, hoping, hoping, hoping to see the tell-tale shimmer of displaced air that signified a Door. Nothing but trees. And more trees. I went further into the wood, squinting hopefully at the gaps between the trees, at the trees themselves, staring until my eyes hurt. Nothing at all. If I ever got back to Ynys Haf, I'd have some words to say about Doors that disappeared. It must surely be somebody's job to see they behaved themselves!

And then – there it was. Even in the darkness the faint, hazy movement of the air was there. I sent out a call to the wolves – *Come back, I've found it!* – and they loped towards me, their shapes huge and threatening, a moving darkness against the shadowy wood.

They sat at my feet, tongues lolling, looking up at me.

'Right. Listen carefully, you two,' I said. 'I want you to go through first – it's nothing to be afraid of, nothing like the huge winds you felt getting here. It's just a short step through Time, and then you'll be back in Ynys Haf. When I say go, you go, all right?'

What about you, Lady? Blaidd asked, his eyes glinting in the moonlight.

'Don't you worry, chum. I'll be right behind you. Now, when I say go, you two get through that door as fast as you can, all right? Don't look behind you to see if I'm coming. Trust me, I am.'

The sound of the hounds was closer now – a matter of yards behind us. 'Right. **Go!**' I ordered, and gave Blaidd a sharp slap on his hairy rump. Blaidd shot forward, his head disappearing into the Door, the rest of his long body fading as if he'd never been there. Brother gave me a long, level glance, and followed him. I heaved a sigh of relief. They were safe, at least. Now all I had to do was get through myself.

I stepped forward, eagerly, and reached the shimmering air that was the entrance to Ynys Haf. Began to move towards the freedom and safety – and was knocked splat on my backside by someone coming very fast the other way.

'Ow!' I landed with a wallop on my rear end. 'I told you not to look back! Just to go through!' I wailed. 'Just turn round and get out of here, will you?'

It wasn't the wolves coming back.

It was Gwydion coming through, hammering through the door like a human battering ram because the wild winds inside it had suddenly dropped, as they do right at the exit, and knocking me titfer-over-teakettle. He tumbled through, tripped over me and sprawled on the leaf mould, looking dazed.

'What are you doing here, you big dope?' I yelled, 'Get back through the Door, quick!'

'Not without you I won't,' Gwydion bellowed back. 'And who are you calling a dope? You, of all people, Tanz! Of all the stupid, senseless, hair-brained, dingbat things to –'

'We can argue later!' I shouted. 'Just get through the door, quick. I'm being followed by –'

Finally reacting to my urgency, he got up, grabbed my hand, and hauled me to my feet. We turned to the Time Door, ready to hustle through it and get out of there before the mob pouring up the hill reached us.

Except. Of course. The Time Door had gone walkabout again.

'This is all your fault!' I snarled at the Dragonking. 'Now look what you've done!'

'Look what *I've* done! Who was it ran off in a huff without even leaving a note, and worried me sick? Who was it threw a tantrum like a spoiled little brat? Who was it bullied the gatekeeper into letting her out of the castle – and without the password? Who was it turned off her aura so I couldn't follow her? If you hadn't used a bit of magic so I could get a fix on you, I might never have found you. What got into you, Tanz? I can't believe you'd do something so utterly stupid!'

I saw red. Bright crimson, scarlet, bloody red. 'Stupid, me? What got into *me?* Well, I like that! Just who, exactly do you think you are, Gwydion?'

'I'm Dragonking of Ynys Haf, that's who I am, and my place is back there running the place, not following half-witted females through Time Doors because they decide to take off in a huff! I mean, you could have ended up just about anywhere!'

'I did! And I was coping just fine before you showed up, so there!'

'Oh, you were, were you? That's why there was a pair of wolves lurking about the Door, was it? You were coping so well they couldn't wait to eat you.'

'They weren't! They were my friends, and I sent them through before me. One of them was the wolf you were

130

chasing, so it's your fault he was here in the first place. And I'd have been back in Ynys Haf by now if you hadn't gone and cannoned into me like that!'

'If you hadn't come here, none of this would have happened. It's all your fault for throwing a wobbler. Anyway, where are we?'

'Camelot!' I snarled. 'IF you really want to know. And all because you went and got in my way, we're about to be –'

'Captured,' said a silky voice behind us. 'Ah, Lady Tanith. I see you've found a friend.'

Medrawd.

Gwydion shoved me behind him and reached for his sword. I put out a restraining hand and stopped him drawing it. I might be mad with him, but I still didn't want to see him used as a pincushion. There were quantities of swords and spears and daggers surrounding us, not to mention several large and hungry-looking hounds.

'I wouldn't bother, Gwyd,' I said, loudly, so that Medrawd could hear. 'You can't fight all of them, so you might as well give up right now. We're outnumbered.'

Quickly, I muttered under my breath. 'Shapeshift, quick, Gwyd. Anything you like that will get us out of here, all right? I'll do the same.'

I felt him tense beside me, readied myself to shift into an owl, take off into the moonlit sky, get away from here. They might fire arrows at us, throw spears, but at least we'd have a chance. If Medrawd got us, I doubted we'd ever see another birthday. I felt the fizzing start in my bones, felt Gwydion squeeze my hand, and –

Nothing happened.

131

17

Medrawd laughed. 'Leaving us so soon, My Lady? Did you really think you'd be able to escape? Oh, no, My Lady. I don't allow my quarry to get away quite so easily. What pleasure is a hunt without a kill? And dear Mama is so anxious to talk to you. She will be devastated if you leave without even a farewell.'

'I'll bet,' I muttered.

'What happened, Tanz?' Gwydion asked, still bemused. 'Why couldn't we shift?'

'Someone's blocking our magic. And I've got a pretty good idea who.'

'Nobody ought to be able to do that! Who is this bloke, anyway?' Then the little light bulb switched on over his head. 'Hang about. Did you say this is *Camelot?*'

'That's right, Gwyd. And this bossy little twerp is Medrawd. Morgan le Fay's blue-eyed boy?'

I felt him relax. Honestly, blokes can be so simple occasionally. 'Ah, Medrawd! He's Arthur's nephew, so that's all right. Friend of the family from way back. Arthur won't let anything happen to either of us. After all, I'm the Dragonking of Ynys Haf, and you're its Lady. We can claim diplomatic immunity and all that.'

I sighed. 'Yes, very clever, I'm sure. But you haven't thought this through, have you? Family connections won't cut much ice, I'm afraid. We're from the future, aren't we? Arthur and Camelot and Lancelot and Gwenhwyfar and all that happened long, long before we came along, right? We haven't happened yet, in this Time. So you can hardly claim family connections, can you?'

'Yes I can. So we haven't been born yet. My great-

great-great-grandmother was, I expect. One thing royalty does is keep records – and I'm royalty. Can't see a problem, personally. After all, Merlin pops back and forth all the time, to sort things out. Arthur means well, he says, but he has a real talent for doing the wrong thing at the right time, and the right thing at the wrong time. If you see what I mean. Anyway, sooner or later Merlin will pitch up and explain everything.' He spread his hands expansively. 'So no worries –'

I sighed. 'But Gwydion, you don't understand, you –'

'Excuse me?' Medrawd had his sword drawn, and raised it to Gwydion's throat. 'Do you mind? Please forgive me for interfering in a personal discussion. Won't you introduce us, Lady Tanith?' Gwydion towered over him by at least half a metre, but Medrawd was as dangerous as a venomous snake – with or without a sword. Gwydion tensed: he doesn't like people pointing sharp things at him. I gave his hand a squeeze to calm him down. Wouldn't help either of us if he lost his temper and Medrawd skewered him. The sword looked very sharp.

'I don't think so, no,' I said, carelessly, trying to be nonchalant, even though I was feeling anything but.

'I see.' Medrawd's eyes glittered unpleasantly.

'I –' Gwydion began, and I elbowed him in the ribs.

'Oof!' he said, folding forward slightly, but at least he shut up.

'So, Medrawd,' I went on. 'Where do we go from here? I am your King's honoured guest, I might remind you, and also Queen Gwenhwyfar's friend – and you are preventing me from going about my lawful business. Neither of them would be pleased.'

'They don't know,' Medrawd said, 'and what the eye

doesn't see, the heart won't grieve over, that's my motto. Arthur rarely sees anything, even if it is under his nose.' Then he smirked.

Oooh. Did I ever mention how irritating I find people who smirk?

'Oh, he'll soon find out,' I said.

'Whatever gives you that idea?' Medrawd asked. 'Do you think I'm going to meekly return you to Camelot, just because you tell me I should? I think not. No, My Lady. I certainly don't intend to put you where you can wheedle favours out of the Queen and my uncle.'

'Me, wheedle? I've never wheedled in my entire life, Medrawd. You, on the other hand . . .' – my heart was thudding, but there was no way I was about to let Medrawd see I was scared – '. . . are the wheedling type. What if I won't go?'

'I shall have to persuade you. That would be quite simple. Before you go anywhere, My Lady, I intend to find out who you are – and where you are from. You say you are from Ynys Haf – and yet this kingdom does not exist on any map that I have seen.' He lost interest suddenly and gestured to his men. 'Enough of this. You know where to take them. I shall return to Camelot before I'm missed. Guard them well. You will suffer if they escape, I promise you.'

I doubted if anyone except his doting mam would miss him. We were grabbed, and despite Gwydion's struggles, he was disarmed, and our hands were tied in front of us so that we could hang on to the wooden saddles on a pair of horses. Hounds milled around us as we were wrestled forward, a snarling mass that snapped at us and each other before the whippers-in beat them back.

Side by side, we were led away, our horses' reins tied to the saddles of Medrawd's men. I could feel Gwydion's temper stoking up, and wondered how to calm him. If he lost it and had a go at someone, he'd end up injured, perhaps seriously, and then I'd have two of us to look after. I decided the straight approach was the best. Forget tact: this was serious.

'Calm down, Gwydion,' I muttered.

'Calm down?' he hissed. 'I'm Dragonking of Ynys Haf. Who does this bloke think he is?'

'He doesn't *think* he is anyone, Gwyd. He *knows* he is Medrawd, Arthur's nephew, and Morgan le Fay's son. He may also know who else he is, but that depends on whether Morgan has shared that with him yet. I don't expect she has, yet, or he'd be even more unbearable than he already is.' Medrawd's ancestry was a bit on the chequered and disorganised side, which, I'm afraid, is where a lot of Arthur's future problems were going to lie. *We* knew all about that, because we had hindsight. They were still living their lives from start to finish. 'Don't forget that in our time you're Dragonking – in this time, you aren't anything. You haven't even been born yet. As Medrawd said: Ynys Haf doesn't appear on any maps.'

'I still don't understand how you ended up here. What's been happening?'

I shrugged. 'I just went through a Door, the way you do, all right? And somehow I ended up in the wrong place. I think the Time Door's on the blink. And before you start rabbiting on about space-time continuum and all that stuff, let's just say I probably wasn't concentrating hard enough, either. I was upset and angry. Anyway, as soon as I realised I was in the wrong place, I tried to go back, but the Door had scarpered. And the wolf you were chasing followed me through, which is why you lost him, so I was stuck with him until I could get us both back. I had to shift him into human form, which must have been how Morgan picked up on my magic so early – she knew a witch had arrived, she just didn't know where until I arrived at Camelot. Then, all she had to do was try to prove it somehow and I was up Poo Creek without a paddle!'

'What did she do?'

'Oh, nothing I couldn't handle. Iron instead of whalebone in my bodices, iron bars and wax dollies and stuff on top of the bed-frame. Amateurish stuff like that, you know.' I was being very calm and collected, although I didn't feel it. I just wanted to make sure Gwyd didn't fly off the handle and knew exactly what we were up against.

'I'm not even going to ask where you thought you were going,' the Dragonking said, huffily. 'Once I've got us out of here, we're going to have to discuss your behaviour over the last couple of days, Tanz.'

Ooooh! That did it. 'I *beg* your pardon?' I said icily.

'So I should think. Well, don't apologise now. You can do that later. Right now, we've got to try to get away.'

Didn't hear the last bit: I was too mad. All my earlier fury had somehow been sort of rehydrated. Instant tantrum: just add Gwydion! '*Me* apologise? Dream on! If anyone ought to apologise, it's you and Merlin!'

'Me and Merlin? Well, I like that! What did we do?'

'If you don't know, Gwydion, don't think I'm going to tell you, because I'm not speaking to you.'

And from then on I maintained a dignified (if miserable) silence until we reached our destination, and so did he. A pair of big fat sulks on horseback.

We got there, but didn't have a clue where it was.

Nowhere near Camelot, that was certain. The countryside ahead of us was black dark, but there was the faintest glimmer of new light showing over the horizon. As far as I could tell we were travelling east, towards the dawn. It was too dark to look for landmarks, so even if we did manage to escape, I wasn't at all sure I could find my way back to where the Time Door should be.

I may have felt more miserable once or twice in my life, but this was pretty close to Rock-Bottom City as far as misery goes.

Eventually, a square, darker shape loomed out of the shadows. It was a large shape: not as large as Camelot or Castell Du, but a reasonably-sized bijou-type castle just right for those odd weekends and whatever prisoners a person might have hanging around that they want to disappear for a while – or (horrible thought) maybe permanently.

The great iron-bound door in the wall was opened – I shuddered at the influence of the metal as we went through – and we were hustled across the inner ward and into a tower doorway. Entering the tower door gave me a moment's hope that it wasn't going to be a dungeon we were going to be locked in. I can't be doing with dungeons. They are damp, dark, and ratty.

But then that hope was dashed, too, because instead of going up the spiral stairs, we went down. And down. And the walls got damper and damper, and the accommodation got gloomier and gloomier, and I got scareder and scareder.

By the time the heavy door, generously studded with iron nails, clanged shut behind us, I had stopped being the brave, proud, adventurous and dauntless Lady of Ynys Haf. I wanted to go home.

At least they left us a lantern with a candle in it. A small candle. And they didn't shackle us to the iron rings set in the walls. But it was still a dungeon. And there was iron in the door and iron on the walls. I stood very carefully in the middle of the room as far away from both as I could get. And shivered.

Gwydion wrapped his arms round me and I had a bit of a howl. Then I remembered I wasn't speaking to him and stopped.

'Well?' he said, and shrugged.

'Well? What do you mean, *well?*'

'Well, what do we do now? Any suggestions?'

'It would be really rather nice to escape. Then perhaps a nice shower, a change of clothes, a lovely hot cooked dinner – roast pork with crackling, maybe followed by a good night's rest in a nice clean bed.'

'I think you're being sarcastic, Tanz.'

'Of course I'm being sarcastic, you big lug! We can't shapeshift – probably because Medrawd or Morgan is blocking us. Oh, and there's iron in the door if you haven't already noticed it – and that means I shall probably be feeling extremely poorly in a very short while. How am I expected to know what to do?'

He sighed. 'Look, Tanz, love. We aren't going anywhere very fast. I know that. But if we can get *us* sorted out, maybe we can stop bickering and being unkind to each other and start working out what we can do to get us out of this mess. So, won't you please calm down and stop shouting at me and tell me what I've done? Please? Will it help if I apologise first, and then you can tell me what I did and I can apologise properly?'

That sort of took the wind out of my sails. He really, honestly, genuinely didn't have a clue, did he? So I thought about it for a bit. He was right. Our priority was to pull together and get out of here, but at the moment I was still feeling hurt and ratty and uncooperative. But it really *was* good to have him with me again. And we had to kiss and make up, or it would get in the way of everything else. I wasn't even thinking straight. 'All right. Apology accepted.'

'Thank you. Now. You want to go into details?'

'Hmph. You really, really don't have any idea at all what I'm upset about, do you, Gwyd?'

'No I don't!' He was still a bit exasperated. 'If I did, I'd say sorry. And I have said sorry, even if I don't know what for yet.'

I scowled. 'Cast your mind back, Gwydion. There we were, having breakfast, right?'

'Right. Good breakfast, too,' he said, wistfully.

'And then? What happened next?'

'Blowed if I know.'

'Think!' I barked.

He took one look at my face and speedily applied himself. 'Well, then Merlin came down late to breakfast. And he was in a particularly foul mood. And he said it was time. He said it in that annoying, significant kind of way he has sometimes. Usually.'

'And?'

'And I said, time for what.'

'And?'

'And he said, time you two got married.'

139

'And?' I could feel my temper building already.

'And I said – I said –'

'Yes?'

'I said "fine". Didn't I? And it is, isn't it?'

'*What?*'

'Well, I've always known we'd get married. You've always known we'd get married. It was sort of accepted, really, wasn't it? It's fine by me.'

'*Fine by you?* It might have been fine by you. But that's not the point.'

He ran his fingers through his hair. '*Then what is the bloody point, Tanz?*'

'The point,' I said, with a great deal of dignity, 'is that you never, ever, even bothered to ask me.'

He stared at me, completely baffled. Then, 'Well, what would you have said if I had?'

'I'd probably have said yes.'

'You probably would. Because you knew it, too, I thought. That we were going to get married some day. So what's the problem, Tanz? I still don't get it.'

'The problem is that *You. Did. Not. Ask. Me.*'

He was starting to get ratty now. 'You just want to get asked, do you? Like some dumb romantic schoolgirl! Is that what all this fuss is about?' he bellowed.

'YES!' I shrieked back, and there we were, eyeball to eyeball.

18

There we were, nose to nose – well, nose to chest, I suppose, since he's considerably taller than me – locked up in a dark, smelly, damp, filthy, rat-infested (I could hear them scuttling in the corners) dungeon.

'Right!' he growled.

'Well, then!' I growled back.

'Right. OK then. If that's what it takes to stop you sulking.' Then Gwydion got down on one knee, grabbed hold of my hand and snarled at me, 'Tanith. Lady of Ynys Haf. I love you. Will-you-please-do-me-the-honour-of-becoming-my-Dragonqueen. That is, in case you misunderstand, WILL YOU MARRY ME? PLEASE!'

'YES I WILL!' I snarled back.

'GOOD!' he bellowed.

Then our eyes met. And I started to giggle.

The giggle turned into a chuckle. I hauled him to his feet. The chuckle turned into hysterical laughter, and Gwydion, at last, joined in.

'That wasn't exactly the proposal I dreamed of,' I said, when I finally calmed down, and was wiping my streaming eyes. 'But I suppose it'll do.'

'I didn't know you were dreaming of *anything*. I thought you weren't that sop-'

My glare shut him up.

'Will it do?' he asked, anxiously. 'Really?'

'Oh, yes. I think so. For now, anyway.' I prodded him in the ribs. 'You can do the romantic bit some other time.'

He rolled his eyes. 'I don't do romantic.'

'Yes you do. You just don't realise it yet.'

'I don't?'

'No. But Gwyd, before we can do the romantic anything, we have to get out of here.'

'So we do. But first things first.'

And then I got kissed. Comprehensively. I stood back, afterwards, a bit shaky round the knee region. 'I thought you said you didn't do romantic!'

He grinned. 'Well, I might. Just occasionally. Don't want you getting above yourself, do I?'

There wasn't an answer to that, was there? Anyway, we did it again, just to make sure.

OK. Mushy bit over. Back to the dungeon.

I looked around me. Deep, dark, damp and doomladen. Typical dungeon, really. 'I don't see any easy way out of here, Gwyd, do you? The floors are stone, the walls are stone, the ceiling is stone. The only way in or out is through the door – which has big fat iron studs. So, any suggestions?'

'We could try to shapeshift; maybe we can do it now that Medrawd isn't about and interfering. Or whatever it was he did. But whatever we shifted into would have to be something that would get us out of here, and the only way out is through that door, as you said.'

He was right, of course. And then I remembered an occasion several years ago where some of the inhabitants of Ynys Haf had been locked up in a dungeon very like this one, when Rhiryd Goch had been a bit troublesome. And we'd beaten him, hadn't we?

'Through the door, Gwydion – or under it!'

'Under it?' Then light dawned. 'Spiders? Or beetles?'

I wasn't keen on shifting into either, actually. Spiders have a sort of nasty single-mindedness that is very unpleasant when you are inside their skins, so to speak, and beetles aren't terrifically bright. Hobson's choice, really. 'Spiders, I suppose. If we must.'

So we concentrated hard. It didn't work the first time – the influence of the iron studs in the door, perhaps – and we ended up half changed, which wasn't a pretty sight. Too many legs and not enough body. We rested a bit (shifting can take it out of a person).

'Right.' Gwydion hauled me to my feet. 'Ready?'

'Yup.' I was about to give it another go, when I had a sudden thought. 'Gwyd, before we shift, we ought to think this through a bit.'

'How do you mean?'

'Well, once we're shifted, we still have to get out of here. And where do we go then? Camelot, I suppose?'

'I can't understand why you went there in the first place. Merlin says there are always problems in these places that turn into legends, you know. It's almost as if the places themselves don't know their own limitations. What's legend and what isn't, sort of thing. Stuff gets overblown and overdramatised, and heaven help any unwary traveller.'

'Like us, you mean? Well, I can't argue with that. But *why* I actually went inside the castle was because of Merlin. He goes to Camelot regularly, doesn't he? He's always popping back to this Time to sort out Arthur's problems, isn't he?'

'Yes. But I can't believe you expected *him*, of all people, to get you out of here! He'd be as likely to make you stay here, from sheer cussedness. Anyway, I thought you weren't speaking to him.'

'I'm not. Wasn't speaking to you, either. But no, I

143

wasn't hoping to meet him exactly – what I was hoping for was to find his Time Door, somewhere inside Camelot. Merlin isn't the most energetic of people, and I can't see him hiking into Camelot from that Door right on top of the hill, can you? What, arrive all hot and bothered, with aching feet? No, not Merlin. I think he's got a private Door tucked away somewhere inside the castle. And I thought, if I can find that, it's bound to be in good nick; he's in and out of it the whole time. But other stuff sort of happened before I managed to locate it.'

Gwydion rubbed his chin. He hadn't shaved for a while, and it made a horrible rasping noise. 'You're probably right. So, what we should do then is shift – if we can – and then head back to Camelot?'

'I think so.'

'It will take a long time to get to Camelot if we're spiders. It'll take forever.'

'Only until we're out of here. Then we can maybe shift into something a bit bigger and faster.'

'Good thinking, Tanz. Ready to have another go?'

Gwydion stood between me and the iron-bound door to shield me from the influence of the metal, and this time the shifting worked. I stretched my eight legs and tried to remember how to walk on them all without tripping and splatting my nose. Then Gwydion got as far away from the door as he could, because being magic the iron still has a slight effect on him, and in seconds he, too, shimmered down into a huge black spider. Not a pretty sight, I can tell you. Only another spider could love him – and this one did!

'Ready?' he said, and we ran for the door. I knew I had to get under it fast as I could, in one swift run, because

144

otherwise the metal would weaken me and I might start to lose my concentration and change back halfway . . . I didn't fancy getting stuck under the door.

The gap was plenty big enough, but the iron's influence was horrible. Halfway under the thick door I could feel myself slowing, affected by the awful iron-sickness. Gwydion grabbed one of my front legs and hauled me out with him, dragging me down the dark, damp passageway and round a bend in the wall.

'Thanks, Gwyd,' I panted. 'I really didn't think I was going to make it. I wouldn't have, without you.'

'Probably not,' he said, smugly. 'See? I can be useful after all!'

'Oh, shut up, clever clogs. It's a long way up to ground level, and if we have to stay spiders until we get up there, we'd better get started.'

We scuttled along passageways and hauled ourselves up flights of stairs. There didn't seem to be any end to them – there hadn't seemed to be nearly as many coming down.

At last we got to the top, and there ahead of us was the door out of the dungeon dimensions and into the daylight. It's a funny thing: if you don't much like spiders as a human, even being one doesn't help. We passed a couple of huge webs and I have to admit I scuttled even faster, then! I didn't want to encounter any other spiders! The door was iron bound, and I was tired, so we rested a little while before going under it.

And then we heard footsteps on the other side, and it opened. A burly man was heading down, carrying a tray.

'Well,' I said. 'Breakfast is served. At least they aren't going to starve us to death!'

'No,' Gwydion said. 'But when he gets down there –'

'We aren't going to be there, are we?'

'So let's get a wriggle on, Tanz.' So we scuttled through the open door and, keeping close to the stone wall, slipped out into the courtyard and the morning sunshine. It dazzled me for a moment, after the darkness of the dungeons, and if Gwydion hadn't hauled me into a handy crack in the wall, I'd have been lunch for a marauding sparrow.

'This is no time to sunbathe, Tanz!' he muttered, as the cheated bird flew off.

'I wasn't sunbathing!' I protested. 'I couldn't see where I was going because my eyes were watering.'

'I think the quicker we shift into something a bit less vulnerable, the better.'

As soon as the coast was clear, we emerged from our hidey-hole, and slipped into a little alcove where no-one could see us. Pounding feet echoing up the stairs from the dungeon told us that our absence had been noted – but for once I thought really fast, shifted back to myself, and when the tough bloke reached the top of the steps, I zapped him between the eyes with a spell that made his eyes cross. He smiled happily, and collapsed in a heap. I used my magic to swing the heavy door shut – hanging the spell onto the woody bits, because the iron was resisting it, of course. But I managed to get it closed, if not locked. And then I shifted back to spider. With any luck he wouldn't be missed for a while.

'So – what are we going to be now?'

Gwydion shimmered, and in place of his sinister, spidery shape there was a large white cat.

'Oh, Gwyd! Just like old times!'

'Don't remind me. But cats come and go as they please and most often no-one notices them.'

'Good thinking, Catman.' I chose black, myself – sleek, slender and a little on the kittenish side. Cat personalities have a nice feel to them – sort of confident, and a bit arrogant, selfish and out-of-my-way-sucker, sort of thing – although the thought of food was never far away, and the image of a fat mouse popped instantly into my head. I licked my lips. And found myself licking a paw to wash my face with.

'Oh, very convincing, Tanz. You make a good cat – easily offended and a bit sharp in the claws.'

I washed my whiskers and started on my ears. 'If I'm going to be a cat, I'm going to do it properly.'

'All the same, I want to be away from here as fast as we can. Sooner or later that guard will be discovered, and then they will start looking for us. And when we get to Camelot, we need to keep away from Medrawd.'

'Not to mention his mother.'

'Oh yes. Morgan le Fay. What's she like?'

I pulled a face. 'Remember Spiderwitch?'

'Ooooh, yes. Do I! That bad, eh?'

'Not at all. Spiderwitch was a sinister lady, right?'

'Yup. Like that, is she?'

'Nope. Worse. Quadruple Spiderwitch. In spades. I doubt you've ever met anyone quite like Morgan le Fay, Gwyd. She's a serious Witch.'

'So are you. I'd back you against her any day,' he said loyally.

'Thanks for the vote of confidence – but then, you haven't met her yet, have you? And don't forget – I'm a Goodwitch. She isn't. So she isn't constrained by any of

147

the Rules – she does what she pleases, to whom she pleases, when she pleases.'

'Oh. Well, let's hope we don't run into her, then. Anyway, if we don't get a move on, it will be breakfast time and our next meal will be on its way down to the dungeons . . .'

'You know when we get back to Camelot, Gwyd,' I said. 'Merlin is likely to have his quarters in the posh part, right? He wouldn't want to go slumming it in the servants' quarters, would he?'

'Not Merlin.'

'So the best place to look will be in the Gate Tower, where Arthur and Gwenhwyfar's apartments are. Merlin's won't be far from them, I'd place a bet on that. He'd want to have easy access to Arthur. I doubt if the Door will be too obvious – he wouldn't want to advertise the way he sneakily comes and goes – loves a bit of mystery, our Merlin. My bet is that his apartments are slightly higher up than the royal quarters – not quite up in the attic, but he does like his tower rooms, doesn't he? And the Door will be concealed somewhere in there. We'll find it, if we look for it hard enough.'

'But first,' I reminded him, 'we've got to get back to Camelot. I think I know roughly which direction it's in – but it will be quicker to find if we're birds.'

And so we stuck our noses round the corner of our little alcove to make sure the coast was clear, shifted into a pair of starlings, and headed for Camelot.

19

I knew we had travelled east – and Camelot was towards the west, so it was a case of heading in the right direction until we spotted the pennants of Camelot flapping in the breeze. From high in the sky it was a rapid journey, and fairly soon we were gliding over the battlements.

Once inside Camelot's walls, however, Gwydion suggested we shifted back into cat-shape again – cats can go more or less where they please, being an independent sort of creature. Castles always had cats – because castles always had mice and rats.

I was intending to bypass Gwenhwyfar's apartments, because I'd already been in there, and hadn't seen anything remotely resembling a Time Door. But Gwydion said we couldn't take anything for granted where Merlin was concerned.

'Did you see the whole apartment?' he asked, and of course I hadn't, had I? Only the ante-room. So we decided to be methodical about it, leave no turn unstoned, and go into each and every one of the rooms.

The Royal Household occupied the best rooms, of course, in the Gate tower, where Arthur would have an overview of the approach roads to Camelot, another down into the courtyard and also out over the river that ran past the castle.

The ground floor was mainly the Great Hall and the sculleries. The Hall at this time of day was populated with half a dozen late breakfasters, men-at-arms hanging around over a mug of beer and a hunk of bread, gossiping, killing time until they had to go on duty or whatever. The serving boys were carrying crockery and stuff to the kitchens, some of the servant girls were seeing to the fires at each end of the Hall, dogs yapping around their ankles and squabbling over discarded bones. We didn't linger in the Great Hall – Merlin certainly wouldn't have his Door there, far too public, even for someone who so enjoyed making an Entrance. Also, we didn't particularly want the dogs to start yapping around *our* ankles and squabbling over *ou*r bones, which is something cats need to think about, in a castle the same as everywhere else!

We scampered up the grand flight of stairs outside the Great Hall to the big anteroom where members of the public with complaints and requests waited for audience with Arthur. We slithered in through the open door and had a good sniff round. Nobody took any notice of us – everyone was too busy plotting and planning, or arguing, or rehearsing the Boons they were going to ask the King, and trying to think up excuses if they were there to be punished, to notice a pair of cats.

There was nothing remotely resembling a Time Door. Trouble was, we didn't know what we were looking for, did we?

When the door opened, we slipped into the Presence Chamber, where Arthur was scribbling with a quill on a parchment, and muttering. A stocky man in a long black gown was leaning over him, showing him another large and official-looking scroll, and Good King Arthur was looking seriously disgruntled about something. I'd half-expected Medrawd or his mother to be around, and it was a relief not to find them there at the King's elbow. Morgan's nose for magic would be a good thing to stay away from if possible! An arched doorway in the far corner of the room led to Arthur's bedchamber. I'd had hopes of that – appearing beside Arthur's bed in the middle of the night would have been suitably impressive to someone of Merlin's way of thinking – but unfortunately he hadn't been quite so predictable and the Door wasn't there.

We slipped out the way we'd come, up a curving flight of stairs to the next floor, where Gwenhwyfar had her sitting rooms. From here on, the stairs stopped being grand and became the familiar narrow and dizzying upward spiral, but cats cope with that sort of thing quite easily. The door to Gwenhwyfar's apartments was shut, but any cat worth its whiskers can get someone to open a door just by hanging round and mewing.

'Yaaaaoooooooowwwwlll!' I said, pointedly.

'Graaaaaooooowwl!' Gwydion added, and the door swung open. Lady Angharad peered out.

'Oh, look at the dear little kitties!' she cooed. 'Come here! Puss, puss?'

Bog off, madam, I thought, *I'm busy.*

'Now come on, Tanz,' Gwydion chided me. 'You have to act like a cat, remember?'

'Do I have to?'

'Yes.'

So I allowed myself to be swooped up and hugged and petted. ''Oo's a boofuls puddytat, den?' she burbled.

I mean, *yuk!*

She rubbed me behind the ears and chucked me under the chin and hugged me to her face, which was nearly as hairy as mine. Also, Lady Angharad, sad to say was not the most fragrant of people. Her gown had obviously hung for a *long, long time* in an exceedingly stinky

151

garderobe. I struggled free of her arms as fast as I could. Meanwhile Gwydion snooped round the walls, sniffing behind tapestries and under furniture.

This room was Gwenhwyfar's, where she and her companions sat and sewed, which was why Angharad was there. I'd been in here before, when Blaidd had been carried up here. Her inner chamber – where, presumably, her bed was – lay through a door in the far corner. Unfortunately that was closed, but I didn't really think Merlin was likely to have organised his comings and goings through Gwenhwyfar's bedroom. He'd said, once, that she was a brainless, flighty little madam, and nothing I'd seen made me disagree with that! But knowing her, knowing what was ahead, I still couldn't help feeling sorry for her.

'It won't be in there, Gwydion,' I said. 'Can we please get out of here before I get cuddled again?'

'We may as well.'

And then the door was flung open and Morgan le Fay was storming across the chamber towards Gwenhwyfar's bedroom. She completely ignored Lady Angharad. I wondered what sort of trouble Gwenhwyfar was in now.

'You don't have to tell me who that was, Tanz!' he muttered. 'The magic comes off her in waves, doesn't it?'

We went up another flight of spiral stairs to the next floor. Lady Angharad's room, and above that Lady Alys's. Surely Merlin's quarters wouldn't be any higher than this – he liked his comfort, did our Merlin, and I couldn't see him toiling up flight after flight of stairs.

And then I noticed a door *set in the outer wall*. It was opposite the door to Lady Alys's room, and I couldn't understand how I hadn't noticed it before. How could there be a door into the outer wall? That would lead right outside, wouldn't it? Anyone going through there would likely fall a hundred metres or so straight down to the cobbles of the courtyard. Gwydion had spotted it, too.

It had an ordinary, innocuous sort of look to it. And there wasn't an iron nail, stud, band or decoration on it anywhere. It was just plain, ordinary, unpretentious wood, and the same colour as the stone wall.

'This has to be it, Tanz!' Gwydion said.

We had a quick listen for footsteps, and a peer around the bend in the downward spiral in case anyone was coming up. There wasn't anything higher, so at least we only had to worry about one direction. We shimmered back into our own shapes, and Gwydion cautiously lifted the wooden latch. It swung open onto a narrow sort of battlement surrounding the tower, barely a metre wide, the pointy bit of the turret with a fluttering pennant rising up in the middle. I glanced over the wall and wished I hadn't. It was a long, long way down. Gwydion edged past me and round the tower out of view.

'Aha!' he said, deep satisfaction in his voice. 'Gotcha! You crafty old so-and-so, Merlin!'

'Found it, Gwyd?' I said, following him round, keeping as close to the inner wall as I could. I don't much like heights!

It wasn't a Door as such: it was just a tall shimmer in the air, but this was it. Merlin's secret way in and out of Camelot. Gwydion grinned at me. 'Let's get out of here, shall we?'

'Oh, let's!' I said, with heartfelt enthusiasm. Then we made our big, soppy, romantic mistake. He stopped, and bent his head to give me a kiss. And then, hand in hand, we turned back to the Door.

And were thrown backwards as the Door opened from the other side, and the Wind's sudden stop tipped Merlin out. Fortunately we managed to get out of the way in time, or he'd have flattened us.

'Oh!' Gwydion said.

'Ooops!' I said.

'And what, pray, are you two doing here?'

'Going home, actually.'

'Got over her little tantrum, has she?' he said nastily, glancing at me.

'Tantrum?' I said, trying to hang on to my temper. *'Little tantrum? You –'*

'We've got things sorted, thank you,' Gwydion interrupted firmly. 'And it's absolutely none of your business, Merlin. Never was, if I'm brutally honest. Now, if you'll kindly stand aside, we'll get back to Ynys Haf and you can get up to whatever mischief you intend to wreak at Camelot.'

'I shall stand aside, certainly,' Merlin said smugly. 'But it won't do you a bit of good. You can't go through this Door for at least twenty-four hours.'

'Why not?' I shrieked.

'Keep your voice down. Do you want to tell the world where I am?'

'Why not?' Gwydion repeated. He seemed to be grinding his teeth.

'Because I come and go here in a mysterious and magical manner, that's why not. I don't want centuries of mystique wrecked!'

'I mean,' Gwydion gritted, 'why can't we use the Door for twenty-four hours?'

'Oh. That. Well, it's an old model – a Mark VII, I

154

believe, maybe earlier than that. Needs a good twenty-four hour charge-up after every use.'

'I don't believe you.' A Time Door needing to be charged up like a battery? He had to be winding us up, didn't he? Getting his own back on us?

'Believe me or not, Tanith, you're more than welcome to try.'

Merlin stood aside, and stretched out an arm, mockingly. We stepped towards the Door. It was still there – although the air seemed to have less of a shimmer than it had. As we reached the Door, it winked out. Gone. Just. Like. That.

'Told you so,' Merlin said, smugly.

I felt like crying and screaming and chewing the carpet.

'So,' Gwydion said. 'What do we do now, Merlin? Any ideas?'

'Of course.' He was wearing his most irritating expression. 'I take you downstairs with me, introduce you as the Future Dragonking of Ynys Haf, and Tanith as the Lady, and you sit down and shut up while I get on with what I have to do. There won't be any problems from Arthur and Gwenhwyfar: they'll just accept you're with me. And then, tomorrow, when the Door is working again, we can all go back.'

'Except,' I pointed out, 'I've already introduced myself to Gwenhwyfar. She decided I was going to be her best friend because she's utterly bored, and we all know where that leads, don't we.'

Merlin raised his eyes heavenwards. 'Oh, dear me. You always manage to do the wrong thing, don't you, Tanith. Ah well. I'm sure I can explain you away if I think about it.'

'You might be able to explain us to Arthur and Gwenhwyfar,' I replied, 'but Medrawd and Morgan have sort of taken a bit of a dislike to me, as well. And Morgan has a pretty good idea that I'm a witch.'

Merlin slapped his forehead. 'Oh, *Bendigeidfran's Bloody Breastplate!* Why me? What have I done to deserve this?'

'Lots, I expect,' I said, evenly. 'And it's your fault anyway, all this.'

Merlin said, 'All what?' in the same instant that Gwydion said, warningly, 'Tanz!'

'Oh, never mind. Anyway Medrawd has already met Gwydion, and locked us both in his dungeon!'

'I can take care of Medrawd, don't you worry your dizzy little head about that,' he said condescendingly. 'And Morgan le Fay, too, come to that. But I can't keep you two out of trouble at the same time. I'm going to have to stow you somewhere until tomorrow.'

'I'm not some sort of a parcel!' I protested. 'I'm not going to just let you stow me somewhere!'

'Might be safest, Tanz, just to stay out of the way. Don't you worry about us, Merlin. We'll take care of ourselves. And we'll meet you back here at noon tomorrow. And then we can all get back. If you aren't here, mind, you'd better be prepared to stay, because we won't hang around. You're probably safer here than we are. You're in the Legends, so you're all right.'

So there, I thought. *Chew on that, Merlin!*

'Come to think of it, mind,' I said, 'you only ever come here when there are problems, Merlin. So what's up now? There didn't seem to be anything much going wrong as far as I could tell.'

156

'Well, what would *you* know?' Merlin muttered, loftily. 'I'm here – not that it concerns you, of course – to try to avert a disaster.'

'What sort of disaster?'

Merlin looked shifty. 'According to my research, Lancelot is due to arrive some time between five and seven tonight. I'm going to try to bend the legend to see if I can prevent Gwenhwyfar from getting involved with him in the first place. It's all nonsense, this love business, anyway.'

'Oh, really?' I said, sizzling again. 'Well, just you –'

'Tanz!' Gwydion warned. Then he frowned. 'But Merlin,' he began, 'you told us – often – that there is no way that anyone can change a legend, and no-one should ever even try. You told Tanith that Cantre'r Gwaelod was going to be washed away in floodwater, and that there was nothing anyone could do to change it. You said we just had to put up with losing all our friends and get on with life, after. What will be, will be, you said –'

'Never mind what I said. I said that *you* couldn't change anything, didn't I? I never said anything at all about me . . .'

20

'But you can't do that!' I protested. 'There's hundreds and hundreds of years of the legends being told and retold by all sorts of people! If you stop Gwenhwyfar and Lancelot falling in love then *everything else has to change*. Besides, how can you – even you, Merlin – stop two people falling in love with each other?'

'Oh, pooh. Love. What's love, after all? Just two people messing around with each other's heads and becoming utterly useless when it goes wrong. Totally ridiculous, the whole thing. Complete and utter waste of time, energy and emotion. Pah!'

Merlin was in his Wise Old Man stage, here in Camelot, and wearing the wrinkles, flowing white beard, traditional long robes and floppy hat – but that was just for effect. He could change his appearance whenever he wanted.

'Oh, really?' Gwydion was using his Quiet Voice which, when you know him well, is quite Scary. 'And is that why you ambled down to breakfast the other day and informed us it was time we got married?'

'Oh, well, that.' He looked slightly shifty. 'Well, it's in the legend, so it has to happen sometime soon, and I'm not doing much round about June – I assume you'll choose June, won't you? Most people do, for some unfathomable reason, although one month is as good as another when it comes down to it.'

Gwydion went very still and quiet beside me.

I butted in, quickly. 'You're free in June, then, Merlin? What about May? And July?'

'Frightfully busy,' he said. 'If you could see the list of things I have to sort out in May and July, you wouldn't even ask.'

'Good,' I said. 'We'll make it May, then.'

'But I –' Merlin stopped talking and scowled. 'Are you trying to be funny?'

'Not in the slightest. But if I may just quote you there, Merlin? *Well*, you said, *it's in the legend.*'

'And your point is?'

'You're saying we *have* to get married because it's in the legend. You said Cantre'r Gwaelod would drown because it was in the legend. And yet here you are, turning up in Camelot trying to fiddle about with a legend. There's something wrong somewhere, Merlin. Do as I say, not as I do? Sound familiar?'

He waved his arms. 'You don't understand, Tanith. By and large, legends can't be changed. What happens, happens. But I've spent years studying the Matter of Brython and all the good that Arthur was trying to do. He has to waste time and energy fighting Lancelot his right-hand Knight and all that, just because of a silly, muddle-headed, disloyal young woman. It's all Gwenhwyfar's fault, of course, the way everything is going to go wrong. If Arthur'd married someone else, someone suitably ugly, maybe none of this would have to happen.'

'All Gwenhwyfar's fault? Really? She kidnaps Lancelot and brutally forces him to love her, does she?'

'Oh, don't be ridiculous! All I'm saying is that if Gwenhwyfar can be just slightly – um – diverted, then possibly none of the consequent problems might happen.'

I was speechless. I opened and shut my mouth like a goldfish. All Gwenhwyfar's fault, was it? When male chauvinist piggery was handed out, Merlin was at the front of the queue with his hand out! No – *both* hands *and* a large bucket! Then I got my voice back. 'And how do you propose to "divert" Gwenhwyfar? Or haven't you thought that far?'

Merlin stroked his long white beard. 'I was going to play it by ear – find some other comely lad to dangle in front of her, so she wouldn't notice Lancelot. According to my calculations, I only have to get her past this evening, and that should mean the legend will be shifted just a little to the right of Time – or is it the left? – and everything should click nicely into place.'

'And where do you propose to find another young man?' I had a horrid feeling I knew the answer before I asked the question. Surely, he couldn't, could he? Not even Merlin would. Silly question, Tanz.

Merlin's lips curved in a nasty little smile. 'I didn't have a clue before I arrived, but since Gwydion is here – Dragonking of Ynys Haf and not exactly too hideously ugly – then –'

I knew it!

Gwydion let out a strangled squawk. 'What? You think I'm going to –'

'Well, it wouldn't be for real, would it? All you have to do is keep her silly little mind occupied just for this evening. You can do it, my boy! You can be quite passable if you put your mind to it. Pay her a bit of attention. It wouldn't mean anything, after all, would it? You could still go on and marry Tanith, afterwards! And any month you like to choose,' he added, generously, 'even if I can't be there to oversee it. So. What do you have to say, Gwydion my boy?'

'Oh, lots,' Gwydion said, calmly. 'But it all boils down, basically, and I expect you'd like it politely, to "no". Not on your life, Merlin! Not even in a parallel universe, in fact. If you're determined to try to change the legend, then you be the distraction. You can change your appearance so you look younger. You do it. But not me. No way. Forget it.'

I slipped my hand into his and squeezed. He squeezed back. *Dat's my boy!*

Merlin looked thoughtful. 'Do you know,' he said, 'I hadn't even thought of that! What a very good idea! Well, they always say, if you want a job done properly, do it yourself. I do believe I shall! After all,' he licked his finger and smoothed a wild, white eyebrow, 'you are still relatively young and totally unsophisticated, whereas I, with my age and experience, can be charming, handsome and, naturally, romantic if I really put my mind to it, I'm sure! Certainly sufficient to convince an empty-headed little baggage like Gwenhwyfar.'

Yeah, right, I thought. I was beginning to get the most delicious feeling that Merlin was going to come a most wonderful, tremendous cropper! *Oh, please,* I thought, *pleasepleaseplease.*

'Yes, indeed. You've hit on quite a good idea for once! I shall be Sir – oh, I'm sure I can think of a suitably romantic name – and I shall just make Gwenhwyfar fall in love with me and it will be the end of all that ridiculous Lancelot nonsense! And once that's out of the way, well, Arthur can get on with the Matter of Brython without bothering his head about his silly little wife.'

Gwydion and I said nothing. We were both, I think, trying to get our heads round the thought of Merlin as the

Romantic Lead. I know I was biting my lip really hard so I wouldn't break into a grin – or, actually, shriek with hysterical laughter and fall on the floor.

'You two try to keep out of sight,' he ordered. 'You'd probably better shift into something unobtrusive and stay hidden. Mice or something. I'll meet you back here tomorrow at the same time. The Door should be charged up and ready to go by then, and I'll certainly have accomplished my mission. And then, with any luck I can forget about Camelot for the next hundred years or so. It's been taking up far too much of my time lately. I'm a busy man, you know!' He bustled between us and headed for the door. Then he stopped. 'Best not change here, perhaps,' he said. 'I'd better make an Entrance with an Entourage so that I'll make a suitable – ahem – *impact* on Gwenhwyfar when I arrive.'

There was a brief fizz of magic and Merlin changed into his namesake and dropped off the battlements, wings spread wide to catch the updraughts.

'Now that,' I said, slowly, 'is going to be some entrance, if I know Merlin.'

'Oooh, yes. I think,' my new fiancé said, 'that Merlin's arrival as the Leading Man is something we should definitely see.'

'I'm so glad you said that, Gwyd. Because I wouldn't miss it for the world.'

Gwydion grinned at me. 'A cat,' he said, 'may look at a King. And a Queen and a Merlin.'

A few moments later, two cats pushed their way out of the door in the wall and padded down the stairs, tails waving. 'It'll be a while before Merlin arrives,' I miaowed. 'And I'm hungry.'

The best place for cats in a castle is a kitchen. Where dogs have to sit around, waiting hopefully for stuff to drop down, or bones to be thrown over shoulders, cats can go up and get it if they're sneaky enough and fast on their paws. We followed our noses to where the food was, off the Great Hall and down a long corridor. The kitchens were warm and busy as an antheap. I sniffed. Fish! And – sniff – chicken! We tracked down the larder, where food was laid out on cool slabs of marble ready to cook for supper. A huge pike, cold and barely caught. I jumped up and took a tentative, ecstatic lick. Gwydion joined me.

'Better not get your teeth into that, Tanz,' he miaowled. 'They'll notice that, and cooks don't take kindly to losing their main course before they get a chance to cook it. Better pinch something they won't miss.'

So we were wise and headed for the offcuts of roast meat left from breakfast and the night before. When we'd eaten, we yowled around a kitchenmaid until she gave in and put a bowl of milk on the floor, still warm from the cow, and we lapped until we were satisfied. Then, being cats, instinct took over and we Washed. It's very comforting, a good Wash, if you're a cat. Then, fed and groomed, we strolled out of the kitchens and back up the stairs, found a patch of sunshine in an empty chamber, curled up together and went to sleep.

We were woken by the sound of trumpets being trumped with enthusiasm, if not a lot of expertise. Gwydion leapt up onto a windowseat and peered out through the arrowslit. I jumped up beside him and nudged him aside so I could see, too.

'Oh, I so do *not believe* this!' I groaned. 'Does he really think Gwenhwyfar is going to fall for *that?*'

163

Gwydion was grinning all over his cat-face. 'All you can say in his favour is that he's the right age, more or less, and has all the right bits in the right places. Apart from that . . .'

'It isn't the bits, Gwyd,' I chortled. 'It's what the bits are wearing! Come on. I need to see this close up. It's enough to –'

'Make a cat laugh. Before you say it!'

Well, as entrances go, this was an Entrance. The two men-at-arms guarding the drawbridge gazed in bemusement at the approaching apparition. In Ynys Haf Merlin usually looked between thirty and forty-ish, depending on what sort of a mood he was in, and was quite at home in jeans and a T-shirt. But now what dress sense he had, had been mugged, beaten up and robbed. A pair of trumpeters led the way (and goodness knows what they'd been originally – possibly hedge-trimmers from the way they played!) and were blowing a fanfare of raspberries and yowls, while Merlin rode behind them on a huge white stallion. He looked like – like –

Can't even think of a suitable phrase. Unless it's 'a nasty accident in a custard factory'. Yellow and red tights, for a start, on long, thin legs. One leg looked like a carrot, the other like a banana. Above that, a red tabard with yellow insignia over a breastplate that was so highly polished that it had obviously never been to war. On his feet were yellow boots with long, curly toes (tied to his ankles with red laces to stop them tangling in his stirrups), and on his head sat a triangular red hat with a glorious nodding plume of yellow feathers. He carried a lance, and by his side dangled a longsword. His nose was so high in the air that if it rained he'd drown. Had we been in human form, we would have been holding each other up and howling with laughter.

'Good grief!' mewed Gwydion hysterically. 'Does he think Gwenhwyfar's going to fall for that?'

'I don't think we need worry about the legend, Gwyd,' I spluttered. 'She'll take one look and won't stop laughing for a week.'

The men-at-arms, trying hard to conceal their grins and not succeeding, stopped Merlin on the threshhold with the customary, 'Who goes there?' Only it came out, 'Ho-ho-hoo go-ho-ho's the-ha-ha-ere?'

I couldn't wait to find out.

'Sir Maelderw of Monmouth, Royal Ambassador from the Realm of Ynys Haf, mai man. Ai present mai compliments to Arthur, Hai King of Brython, and demarnd admittance,' he announced, in a voice that was just a little bit shrill – surely not? Was Merlin nervous?

One of the guards dabbed his eyes and tried to wipe the grin off his face. 'P-p-pass, Sir Maelderw!'

Maelderw? Oak Prince? Woodentop, possibly.

The men-at-arms stood aside, at attention, their faces red. Merlin rode his big white horse into the inner ward. He didn't seem to know what to do with his lance. The top of it caught on the bottom rung of the portcullis, which almost yanked him backwards off the horse. In the end he let go of it, and it clattered to the cobbles and lay there. Behind his back the men-at-arms were shaking with laughter and trying to muffle their guffaws.

Watching Merlin get off his horse was like watching a very clumsy cat-burglar climb down a very smooth, very high wall. In the end he had to swing both legs onto one side, turn on his stomach and slither off.

Merlin hit the cobbles, staggered and straightened himself. He pulled his tabard down over his bottom and stalked towards the door into the Great Hall. Halfway there he tripped on his longsword and had to hold it up out of the way of his feet. As soon as he was out of sight inside the building, Gwydion and I streaked down the stairs to be there when he arrived.

In the Great Hall, servants were setting the tables for the noon meal. Merlin (knowing the way perfectly well, of course, which Sir Maelderw wouldn't have – he hadn't thought of that!) set off towards Arthur's chambers. We followed the carrot and banana legs.

We were halfway up the grand staircase when I realised I wasn't paying enough attention to what was going on around me. Morgan le Fay was coming down as we were going up. I sent a quick thought to Gwydion, who glanced up at her. I tried simultaneously to hug the wall and make myself as inconspicuous as I could. She glanced at me, looked away – and then, just as I thought I was safely past her, bent down and grabbed me by the scruff of the neck. I yowled, and Merlin turned. But all he saw was Morgan dangling a small black cat from her hands.

Gwydion tensed to spring at her.

Don't attack her, Gwyd! I begged. *She'll take you apart if you so much as scratch her. Don't worry. Just stay close. I'll get away as soon as I can.*

Because I was thinking, right, *Morgan thinks she's got hold of a stray moggie. She'll play with me a bit, give me some kitty treats, and then get bored with me, yes?*

I wish.

166

21

I was borne upwards – not the way most people carry a cat, nestled in their arms, but at arm's length by the scruff of my neck. It doesn't hurt, being lugged around like that – but it's uncomfortable and not particularly dignified. Oddly, she was wearing leather gloves.

She carried me into her apartment, and leaned against the heavy door to close it behind her, shutting Gwydion out. Then she raised me, turned me so that we were face to face, and smiled. It wasn't at all a friendly smile. It was a smile that had elements of satisfaction and triumph written all over it. And a lot of sharp teeth.

'Did you really think, Witch, that I wouldn't find you in the end, wherever you tried to hide?'

Oh, &*^%$(* I thought.

'I can *smell* a witch. I can *feel* a witch. I can *sense* a witch. And you, my dear, are a witch.'

But luckily, while she was smelling and feeling and sensing me, she hadn't noticed Gwydion.

'But Lady of Ynys Haf, I'm afraid there is room for only one witch at Camelot, and that witch is Morgan le Fay. And therefore, you must be –' here she smiled even wider, '– elim-in-a-ted.' She got a lot of syllables out of that one word. Nasty ones.

No need to get all territorial, I thought. *If you want me to go, just say the word, and I'm out of here.* Now that I knew where the Time Door was, and Merlin was here, and Gwydion was outside, I'd stopped worrying. Gwydion would rescue me. The minute she put me down, I'd be streaking for safety. It would be a pity to miss seeing Merlin make a complete prat of himself – but Gwydion would tell me about it later. So I wasn't worried. Not at all. Not right up until the moment she – opened the door of a small iron cage and shoved me inside. So that was why the gloves. So she wouldn't have to touch the iron. It was so small that I couldn't turn round in it, or even sit up. I had to lie down, my paws tucked under me. Completely surrounded by the horrible, sickening feeling of iron bars. I slitted my eyes, already feeling ill.

'Did you know,' Morgan le Fay said, peering at me from a safe distance, a satisfied smile on her face, 'that if a witch can be caught in a shifted shape, and kept in that shape, then all her magic can be distilled into the most wonderfully powerful potion?'

No, actually, I didn't. And to be honest I don't much like the sound of that 'distilled' . . . Gwydion! Can you hear me, Gwyd? Gwyd!

'I hear you, Tanz. Where are you?'

She's put me in an iron cage, Gwydion! I can't bear it. I'm already getting weaker. Find Merlin! Get me out of here!

'Don't panic! I'll be back as soon as I can.'

What, me panic? You bet I'm gonna panic!

'From the fear in your eyes, Witch, you know the fate that awaits you. Oh, I shall so enjoy this. With the potion I shall distil from your magic I can rule Arthur – and through him rule all Brython!'

Basically, I was still trying not to think about that distilling business. I hoped that was just a figure of speech. But then she walked away and began to set up a weird piece of equipment. I watched in horror as she found a cauldron, filled it with water from a large ewer and set it over the fire. The cauldron had a lid, (a heavy lid) and a tube led from it, twirled round and round like something out of a Frankenstein film, ending up in a large bottle. The bottle was on a stand, and near it was a small brazier with hot coals, waiting.

And I had a strange feeling that she wasn't going to be cooking a nice chicken and mushroom casserole. It was going to be me . . .

If I lived that long. Already the iron cage was having its terrible, weakening effect. If Gwydion didn't hurry, I'd really be in the soup – literally.

Morgan le Fay sang as she worked . . .

I just hoped Gwydion could attract Merlin's attention.

He could shift and rescue me, but that might prove fatal if Morgan set eyes on him – she might get Gwydion too, and boil both of us. If only he could find Merlin and bring him. Fast. The door opened.

'Ah, Medrawd,' my captor said brightly, 'just in time!'

'For what?' he muttered. 'What are you plotting now, Mother?'

'*I have the Witch!*' she said, hoarse with excitement. 'And she has shifted! Look!'

Medrawd pottered over and peered at me in the cage. Poked me with a bony finger. 'Doesn't look much like a witch. It looks like a cat. A scrawny sick one.'

'Trust me, that's the Witch. I have to move fast before the iron kills her, but I have her! Now I can make that potion. I've waited so long for this opportunity.'

'Pah!' Medrawd spat. 'Do you honestly think that boiling a witch to the bare bones and distilling the liquid will really make you so powerful? It's an old witch's tale, nothing more. It will never work!'

Morgan le Fay looked at her son through narrowed eyes. 'Oh, it will work, my boy. Believe me, it will work. This is a powerful witch, and a young one, too, and *still alive!* The potion will give me the power to rule the world, let alone Brython!'

Medrawd flung himself into a chair and pulled on his bottom lip. 'Some fool has just appeared, uninvited. Maelderw of Monmouth, his name is, apparently. He's dressed like a clown, and he's closeted with my uncle and Gwenhwyfar. Who has just announced that henceforth she wants to be called Guinevere, because it's more modern. The girl is a half-wit.'

'The easier to rule her, when the time comes, Medrawd!' Morgan hissed. 'When Arthur is dead and you are Crown Prince and I am Queen – she will be nothing at all. If I allow her to live, that is.'

The look Medrawd gave her didn't hold out much hope for a future of harmony and peace. 'Can't come quickly enough for me,' he muttered. 'I'm sick of having to be polite to my uncle with his stupid ideas of honour and the rights of the common man. When I am King, I shall – '

'Not King, Medrawd – while I live you shall be Crown Prince.'

'Oh, all right, when I'm Crown Prince and you're Queen, we shall be *everyone's* better, and stupid common people shall have no rights at all. I shall kill them all, if I want to. And Gwenhwyfar – oh, I beg your pardon, *Guinevere* – is making sheep's eyes at some knight that has just arrived.'

'This – what did you say his name was? – Maelderw?'

'No. Another one. Some Frenchman, du Lac or

170

something. Pompous ass. Ugly as sin, but tall and strong and young.'

'And straight, no doubt, as you are not,' Morgan said calmly.

'That's right, *Mother dear*, rub it in! It isn't my fault that I was born with a twisted body.'

And your mind's got a couple of kinks, too, I thought dismally.

'Indeed it was not, my boy,' Morgan agreed. 'But never mind. When you are Prince no-one will dare mention your shortcomings ever again.' She stripped off her gloves and patted his face. 'Is the water boiling yet?'

Medrawd peered into the cauldron. 'Almost. A few minutes more and it will be a full, rolling boil.'

'Then we can begin!' She sounded as excited as a kid going to a party. And she was talking about gently simmering me for a couple of hours! Still, to get me in that pot she had to get me out of the cage, first, didn't she? And I might be weakened, but I wasn't giving up without a fight. I got my claws out.

'Bring me the Witch, Medrawd!'

He hauled himself out of the chair and came over to where I lay, trapped in the cage. I tensed myself ready.

He unlocked the cage door and reached in to grab the scruff of my neck to drag me out, just as Morgan said, 'Bring the cage here! Don't risk taking her out!'

Too late! Medrawd's hand was already in the cage, and a split second later – even though I was slowed and hampered by both the size of the cage and the iron – my claws were buried deep in his hand. And my teeth in his wrist. I bit down with all my strength and tasted blood. Yuk.

He let out a yell and yanked his hand back, trying to

171

shake me off, but I hung on until he'd dragged me out of the cage. As soon as I was out, I let go and leapt to the ground. I couldn't get out of the room, but I could keep out of their reach if I kept moving – and keep away from the iron in the cage, which would still have a weakening effect on me even if I wasn't inside it any more. I did the one thing neither of them expected – shot straight at Medrawd, climbed up his velvet doublet, and dug my claws into his face in passing. He screeched and tried to shove me away from him, but I was too quick. I leapt off the top of his head, caught a tapestry on the wall and climbed it. It's amazing how fast a person – or a cat – can travel if they are really afraid! I went up like a sky-rocket, got to the top and made a mighty leap onto the beams supporting the ceiling. It was dusty up there, but I was well out of their reach.

I crouched, pulled my paws under me and wrapped my tail around my body, trying to get my breath back and recuperate from the effects of the iron. Luckily I hadn't been in it for very long.

Down below, Morgan was beating her son around the head with her wooden spoon.

'You stupid, stupid fool! I told you to bring the cage? You should have known the Witch would try to escape!'

'I already had the door open!' Medrawd wailed. 'How was I to know she was still alive enough to attack me! Look at me! She's clawed me half to death! I'm bleeding! Stop hitting me, Mother! I'm going to be King one day! You shouldn't treat me like this, it isn't right!'

'Isn't right? *Isn't right?* Are you really such a fool that you can't do a simple task without ruining everything? Without me to guide you, you'll never be King! Now stop whining and get that cat.'

Medrawd, his face oozing blood where my claws and teeth had gone in, peered up at me. 'I can't reach it, Mother. It's right up in the roof beams!'

Morgan le Fay sighed. 'Then I suppose I shall have to do it myself. It's always the same, isn't it Medrawd?'

Right, I thought, *you go and get a nice, tall ladder, and try to get me down, chum. I'll scratch your eyes out if you so much as lay a finger on me! Nobody's putting me in a stewpot without a fight!*

I slitted my eyes and watched her, quite comfortable on my beam.

I was so relieved to get away that I'd completely forgotten she wouldn't need a ladder, would she? She was a witch, too, wasn't she?

Morgan le Fay's outline suddenly blurred. I tensed. What was happening? Then her body wavered, she shrank down, and dropped onto all fours.

Hang about! This was cheating! There was no way that a witch was allowed to shift into something that didn't exist in the place in Time that they were currently occupying. Not fair!

I mean, a full grown black panther is overkill up against a sweet little kittycat, right?

Right.

But all the same, there was a very large black panther currently pacing below me, tail lashing furiously. It snarled, and teeth like ivory daggers flashed in a crimson mouth. It gathered itself onto its haunches ready to spring, and I wanted to shut my eyes, because it would only take one bound for it to reach the tapestry, and a little leap to reach me. And a little chomp to eat me.

Morgan sprang, claws extended, and hit the tapestry

173

just below the hooks that attached it to the wall. The claws went into the fabric – and the whole lot came away and crashed to the floor, wrapping the panther up in dusty, heavy material. Strong enough to bear the weight of a cat – but not a panther. It took Morgan a while to struggle out – and I noticed that Medrawd didn't do much to help – but then she was free.

And shifting again.

This time, she shifted into a bird. A large bird. A very large bird. An eagle owl, which has something like a two metre wingspan. Fierce orange-red eyes in the pale facial disc fixed on me, and the ear tufts pricked upwards. Morgan spread her brown-and-buff rounded wings, and took off. It was barely a hop up to the beam, and she was only feet away. She folded her wings again, her fearsome eyes fixed on me. She could kill me with her talons. Except, of course, that she didn't want me dead, did she? She wanted me in the pot, alive and casseroling for four hours on Gas Mark 6.

Well, I wasn't going to sit there and get caught. With the strength of pure terror I leapt straight up in the air and over her head, landing behind her. The head swivelled right round to look at me, and she spread her wings again. Frantically, I looked around. Now that the tapestry was lying in a heap on the floor, I couldn't get off the beam unless I shifted into a bird. I couldn't go up, because the roof timbers were there. I had two choices. Shift and do battle, or prepare myself for a very hot bath . . .

22

I wasn't sure I had the strength to shapeshift after being so close to iron, even for a comparatively short time. As well as that, my subconscious was doing a bit of a Job on me. I knew, deep down, that Morgan le Fay was far more powerful than I was. I only had Good Magic to call on: she had all the powers of Darkness. I wasn't mad any more, I was scared. No. Scrub that: make it mortally terrified. I wasn't entirely confident I could shapeshift – whether the iron would let me, and whether, if I did, Morgan would somehow prevent me. Only one way to find out. I gathered my strength and concentrated. I felt the familiar fizzing in my veins, but – it didn't seem nearly as potent as usual. I fought back the urge to do a really good Panic and concentrated harder. It seemed to take forever, but at last I felt myself begin to shrink. My nose lengthened into a beak, my arms stretched and curved into wings. As soon as I was in full sparrow shape, I took off. It could have been a really dumb mistake, shifting into a bird when there was what was possibly the most fearsome predatory bird of all sitting a metre or so away from me. But I gambled on the hope that its wing span would be too great for it to fly easily in that small chamber, so it wouldn't be able to get me if I was fast enough.

I darted round the room, my heart thumping with fear, skimming Medrawd's head, so that Morgan le Fay couldn't get at me properly without harming Medrawd – I hoped she had enough mother-love to worry about that! Medrawd reached up to grab me, and from the corner of my eye I saw Morgan spread her wings and prepare to drop from the beam on top of me. I did two quick circuits of the room – looking frantically for a way out, and then I gratefully spotted an arrow slit and hurtled through it, clouting my wing on the stone surround in my panic. I risked a glance over my shoulder as I reached safety. Well, perhaps not safety just yet.

Morgan had shifted into a sparrowhawk and was scorching the airspace in pursuit. Have you ever had one of those dreams where you're being chased by something big and nasty, *and your legs don't work any more?* It was just like that. My wings felt stiff and useless with pure terror, and I had to concentrate really hard on moving them. I felt as if any second, vicious talons would sink into my soft wing feathers, and I'd be an ex-Tanith. I got them going in the end, and hurtled round a tower, in through another arrowslit and down the spiral stairs, a furious, deadly Morgan still hard on my tailfeathers. If I could only find Merlin and Gwydion! I could feel her gaining on me.

A quick, panicky circuit of the Great Hall: no Gwydion, no Merlin. Oh, help me, someone! Mad swoop up the wide state staircase to Arthur's audience chamber, Morgan swooping after me: the door tightly shut. Up another flight to Gwenhwyfar's apartments. Sounds of music and laughter from inside. Once again, the door was tightly shut, but outside Gwydion was yowling and scratching frantically to be let in. Maybe for once even the Dragonking was panicking.

'Quick, Gwyd,' I panted, 'shift and follow me. Morgan le Fay is after me!'

He didn't need telling twice: he shot from cat into

sparrow feathers so fast the air around him popped, and came after me. I didn't go downstairs – I knew where the sparrowhawk would be heading – but up, until we came to an arrowslit that opened onto the courtyard. We shot through the narrow space, round the tower until we came to Gwenhwyfar's quarters, and hurtled in through the arrowslit in the garderobe. We didn't hang about – we kept right on going, straight into her private sitting room, pure terror speeding us. I could feel my little insides hammering so hard I thought I might have a birdy heart attack. We zipped into Gwenhwyfar's apartment –

Where Merlin in his banana and carrot outfit was looking daggers at a tall young man who wasn't paying any attention to him at all. I glanced over my shoulder: the arrowslit was too narrow to let Morgan in: the hawk hovered furiously outside, its curved beak opening and shutting threateningly. But it wouldn't be long before she shifted into something else and joined the party. We had to think of some way to escape before she did. Whatever shape she was in, she was lethal, and whatever shape we were in, we wouldn't last long if she caught us.

For the moment, however, we were safe. I looked around me. Gwenhwyfar was batting her eyelashes so hard at the newcomer that I could feel the draught from where I was perched on the top edge of a wall-hanging. The young man, in fairness, wasn't taking any particular notice of her, but was looking acutely uncomfortable in his skin anyway. He looked as if ladies' drawing rooms weren't his natural habitat – the sort of man more at home on a battlefield, or in an armoury or tiltyard. I know I'm female – but good grief, I despair of my sisters occasionally! I mean, just *listen* to the conversation!

'Sir Lancelot,' Gwenhwyfar trilled, '*dooo* tell us what the French court is like! What *aaare* the current fashions? Are the gowns as fine as they are here? Are the ladies,' and she tittered and simpered, 'all much more beautiful than the ladies of our court here at Camelot?' She was, of course, expecting him to say something totally creepy like, 'Could any woman be more beautiful than you,' etc etc. He didn't.

'Couldn't say, Highness,' Lancelot muttered. I don't even think he was being diplomatic. I think he was just one of those blokes who wasn't at ease around people in general and females in particular. Merlin, on the other hand, was still Trying . . .

'How could they be?' Merlin put in, striving to get noticed. 'No-one on earth is as gracious and charming and beautiful as our own dear, lovely, adorable Queen Gwenhwy – '

'Guinevere!' she snapped. 'I've told you twice already, you stupid man.'

If I hadn't been so scared, I might have laughed, because Merlin's master plan was rapidly coming apart at the seams. There was no way Gwenhwyfar was going to even notice Merlin with Lancelot around. I mean, it was the difference between Mr Bean and Johnny Depp. Gwenhwyfar totally ignored him. She tapped Lancelot on the knee and smiled coyly up under her eyelashes.

'Oh, come now! You must have an opinion, dear Sir Lancelot! Is the French Queen as pretty as me?'

Oooh. Was anyone really dumb enough to ask a question like that?

Lancelot frowned. He was perspiring, and I felt quite sorry for him. 'She's a bit taller, Highness. And a little wider. And her nose is a bit bigger.'

I could see Gwenhwyfar translating this into, 'She's tall and fat and has a big nose. She isn't as sweet and small as you, and you have a dear little nose'. She lowered the eyelashes and managed a blush. 'Oh, Sir Lancelot! You flatter me outrageously.'

'Do I?' The poor chap looked thoroughly confused. 'I'm sorry, Highness. I didn't mean to.' Confused and panic-stricken, obviously aware that flirting with the King's wife was not a wise diplomatic move. Little did he know what the future held for him. Hindsight is a terrible thing, especially when you're watching it happen.

Then my attention snapped away from the conversation. A third sparrow slipped into the room. My heart, which had slowed, speeded up again. I felt sick. Morgan. She wouldn't stay a sparrow for long. She'd shift, and then there'd be trouble.

'She's inside! What shall we do, Gwydion?'

'We could shift back to ourselves. Merlin would have to help us then.'

'Not without blowing his own cover! He daren't do that. He'd be a laughing stock for the rest of his life, every time he came here. All his authority would be gone, and the legend would be thoroughly messed around – but in a different way to what he planned.'

'Then we have to attract his attention somehow, get him outside so he can shift into himself and –'

'And what?'

'Well I don't know, do I? We can't get away from here for ages – not until tomorrow, when the Door is ready. But it's Merlin's fault we're here.'

'No it isn't.'

'If you hadn't . . .'

'Shut up, Gwydion.' I didn't want to be reminded that if I hadn't gone off in a huge huff, neither of us would have been here in the first place to watch Merlin make a fool of himself. If I said it was Merlin's fault, then it was Merlin's fault, and no argument. Especially not now, when there were lives to save. Ours.

'We'd better attract his attention then. Come on.'

We dropped off our beam and slipped down into Merlin's line of sight. I flew backwards and forwards, hoping the flicker of movement might attract his gaze. Surely he'd realise that a pair of sparrows fluttering around the room wasn't normal?

Except that he was occupied with Gwenhwyfar, and when he wasn't looking at her, he was looking sourly at Lancelot. I'd reckoned without Merlin's ego. Gwydion flapped, too, but Merlin didn't notice him, either. The third sparrow dropped to the ground, behind a chair out of sight. I watched the chair nervously. Sure enough, out from behind the chair slunk a large tabby cat, green eyes fixed on me. It licked its lips, yawned, and I saw needle teeth. I flew up onto the beam again, followed by Gwydion, and watched as the cat began to make its way towards a tapestry stretching from floor to ceiling. This one wouldn't break, but as birds, at least we could fly away from it. But how long could we keep going?

'Aaaatchoooo!' Lancelot suddenly sneezed. 'Chooo!'

'Oh dear, Sir Lancelot!' Gwenhwyfar smarmed. 'Have you taken a chill? Are you ill?'

'No, Highnessaaaaachoooo. Is there a ca-ca-atchooo! in the room? I'm afraid that I always sneeze whenever I am near a cat. I'm so sorry – atchoo! Aaatchoooo!'

'There was a cat here earlier,' Lady Angharad said.

180

'Perhaps it's still in the room.' Everyone began cat-hunting, including Merlin, and Morgan le Cat was quickly spotted halfway up the tapestry.

'There it is!' Gwenhwyfar carolled. 'Get the horrid thing out, someone! Quickly!'

'Aaaachooo!'

She took the opportunity to pat Lancelot comfortingly. She was having difficulty keeping her hands off him.

Merlin reached up and scooped the cat off the tapestry, hoping to earn some brownie points, but all he got was a set of sharp teeth in his wrist from Morgan. He almost dropped her, but hung on.

'Well done, Sir – ' Gwenhwyfar had obviously forgotten his name already. 'Put it outside, will you? There's a good chap. Oh – and while you're about it, would you please fetch some wine?'

Merlin's face was a study. Here was he – the Merlin of Brython – being used as an errand boy while Gwenhwyfar flirted with his rival. And there was absolutely nothing he could do about it because he was in disguise! However, as he walked towards the chamber door, I saw his back suddenly stiffen. He'd realised he had something magical in his hands. Luckily, his ability to detect magic wasn't diminished by the banana-split and carrot tights and curly toes!

Thankful for small mercies, I swooped outside with him before he got the door closed, but Gwydion had to fly out of the arrowslit and go round the long way. Morgan's malevolent cat-eyes fixed on me, but she wasn't struggling to escape any more, and allowed Merlin to carry her outside into the courtyard. She was obviously expecting him to release her once they were in the open air – but he held on, and carried her through into another tower. Morgan could have shifted back at any time, but perhaps she didn't know who her captor was.

Merlin went up a flight of stairs until he came to a small door. He held Morgan le Fay securely under one arm while he opened the door and went inside. Unfortunately, shutting us out. No matter. We could still get inside.

Swiftly we shifted into ants and shot under the door. Inside, Merlin was still holding tight to Morgan.

'I know that you are not a cat,' he said, sternly. 'I command you to show yourself in your true shape.'

Ha! Get out of that one, Morgan le Fay! Magic fizzled high in the roof beams as Morgan was unwillingly forced back into her own body.

'Ah. Morgan. Of course. I should have known.'

'You have the better of me, Sir Knight,' Morgan hissed. 'Who are you to command me?' She eyed him up and down. 'No-one important could look so ridiculous. And yet you have sufficient magic to make me appear in my human form. You cannot have any real power, for all you have commanded me this once. Who – what – are you? Some third rate wizard?'

Gwydion and I mingled our antennae ecstatically. Oh, now we'd see some fireworks. Because Merlin had really got himself in a tangle, hadn't he! He was masquerading as someone he wasn't, and he'd managed to run up against Morgan le Fay. He had two choices: back off and lose face, or show himself in his true shape as Merlin – and lose even more face. If Morgan le Fay discovered who he really was and what he was doing there, he'd never hear the last of it. His authority in Camelot as

Arthur's chief adviser and court magician would be totally shot, forever.

We watched a mixture of emotions shift across Merlin's face. Indecision and even the tiniest trace of panic.

'Well, little man?' Morgan sneered.

Little man! If that didn't do it, nothing would!

Merlin drew himself up to his full height, and looked down his nose. 'Madam,' he said, 'you don't have the faintest idea of the risk you take by challenging me.'

Morgan walked round him, taking in the skinny legs and the ghastly tights and the pointy shoes. 'Whoever you are, *little man*,' she said calmly, 'be aware that I could annihilate you in seconds. Be afraid. You have no idea how much trouble you are in – little man.'

'I think you should watch your words, madam,' Merlin said warningly.

'Oooh! The end of his nose has gone white!' Gwydion said ecstatically. 'When I was a kid, whenever his nose went white I used to run for it. He's *that far away* from losing it entirely! Explosion any time now!'

Merlin's voice was chilly, too. Straight out of the freezer, actually. I could hardly wait! All the annoying things Merlin had said and done over the last several years were being avenged. Because Merlin was well and truly in a cleft stick, up a gum tree *and* seriously in the you-know-what also. Morgan would make him suffer somehow. He was in a lose-lose situation and no mistake!

'Don't get too excited, Tanz,' Gwydion warned. 'Merlin is our ticket out of here. Maybe . . .'

'I know,' I groaned, and I did, unfortunately. 'We're going to have to help him, aren't we?'

''Fraid so.'

183

23

'How?'

'Dunno yet. Let me think about it a bit.'

Morgan le Fay was still regarding Merlin as if he was some particularly unpleasant species of bacterium. 'Nothing to say, little man?' she taunted. 'What shall I do to you? Would you like to spend the rest of your life grubbing in the lily pond and siring tadpoles?' She was walking round him, her arms folded.

The end of Merlin's nose was getting whiter and whiter, and a red spot had appeared on each cheek.

'Any minute now he's going to blow!'

'We have to create a diversion, Gwyd!'

'Right! Diversion. What?'

I scuttled a little further into the room, and while Morgan's back was towards me, I shifted. One creature I've never yet changed into was a dragon, and I went for broke. I almost filled the room. I was huge and red and had the worst case of indigestion I've ever had. I could feel a burp stuck halfway up my long, scaly neck and I straightened it out to see if it felt any better.

What it did was release the burp . . .

Oops! Fire shot out of my mouth and, across the room, tapestries burst into flame. Merlin's stupid hat blew off, the feathers catching fire, and he staggered backwards, his mouth falling open. Morgan looked startled, gasped, and stopped concentrating on Merlin.

I sent a quick thought to him.

Hop it while I've got her distracted, Merlin!

He stared at me for a second, blinking, and then shot

out of the room and down the stairs. Even Merlin knows when it's a good idea to run for it. Good thing his shoe-points were attached to his ankles, the speed he was travelling!

Morgan narrowed her eyes and glared at me. 'Ah. I assume the Witch has shapeshifted? A dragon is quite impressive, dear, for a beginner, but don't forget –'

She could of course challenge me, make me shift back to myself. But only if I was there to hear, and I certainly didn't intend to hang around long enough to let her get the words out!

'Quick, Gwydion!'

I changed rapidly into a wasp and shot past her ear. She swatted at me, but missed.

'I command –' she shrieked, but I'd gone!

Gwydion scuttled outside the door again. Wasp isn't a nice shape to be in – I was a black and yellow bundle of spite, most unpleasant. I shifted to a bumble bee instead – much more comfortable – and Gwydion did likewise. Then we flew off in search of Merlin.

He hadn't gone far. He was sitting on the roof-walk near the Time Door, gnawing his fingernails. We buzzed alongside him and shifted back.

'I suppose I should thank you,' he said, grudgingly. The end of his nose was returning gradually to its normal colour.

'You should,' I agreed. Oooh, I love a bit of nice, cold revenge occasionally! He really should have grovelled, apologised, been thoroughly effusive and all the other stuff he so rarely did.

He didn't, of course! Altogether too much to ask, gratitude, from Merlin!

'That could have been quite nasty if it had gone wrong, Merlin,' Gwydion commented mildly.

'Not at all! I was in complete command of the situation the entire time.'

'Yeah, sure you were. Right up to the point when she was going to turn you into a frog.'

'As if she could have done anything at all to someone with my powers! If you hadn't intervened, I should simply have . . . have . . .'

'Appeared in your usual Camelot guise and zapped Morgan?'

'Of course. She'd have had the shock of her life.'

'Oh, she would. She'd have been absolutely gobsmacked that you could even think of changing the Camelot legend so that Gwenhwyfar doesn't get involved with Lancelot. Not that she knows what's going to happen yet, of course. And once she'd got over realising you weren't Sir Muddlehead of Monmouth or whatever your name is, but Merlin in disguise, she'd have been absolutely ecstatic. Now *that* would have changed the legend, and no mistake. I can see the headlines now: *Merlin scuppered in takeover bid by Morgan le Fay.*

Merlin looked shifty. 'It might have worked!'

'And then what would happen to Camelot? Would Arthur go on to old age and grandchildren and happiness and peace all over Brython forever and ever? I don't think so, Merlin. There are too many other possibilities, even if you take Lancelot out of the equation, you can't get rid of Morgan and Medrawd as well, can you? And it's Medrawd who causes the most trouble, not Morgan. Most of the trouble she causes has already been accounted for –

186

producing Medrawd, for instance. And then there's Gwenhwyfar. If it isn't Lancelot, it will almost certainly be someone else she falls in love with. She's a dingbat. Merlin, she's a total dingbat!'

'She certainly doesn't have much commonsense.'

'What, because she didn't fall for you? She fancied Lancelot more?' I admit it. I couldn't help it. I chortled.

'That has nothing at all to do with anything,' Merlin said huffily. 'Nothing at all whatsoever.'

'Oh, really?'

'Really,' he said, and I noticed the tip of his nose was going white again. So did Gwydion.

'Tanz!' he muttered, and (reluctantly) I backed off. No point in rubbing it in too hard – but it was nice to have Merlin on the back foot for once.

'So. What are you going to do now?' I asked.

'Well, I'd like to go back to Ynys Haf – but we can't until tomorrow. As I see it, I have two choices. Either I stay hidden, or I become the Merlin they are used to seeing and make a surprise visit. And since Camelot is a difficult place in which to hide, I had better shift into Wise Merlin Mode.'

He did a brief thing with arm-waving and muttering, and his outline blurred. The ghastly yellow and red outfit disappeared (thank goodness!) and his face wrinkled and became old and wise-looking. A long white beard sprouted from his chin and travelled down his chest almost to his belly-button, and he smoothed it down over his black velvet robe. A small skull-cap sat on his thick white hair, and his eyes glinted under white eyebrows like hairy caterpillars. It was really weird, seeing him in this old man guise. Quite creepy, actually.

'And what about you two?' he asked, straightening the sleeve of his robe.

'What about us?'

'I don't think it would be a good idea for you to try to stay hidden. Now that I am here in my usual guise, you might as well stay with me. I can protect you better if you're out in the open – at least until tomorrow.'

'And that way perhaps we can get fed,' Gwydion muttered. 'My stomach thinks my throat's been cut.'

'If you get too close to Medrawd, Gwydion my boy, you may find that your stomach is perfectly correct!' He smirked. Nothing keeps him off balance for long.

'So – who are we going to be?' I asked.

Merlin raised his eyebrows. 'Who else but the Dragonking and Lady of Ynys Haf?'

'The Dragonking,' Gwydion said, grinning at me, 'and his *fiancée*, the Lady of Ynys Haf.'

Oh yes! I dimly remembered being proposed to. Which logically makes me a fiancée, doesn't it!

'Oh. Got that sorted out, have you? Good thing, too. Ridiculous fuss to make, Tanith. Utterly ridiculous. Of all the brainless things to do, running off like that and worrying everybody. Totally illogical. Typically female. Can't imagine what got into you.'

'You can't imagine –'

'Tanz!' Gwydion warned. 'Not now, all right?'

I subsided. I'd get my revenge on Merlin sometime. Soon. 'Better smarten ourselves up a bit, then,' I decided. I produced a gorgeous apple-green gown and headdress, then changed my mind and made it amber, then remembered I'd worn brown the night before, went for gold instead and back to pale green.

'Why does it take women so long to get changed?' Merlin sighed. 'Gwydion, you'd better look tidy, too.'

Gwydion produced a neat tabard and hose, and some soft leather boots. He also, I noticed, magicked himself a small and wickedly sharp knife to slip into his right boot, as well as the one openly on display at his belt.

'Expecting trouble, Gwyd?' I asked.

'You never know. With Medrawd around, I'd rather be prepared. It seems a good idea to take precautions, just in case.'

I couldn't argue with that. I wished we could just get away from here – but since we couldn't, the best plan would be to stay close to Merlin.

We checked that the coast was clear, and then the three of us sneaked into Merlin's chamber – which, true to form, was right at the top of one of the other towers. I don't know why Merlin always likes to be so high up. Maybe he feels he's mentally so far above the rest of us, he ought to be physically above us all as well!

At supper time, we joined the crowd heading for the Great Hall. I would have happily lurked at the edges of the huge room, but Merlin was having none of it, and strode up the little steps onto the dais where everyone was standing beside their chairs, awaiting the arrival of Gwenhwyfar and Arthur. I did a quick count and realised that there were more bums than there were seats available on the dais. Good. Maybe Gwydion and I could sit in the body of the hall instead.

Arthur and Gwenhwyfar appeared, the Queen in a deep red robe, closely followed by Medrawd, who glared furiously at me. I couldn't resist giving him a little finger wiggle. Lancelot pootled unhappily behind them all, and

Gwenhwyfar kept glancing over her shoulder at him, still batting her eyelashes. Arthur, bless him, didn't notice – that was his trouble in the long run, wasn't it? – he didn't notice. Not even when all manner of misbehaviour was going on under his royal nose. Poor Lancelot was getting increasingly uncomfortable.

'Merlin!' Arthur said, spotting him. 'I had no idea you were here!' He pretended to be nervous. 'Oh, dear. What have I done wrong this time? Passed an erroneous law? Broken one of your Rules? I'm sure you will tell me in time. You usually do.'

'I'm sure I shall, Your Grace,' Merlin replied smoothly. He inclined his head towards Gwenhwyfar. 'Highness.'

'Merlin,' Gwenhwyfar replied, distantly. She didn't look ecstatic to see him. 'I see that you have Lady Tanith with you. My Lady, I looked for you this afternoon, and could not find you. I was not aware that I had given you permission to leave court.'

Who did she think she was? My temper started to rise, but then I remembered: she was Gwenhwyfar, High Queen of Brython, one of the three gentle gold-collared Ladies of Brython, her status divine. Despite appearances, she outranked me.

'Highness, Lady Tanith's absence is my fault, I fear. I have been in her company for most of the day. You may not know, because perhaps Lady Tanith has been too modest to enlighten you, but she is the Lady of Ynys Haf, a small kingdom but one of great richness, lying near the sea to the west of here. Great richness, but sadly it has yet to achieve total peace.'

I pricked up my ears at this: we weren't at total peace?

Well, I suppose that was true. But we nearly were, thanks to Gwydion.

'And this, Your Majesty,' he indicated Gwydion, 'is Gwydion, Dragonking of Ynys Haf.'

Arthur nodded at us, Gwydion bowed, and I dropped a curtsey.

'And what,' Arthur enquired, 'are your companions doing here in Camelot?'

Merlin was good, I'll give him that. He thought almost as fast on his feet as I do occasionally!

'They are here, Your Grace, so that they may see at first hand the great and wondrous work you are doing to achieve peace and harmony throughout Your Realm. To learn how they, too, can make their homeland fair and just for all.'

Arthur smiled. 'You are welcome at Camelot – although Lady Tanith, you should not have been so modest when first you came before Us. You have arrived on a memorable day, my Lord Gwydion.' He gestured towards Lancelot, who was standing looking extremely uncomfortable at the way Gwenhwyfar was gazing worshipfully up at him.

'Today my court has been graced by Sir Lancelot du Lac, who has come to swear fealty to Us and to Our Realm. His sword will, We are certain, be a worthy addition to Our Knights of the Round Table, and his presence will add to the harmony of Our court.'

Too true, I thought. *But not the way you mean it.*

'Now,' Arthur said. 'We shall be seated.' He beckoned a servant over and the man scuttled away to find some extra chairs. Very thoughtful, Arthur. Good thing he couldn't see Medrawd looking daggers at him. 'Dragonking, perhaps you will sit here on my right, and your Lady shall take her place next to my dear wife, if that pleases you?'

'It may please *them*,' a voice said, 'but it does not please me. Would Your Grace knowingly entertain a witch?'

Oh, shut up, Morgan! I thought. She might at least have waited until we'd eaten.

24

'A witch?' Arthur looked startled. 'Sister, you accuse the Lady of Ynys Haf? She is Our guest! I would hope that you have proof!'

'Of course.' Morgan drawled. Her gaze drifted over me. It said, more or less, *Get out of that one!* 'Many strange things have happened since this lady arrived – wild birds inside the castle, cats invading our chambers – and the mysterious disappearance of your entire menagerie. Who but a witch could be responsible?'

Arthur gazed at me, frowning. 'Lady Tanith, this is a serious accusation my sister makes. Is this true?'

Now I had to think *really fast*. I felt Gwydion tense beside me, and sensed that Merlin was about to put his oar in. On current form, it might be better if he didn't. The problem was that as a Goodwitch – *I couldn't lie!*

Fortunately, my feet are used to being thunk on fast. 'Your Grace, I am no more a witch than the Lady Morgan.'

'Oh, well done, Tanz!' Gwydion muttered. 'Good thinking. Nice one.'

Arthur, of course, was perfectly aware that his sister was not as quite as immaculate as the driven snow on the subject of witchcraft. Arthur probably had his faults, but he was painfully honest. He opened and shut his mouth helplessly.

'And since,' Merlin interjected softly, stating the obvious, so that only Arthur and those closest to him could hear, 'the Lady Morgan your sister is *obviously* no witch, Arthur, then neither can the Lady of Ynys Haf be. To accuse one is to accuse the other.'

Gwenhwyfar looked from one man to another. She knew

perfectly well that Morgan was sinister and scary, even if she had no idea quite how bad she was. I could almost see the wheels ticking round in Gwenhywfar's head.

Now if she'd only kept her big mouth shut, we might have all subsided into a guarded truce, eaten our suppers and maybe even finished the evening unscathed. But no. Gwenhwyfar was out to impress.

'I think,' she said, smiling sweetly at all concerned, 'it should be trial by combat!'

My jaw dropped. *Trial by combat?* What was she bleating on about? Was I supposed to fight Morgan? What with? Magic or swords?

Arthur turned to her. 'Trial by combat? What do you mean, my precious?'

Gwenhwyfar smiled triumphantly, centre stage once more – and able to show off in front of Lancelot how erudite she was. 'Well, if Morgan is really accusing Tanith of witchcraft, then shouldn't their champions fight? In trial by combat, whoever is the winner proves who is right and who is wrong. Tanith is my friend, and I am absolutely sure that she isn't a witch.' She looked knowing. 'I'm sure I would have sensed if she were.'

Right. She was so self-centred that she wouldn't sense a brick if it clouted her on the head.

She smiled sweetly at Morgan, who narrowed her eyes nastily back. 'And dear Tanith is new here at court, and doesn't know hardly anybody, and because I am Queen, I shall choose her champion for her.' She glanced over her shoulder flirtatiously. 'And I choose Sir Lancelot, who is Arthur's newest and bravest knight. And who shall be your champion, Morgan?'

Medrawd leapt to his feet. 'Of course, I shall fight for my

mother,' he said. He couldn't really do anything else. Morgan looked bored, and I almost felt sorry for Medrawd: whatever he did I had the feeling he wouldn't impress her much. Of course he wouldn't fight fair. He was so sneaky and twisted that he'd meet himself coming out of a revolving door. And Lancelot might be fatally wounded in this encounter, because he was Good, and would fight according to the Old School Rules and all that. Which was a real handicap if he came up against someone like Medrawd.

The other problem, of course was, if he got killed, that would mess up the legend as effectively as it would have been messed up if Merlin's idiotic plan to make Gwenhwyfar fall in love with him had succeeded. Lancelot was supposed to be the finest knight of all those seated at Arthur's Round Table – but he certainly wouldn't want to go and kill the King's nephew as soon as he got to Camelot, would he? It put him in a terrible situation, and from the expression on his face, he knew it only too well. It didn't look good for any of us, actually. Merlin's face was still, and I couldn't properly read his expression – but I thought there might be a trace of panic in there somewhere! At least, I hoped it was panic. What if it were curiosity and anticipation?

A voice came from behind me. 'Excuse me, Your Grace?'

Arthur looked at Gwydion and nodded permission to speak.

My will to live went into my boots. What now? Oh, Gwyd, please don't –

'Your Grace, Lady Tanith and I are to be married. I can't possibly allow Sir Lancelot to fight for my future wife's good name. I beg leave to be her champion.'

I wanted to smack him. 'Gwydion, what on earth –'

'Shut up, Tanz. Think about it! It's the only way.'

I knew it already, which was the problem. Gwydion *had* to fight Medrawd; there was no other option. Gwydion couldn't risk Lancelot getting killed. If Medrawd died, then that would change the legend, yes. Without Lancelot, the Gwenhwyfar problem wouldn't exist, that was true. But nevertheless Medrawd would find some other way to bring Arthur down. Either way the legend would be changed, but if Medrawd died instead of Lancelot, then the chances were that Arthur's wonderful dream for a peaceful, law-abiding, fair to everyone kingdom might succeed. So Medrawd's death was a marginally better outcome than Lancelot's. Add to all that commonsense the fact that Gwydion was both brave and a bloke: of course he'd want to stick up for me.

Gwydion was absolutely right to challenge Medrawd. Except, of course, that of the three of them, Medrawd, Lancelot and Gwydion, Gwydion was *the only one who was expendable to the legend*, because Gwydion didn't exist in this Time, did he? He hadn't been born yet.

But he wasn't expendable to me! 'Gwydion, you can't!'

'I have to, sweetheart,' he said softly, and touched my face. 'It's the only way. Don't worry. I'll be fine.'

I gave him a Look. 'You'd better be, chum. I'm not prepared to train another husband-to-be.'

'Very well,' Arthur agreed. 'It shall be trial by combat. Tomorrow morning, in the tiltyard.'

Maybe we could escape in the night. Maybe we could get away before the fight. Maybe –

'Your Grace,' Medrawd said. 'It would quite spoil my

appetite to eat supper with someone I am about to exterminate. I would rather fight here and now and get the business finished. But –'

'But when my son kills this – foreigner,' Morgan leaned forward, her eyes glittering, 'and proves that the girl is indeed a witch, and my accusation is true, then I demand that she shall suffer the usual penalty.'

Oh, great. I wondered what the usual penalty was in this day and age: dangling by the neck until I was taller but deader? Barbecuing?

Gwydion met my eyes. His face said, *Don't worry. It will all be all right.*

Oh sure. If you don't win, you'll be dead and I'll be next. Fan-blooming-tastic.

Arthur inclined his head in agreement. 'Very well. It shall be now. Choose your weapons if you will.'

'Swords,' Medrawd spat, glaring at Gwydion, and gestured to his servant, who scurried away and returned bearing an ornate sword, its handle studded with jewels and intricate bits of wrought iron. Medrawd drew the sword from the scabbard and swished it about a bit. Light glinted off the blade. It looked horribly sharp.

'What are you going to do, Gwydion?' I whispered. 'You haven't even got a sword!'

He grinned. 'I'll have to borrow one, then, shan't I?'

'I would be honoured if you would take mine, Lord Gwydion,' Lancelot murmured. 'I understand that you wish to protect your Lady's good name, but I should have been honoured to be her champion.' He probably would have, too. He was sufficiently Good, Kind, Virtuous – and Stupid.

Gwydion took the proffered sword and hefted it.

'Is it all right?' I asked, anxiously. 'Because if it isn't, I –'

'You'll what, Tanz?' he whispered. 'Magic me another? Oh, great idea! We won't need to bother with trial by combat then, will we? No, honestly, this is fine. Here. Hold my dagger.' He passed me the little ornamental knife that hung at his waist and took off his velvet doublet.

A space was cleared in the centre of the Great Hall, and Medrawd and Gwydion took up positions opposite each other. Small boys hurriedly returned hot dishes to the kitchen and scurried back to watch, fizzing with excitement. Nothing like a good duel to the death to add a bit of interest to a dull evening!

'When you are ready,' Arthur said, 'you may begin. But if We decide to end it, you will obey without question.'

I felt hopeful suddenly – then remembered that Medrawd was his nephew; Gwydion was someone he'd only just met, and that Gwydion, being Gwydion and honourable, would probably try very hard not to kill Medrawd, because of the legend. It was a No Win situation to end them all. I felt horribly sick, and my head was thumping. This whole business was *my fault*. If I hadn't thrown a wobbler and decided to go home to Mam, none of this would be happening. Oh, what had I done? Talk about Gwydion being dumb – I was twice as bad.

Arthur held his kerchief in the air and then dropped it. The tension in the Great Hall was like a spring, wound tightly and ready to pop.

Medrawd held his sword towards Gwydion, the point

making small, dangerous circles in the air. I knew Gwydion practised regularly with his swordmaster, and that he was pretty good, but was he good enough? I just didn't know. It briefly crossed my mind to magic us both out of there – but Gwydion would never forgive me.

He stood calmly, completely motionless, watching Medrawd. The other man danced about in front of him. Medrawd was shorter than Gwydion, but that didn't make too much difference in swordfighting except for the longer reach. But if Medrawd were more skilful than Gwydion, Gwyd's longer arms wouldn't help much.

Suddenly, Medrawd sprang, his sword slashing sideways at Gwydion's neck. Gwydion wasn't there. I expected him to parry, to thrust back, but he didn't. He just stepped calmly to one side, very fast, so that Medrawd shot past him and had to turn to face him again. Back to the circling sword-point again. Medrawd's eyes narrowed and again he attacked.

And again, Gwydion was elsewhere. So far, Gwydion hadn't attempted one whack at his opponent. He hadn't even raised his sword. Surely he wasn't just going to keep on dodging?

He *couldn't* kill Medrawd because of the legend. And anyway, because he is Gwydion, he wouldn't kill anyone if he could possibly help it. He isn't that sort of person.

Again and again Medrawd hurled himself at Gwydion, and again and again Gwydion dodged. The watching court was beginning to smile, then titter behind their hands, but as the one-sided fight went on, they began openly to laugh. Medrawd, of course, interpreted this as laughing at *him*. Which made him more erratic, more frantic, more angry by the second.

199

'Coward!' he panted, as Gwydion dodged his thrust once more. 'Fight! If you don't fight, you are admitting the truth – your Lady is a witch. I shall kill you, coward. And after, I shall enjoy watching her die!'

'Oh, I don't think so,' Gwydion said, his face calm, his voice friendly. Suddenly his sword came up, and he thrust back at Medrawd. Medrawd hadn't been expecting it, and stumbled. His arm went wildly up to parry the blow, and in an instant Gwydion had hooked the point of his sword into the intricate, bejewelled, vain and useless decoration on the hilt of Medrawd's. The sword went flying into the air, and every eye followed it as it clattered to the floor. Medrawd tripped and fell. Disarmed, he glared up at Gwydion. Who, by rights, should have finished him off once and for all. It was Gwydion's right, and in trial by combat it was tradition that the ending was the death of one or other combatant. But I knew he wouldn't kill Medrawd. Instead, he put out a hand to help his opponent up.

Then he glanced towards Arthur, sitting on the dais in his high-backed chair. 'Your Grace, I won't shed blood when there's no need. If Medrawd will yield, I shall claim victory, and My Lady Tanith's good name is safe.'

'So be it,' Arthur said. 'Medrawd?'

Medrawd really didn't want to admit defeat. The conflicting emotions – admit defeat and stay alive, or dig in his heels and get extremely dead, flitted over his face. Then, expression thunderous, he muttered something under his breath.

Gwydion again offered Medrawd his hand to help him up, but Medrawd ignored it.

Arthur frowned, but said nothing. Then, 'Let this be an

end to it. Let us eat.' He ignored Medrawd, and beckoned Gwydion to join him at the high table. Merlin, beside me, let out a long, shaky breath.

'The boy did quite well,' he said. 'I knew he would. After all, didn't I educate him? A pupil is only as good as his tutor, and if I say it myself, I am an excellent one.'

I buttoned my lip. I was shaking so hard that if I said anything, I'd probably burst into tears. And I'd certainly give Merlin a piece of my mind. A big piece.

I turned to take my place beside Gwenhwyfar – I still wanted to shake her until her teeth rattled – but turned at a sudden scuffle behind me. Medrawd had produced a hidden knife and had launched himself at Gwydion.

'Gwydion! Look out!' I screamed, and Gwydion turned just in time. The knife went into his left shoulder rather than his back. He gasped, cried out and fell, and Medrawd flung himself on top of him, the knife raised to stab. I saw Gwydion suddenly heave upwards, throwing Medrawd off. And then Gwydion was on top of him, one hand gripping Medrawd's knife-hand, and the other holding his insurance – the knife he had earlier tucked into his boot.

'A cowardly act, Medrawd,' Arthur boomed. 'Dragonking, my nephew's life is yours to take.'

It must have been a tremendous temptation, even for Gwydion, to slit Medrawd's throat and be done with it – but there was the legend to consider, wasn't there? And Merlin, despite his own recent antics, had drummed that into him – into both of us.

He squeezed Medrawd's wrist until the knife clattered to the flagstones. Then Gwydion got up, holding his damaged arm, and kicked the knife into the far corner of the hall. Blood seeped between his fingers and he staggered slightly.

'Take Medrawd to his chamber and keep him there,' Arthur thundered. 'Medrawd. We should banish you for this night's work.'

'But you can't ban- –' Morgan began. Then her face changed. 'Of course, Your Grace,' she said softly. Her eyes flicked to me. She was smiling, but the smile didn't get anywhere near her eyes. 'Lady Tanith, please – bring your champion to my apartment. I shall treat his wound personally. I have a miraculous ointment.'

In a parallel universe, chum! I thought, and smiled sweetly. 'I'm sure you do, My Lady, but I also have ointments, and the Merlin will also attend him.'

My wounded hero, ancient legend preserved, tottered towards the door. 'Your Grace,' I said, turning back, 'may food be sent to Merlin's chamber for us, please?' I wasn't feeling sick any more. I was starving! I saw an eager glint appear in Morgan's eyes, and remembered the variety of poisons available to a determined practitioner of the Black Arts. So before Morgan offered to cook us something tempting, I went on, 'Sir Lancelot – perhaps you would bring it? I should like to thank you personally for your kindness.'

Lancelot bowed. He was grateful for any excuse to leave the high table. I think Gwenhwyfar's attention was worrying him. And I could be sure that any food Lancelot brought would be untouched by inhuman hands!

25

By the time we reached Merlin's chamber, Gwydion was almost collapsing. His sleeve was wet with blood, and the adrenaline from the swordfight was baling out of his body and leaving him weak as a wet paper bag. He managed to get to the bed, and fell on it face down, groaning.

'Oh, Gwyd!' I knelt on the bed beside him and peered at the bloody slit in his doublet. 'Is it bad?'

'How should I know?' he moaned. 'It just hurts!'

'Get out of my way,' Merlin commanded, rolling up his sleeves. 'Get me a pair of scissors and some hot water and bandages.'

I looked wildly round the room. 'Where from?'

'You're a witch, aren't you? Isn't that what all the fuss has been about?' Merlin snapped. 'Act like one!'

Oh yes. Right. At this point it hardly mattered that I'd be exposing my magical aura for Morgan to detect. I magicked scissors, tweezers, hot water, bandages, sticking plaster and gauze onto the side table, and added antiseptic spray and some antibiotics. I didn't care if most of it hadn't been invented yet. I only wished I could cure Gwydion magically. But it wasn't in the rules for witches. We could make lotions, potions and pills and stuff and use them to cure – but I couldn't wave my arms and mutter a bit and cure him instantly. Apparently healing the human body isn't in the job description!

The Wizard took the scissors and cut Gwydion's tunic away from the wound. He peered at it over his half-moon glasses. 'Not too deep. Just a scratch, really. That's a relief. Good thing you turned when you did or we might be looking at something much worse.'

'I wouldn't have if Tanz hadn't yelled,' Gwydion muttered. 'Ouch. Do you have to prod quite so hard?'

'Yes. Have to get the wound clean, so you'll have to put up with a bit of discomfort. You're right, it was a good thing she warned you. Mind you, if you'd skewered the wretched, cowardly little worm when you had the opportunity, this wouldn't have happened.'

'So, all my own fault then,' Gwydion muttered.

Little red sparks were whizzing in front of my eyesight. 'And what about the legend, Merlin?'

He waved a hand carelessly. 'Oh, Medrawd would be no loss at all to the legend. In fact,' – he squirted an aerosol antiseptic into the wound – 'it would have been an interesting experiment to find out what –'

Gwydion rolled over and sat up, the candlelight gleaming on the blood trickling down his arm. 'Merlin, how can you of all people say that? You spent the last goodness knows how long drumming into Tanith and me that legends are sacrosanct. So what's new? What haven't you told us? Did somebody make new rules and you forgot to mention it?'

Merlin looked shifty. 'I don't have to explain anything. I'm the M-'

'We know exactly who you are. The Merlin of Brython. But I think you owe us an explanation all the same. How come it's suddenly one rule for you and another for everyone else?'

'Oh, all right,' he said sulkily. 'I've been doing quite a lot of research lately – I *am* a research scientist, you know – I have all sorts of degrees from all sorts of universities all over the world. I came across this astrological chart, an old and unusual one in my great-great-great-

204

grandfather's archive – thousands of years old, of course, long before Arthur and Gwenhwyfar or Guinevere or whatever the silly girl calls herself.' Merlin squirted some more antiseptic into the wound, stuck some butterfly plasters across it and began to wrap it in bandages.

'And?'

'And of course there wasn't any legend, not then. How could there be? Arthur hadn't happened yet, had he, or that sword in the stone business and all the rest of it, and of course a legend can't happen until there's a living person to make it happen. Then, of course, it needs another person to pass it on – and embroider it, that's what usually happens, which is why legends get totally out of hand and above themselves. But this scroll that Great-Great-Great-Grandad left actually *foretold* Arthur and Lancelot and Galahad and Gwenhwyfar. And in *that* version of the legend *there was no Medrawd*. And also, Gwenhwyfar and Lancelot just stayed jolly good chums, adored Arthur until the day he died, and meantime they all lived happily together at Camelot. In Grandad's scroll, the whole Matter of Brython was wonderfully organised. The barons got dutifully into line or got punished, democracy ruled, and Arthur lived a long, fulfilling and virtuous life! There was none of that nonsense with Lancelot and Galahad and the Grail, and Black Knights and rescuing ladies from hot baths – it was just a straightforward story with rather a happy ending. Certainly nothing much to make a legend happen. So then I started thinking . . .'

Merlin finished off the bandage with a neat strip of sticking plaster (I got Mr Bump ones!) to keep it in place. No-one would notice the twenty-first century invention under Gwydion's clothes, anyway.

Gwydion, tied up like an Egyptian mummy, groaned. 'You started thinking that maybe the foretold version was the *right* one, and the legend had got it all wrong somehow, and so maybe you were just the person to go back, straighten everyone out and put things back on the right track again? Am I right?'

'Of course! I mean, who else? I am the obvious person. No-one but me has such a clear overview of the situation both Once and Future, and when the Before clicked into place so clearly, then – well, logical, wasn't it? And my way, it avoids so much unpleasantness!' He beamed and spread his hands. 'As I say, totally, utterly logical.'

Gwydion closed his eyes and leaned back on the pillows. 'Logical!' he muttered despairingly.

I got a cloth, wet it and washed the blood off his back and arm. 'It never occurred to you, Merlin, that the foretold version might possibly be wrong?'

'Of course not. My great-great-great-grandfather was always right! As am I.'

He really was the most infuriatingly arrogant man it had ever been my misfortune to meet.

There was a rap at the door and Lancelot came in, a covered tray in his hands.

'Thank goodness!' I fell on the food. 'Oh, this chicken is gorgeous. Want some, Gwyd?'

'If you can spare it. Lance, have you eaten? There's loads here.'

Merlin reached out and grabbed a chicken drumstick, bit into it and then waved the remnant at Lancelot. 'It must seem very strange to you, Arthur's court, young du Lac. I don't expect you're used to such outrageous goings on, are you?'

Lancelot finished his mouthful. 'I've never been to Brython before. Never left France before, actually.'

'And now,' Merlin said, with careful nonchalance, 'here you are, Lancelot, pitching up at Camelot, all ready to die for Arthur. If you must, that is.'

'Mmmhm.'

'Tell me, Sir Lancelot –'

'Oh, Merlin – Your Eminence – Lancelot, please. I am no-one, compared to you.'

Your *Eminence?* Oh, per*lease*!

Merlin smirked. He probably agreed with that remark, the pompous twonk! 'Do tell me, Lancelot,' he went on, 'what are your first impressions of our dear Queen?'

Lancelot choked on his mouthful, and I thumped his back until he could speak again. 'To tell you the honest truth, sire, I am more afraid of Queen Guinevere than I am of facing a horde of enemies in mortal combat!'

'And quite rightly too . . .' Merlin murmured, 'bearing in mind –'

'Merlin,' we said, together, 'stop it at once!'

Lancelot looked bemused.

'Just a private joke,' I explained. Except it wasn't really funny, was it? Poor Lance. Poor Gwenhwyfar. Poor, poor Arthur, for whom everything would go so spectacularly and horribly wrong.

When we'd finished eating, and Lancelot had taken the tray back downstairs, we settled in for the night.

'The Door should be fully charged and ready to use by about midday with any luck,' Merlin said. 'This time tomorrow we shall all be safely back in Ynys Haf. And let this be a lesson to you, young lady,' he said, looking severely at me over his silly little spectacles.

I opened my mouth to howl at him, but Gwydion gave me a *shut up* sort of prod. So I did. I'd get my own back sooner or later. There was one legend Merlin didn't seem to be at all aware of, for some reason. It had a young lady by the name of Nimue in it. Perhaps the one future he *couldn't* foretell was his own. I had a quiet chortle. Boy, Merlin was – eventually – going to get his comeuppance *in spades!*

'It will be nice to get home,' Gwydion said sleepily.

I actually had other ideas, but didn't intend to share them with Gwydion while Merlin was in earshot!

Gwydion, being wounded, had the bed, so I magicked up a couple of air mattresses (and a blower-up – I'm not stupid!) for Merlin and me. They were quite comfortable, and certainly beat sleeping on the floor. Merlin lay on his back on his, long beard draped over his blanket, his robe hanging neatly in the garderobe. I was just drifting off to sleep when I had a thought.

I thought about it some more, decided I was probably overreacting, then I did what the thought suggested anyway. No harm in taking precautions, is there? Then I fell asleep.

Despite being absolutely shattered after the day's excitement, I was woken in the early hours by Merlin snoring like an express train hurtling through a tunnel. He was over the other side of the room so I couldn't prod him to shut him up. So I got off my mattress and stumbled half-asleep across the floor towards him. I felt like giving him a good hard kick in the ribs for all sorts of reasons, let alone the snoring. I was halfway there, just passing the bed with Gwydion peacefully slumbering on it, when what I had done before dropping off proved that I'd been so wise.

I'd had this feeling that it was just possible Morgan or Medrawd hadn't given up, and might try to nobble us while we slept. So I'd put a burglar alarm on the door. And now, someone, very quietly, was trying to open it . . .

I wasn't worried. The door creaked open a couple of centimetres – and the world exploded into sound. Bells, whistles, catcalls, rockets going up, firecrackers, you name it, it was New Year's Eve and Bonfire Night all rolled into one. It was a really good noise spell. Merlin shot out of bed bolt upright, and Gwydion sat up, yelping in pain.

I yanked open the door to reveal Medrawd, ashen-faced, cowering away with both hands over his ears. People were running from all directions to see what the racket was about, and Lancelot pounded up the stairs in his nightshirt, his sword in his hand.

'Lost your way, Medrawd?' I asked him kindly. 'Your quarters are in the gatehouse tower, I think you'll find.'

'Let me show you the way,' Lancelot said grimly, grabbing him by the scruff of the neck and dragging him down the stairs.

I shut the door behind him. 'Thought that might happen,' I said smugly. 'Medrawd isn't one to give up easily.'

'I almost had a heart attack,' Merlin complained. 'You should have warned me!'

'Good thing you thought of it, Tanz,' Gwydion yawned, sinking back onto the bed. 'Do you think he'll try again?'

'I doubt it,' I said. But then I had a thought. 'But his mother might. And she doesn't have to come through the door, does she?'

Merlin gave me a long look. 'You may be right. The

woman never does know when she's beaten. We'd better take it in turns to stay on guard.'

'I'll take first watch,' Gwydion said drowsily. 'I'm fine, really I aaaaaahhhm.' He was asleep almost before he finished speaking.

'No. I will,' I said. I got a hard, straight-backed chair so I wouldn't fall asleep, and sat on it. 'I'll wake you if I start to doze off, Merlin.'

He didn't argue, and was soon snoring again.

I sat there for what seemed like hours. It's deadly boring, being on watch in the middle of the night. In the end I magicked up a book and one of those clip-on torches so I could see to read. But I started getting too involved with the story (as you do!), and my senses were going off-duty. I needed to be alert and watchful in case Morgan le Fay tried to get at us.

I disappeared the book and tried to get comfortable on the hard chair. It had a slithery seat, so if I relaxed, I sort of slipped towards the floor. My back was aching, and I was beginning to think it might be a good idea to wake Merlin and let him take a turn, because his snoring had gone from prize pig to prize-pig-plus-whistle-and-snort when –

26

A faint reddish glow appeared in the corner of the room by the window, as if someone was holding a torch with the beam hidden within cupped hands. But then it sparked, faded and was gone. I was at full alert now: aware of every sound, although I tried to keep as still as I could. I knew that something was happening, or was about to happen, and I wanted the element of surprise if push came to shove. Whoever it was (like, guess?) wouldn't expect anyone to be awake. Every sense was paying extreme attention, every nerve was standing on end and twitching. For a while, there was nothing, and then I heard a small sound.

I couldn't identify it, and frowned to myself in the darkness. It was a sort of rustly, scraping noise, as if something was moving in the rushes on the floor. A dry, slithery sort of sound: I could hear it, but I couldn't place exactly where it was coming from. Down at foot level, certainly, but moving – and I couldn't tell in which direction. There was a candle and a tinderbox beside the bed, but to reach them I'd have to cross the floor, where the strange sound was coming from, and something told me I would be safer staying exactly where I was. And maybe tucking up my feet, too . . .

And so I conjured up a moon. A large one, to flood the chamber with silvery light, illuminating every dark corner. I blinked in the sudden brightness, and my eyes watered. I scanned the floor, but I couldn't see anything moving down there. The rushes were still. I couldn't hear the sound any more, either. So what had it been and where was it now?

Merlin sat up suddenly, blinking in the light. 'What on earth are –'

'Quiet,' I hissed. 'Keep still, Merlin. I think I heard something moving on the floor.'

Merlin sighed and squinted around him. 'Your imagination is working overtime, Tanith,' he grumbled. 'There's nothing there. Unless it's a rat or a mouse. Put out the light, for goodness sake. Really, at my age, I need my sleep.' As if he couldn't be any age he chose to be. He lay down again, turned on his side away from me, and was soon snoring.

I kept looking. I knew there was something. I could feel magic in the room, like a prickling in my skin, or a greasy film on every surface, unpleasant, because it wasn't good magic. I couldn't see it, but I knew it was there.

I glanced at Gwydion, flat out on the bed. He lay absolutely motionless: even the sudden light hadn't woken him. Then, out of the corner of my eye, something odd caught my attention: one of the ornately carved bedposts seemed somehow thicker, darker, more solid than the other three.

I got up, walking cautiously, taking care where I put my feet. I was barely half a metre away from the bed when –

The bedpost moved.

It sort of melted, dissolved into itself, flowed downward, changed, and slithered across the patchwork cover towards Gwydion's sleeping form.

I wanted to scream, but I couldn't even get a squeak out. Horror crawled up my spine and goosebumps rose all over me. The bedpost had become the biggest snake I had ever seen in my entire life – not that I'd seen many, except in the zoo. It was over two metres long, and thick around as my arm. Up its back was a dark, zig-zag stripe against the grey-silver scales.

An adder, and many times the size of the adders that basked on smooth stones in summer in Ynys Haf. This was not real, couldn't be, even here in Ye Olde Middle Ages. Adders were never this size, even then.

A normal-sized adder could not kill a fully-grown man unless he was extremely unlucky – but a reptile this size most certainly would. And it was heading for Gwydion's throat. Adder venom injected directly into the jugular would kill him in minutes.

If I shouted to wake him, he would inevitably jump awake, move suddenly, and the adder would instantly strike. If I didn't, the snake – which was certainly some creation of Morgan le Fay's – would kill him anyway. I tried frantically to think of a spell that would zap the snake, but my mind was blank and I panicked as the thing slithered closer and closer, sliding up and over his feet, his legs, the movement mesmerising. If there's anything that scares me more than spiders, it's snakes.

And then Gwydion stirred, moved slightly, yawned. The snake coiled up on itself, the blunt, diamond-shaped head turned towards him, rearing back ready to strike –

And without any further thought on my part, suddenly my right arm shot out, grabbed the snake by its tail, and snapped it like a whip.

Crack.

And then I dropped it, leapt onto Gwydion's bed and danced around, screaming my head off. 'Oh, oh, that was so gross! Oh, I'm going to be sick!'

Once again Merlin shot grumpily upright. 'Tanith, for goo-'

'It's a snake, it's a snake, it's a snake!' I collapsed in a heap, sitting up as far away from the edge of the bed as I could get. 'I touched it, I touched it!'

Gwydion was sitting up, wincing, gazing at me blearily. 'Don't panic, Tanz, it's probably only a grass snake,' he began, and then he saw where I was pointing and his eyes got big and round. 'Ooh,' he said.

On the floor the snake was suffering severe whiplash. I had broken its back and it was dying rapidly. It twitched feebly, and then was finally still.

'I killed it, I killed it!' I babbled.

Merlin got up, slowly, and peered at the snake. For once he said absolutely nothing.

Gwydion's good arm reached out and hugged me. 'What did you do?'

'It was going to bite you, Gwydion! So I grabbed its tail and sort of snapped it. I caught it by surprise.'

'How did you know to do that?' he asked.

'Um. Don't know. Yes I do. It was in an old cowboy film I saw. John Wayne, I think.'

Gwydion went pale. 'That was probably a rubber snake and a stunt man, Tanz! I doubt anyone ever killed a snake like that and lived to tell the tale!'

'Now you tell me. Well, this time it worked.' I peered over the edge of the bed. The snake was dead – but it had straightened out. It was dark brown, now, all trace of zig-zag markings gone, intricately carved – and wooden. 'It's turned back into a bedpost,' I sniffled. 'It wasn't real.'

'It was real enough,' Gwydion said. 'Real enough to kill, the size it was.'

'Morgan!' Merlin muttered. 'I must do something about that woman some day.'

'Do it soon,' I suggested. 'And permanently. And painfully, if possible. I owe her one. No, lots.'

Merlin picked up the bedpost and tried to fit it back into place, but it was cut top and bottom – at the top the break was long and pointed, like a snake's tail, and at the bottom it was the blunt shape of the snake's head. He shook his head. 'Ruined, I'm afraid.'

'Oh, give it to me,' I said, turned it the other way up to make it fit like the last piece of a jigsaw, held it in place and muttered a joining spell. It worked. I could think straight now the snake was a bedpost again.

'I wonder what time it is?' Gwydion murmured.

'Nearly morning, I think. I peered out of an arrowslit towards the east. There was a pink smear of dawn creeping above the horizon.

'Is it breakfast time?' Gwyd said, hopefully.

'Feeling better, are we?'

'Much. Bacon and egg and sausages and mushrooms and fried bread and –?'

'Coming up. What about you, Merlin?'

'And kidneys and black pudding and baked beans. Oh, and coffee. With cream.'

'What's the magic word?'

'What –? Oh. Ha ha. Joke, eh? Getting your sense of humour back, Tanith! *Please*.'

I produced breakfast and a big table to eat it from, chairs and cutlery. And a huge cup of tea and some freshly squeezed orange juice and bread-and-butter and HP sauce and tomato ketchup. It might have been a heart-attack-on-a-plate type breakfast – but when you've

215

been terrified out of your wits, you get hungry. At least, I do.

By the time we'd finished, and I'd magicked the debris away (never any washing up with magical breakfasts!) the sun was fully up.

'I do hope that Time Door is going to be working properly again,' I said. 'I don't think I can take much more of the Morgan and Medrawd show.'

'Oh, it will work,' Merlin said loftily. 'Don't worry about that. You'll be back in Ynys Haf in no time.'

Gwydion grinned at me, and I grinned soppily back. He bent down and gave me a kiss.

'Oh, for goodness sake!' Merlin growled.

'Don't be such an old misery, Merlin,' Gwydion told him. 'Or we won't ask you to the wedding.'

'Oh, yes. The wedding. I needed to talk to Gwydion alone . . .'

'Are we just going to disappear from Camelot and let Morgan and Medrawd get away with this?' I asked.

'You are,' Merlin said. 'But I shall stay on for a while longer. I want to make certain Medrawd spends a considerable length of time out of royal favour. And as for Morgan – sooner or later she'll get what's coming to her. It's –'

'In the legend,' we chorused.

Merlin scowled. 'I doubt she'll be able to resist coming to check that we're all conveniently dead. We only have to wait. She's bound to turn up sooner or later.'

'You think so?'

'Oh yes. She will want to inspect the bloated corpses to make certain – she can blame it on ingrowing witchcraft, then – yours. Our Morgan leaves nothing to chance.'

216

'I don't understand why she hates me so much,' I said, thoughtfully. 'Medrawd, now, that I can understand. He's just what Mam calls a Nasty Piece of Work, who is evil because he likes it, and he hates Arthur for all sorts of reasons – not least for staying alive when Medrawd wants to be King. But Morgan? She's a powerful witch. Why would she even notice me? What did I ever do to her?'

'Came to Camelot, Tanith,' Merlin said drily. 'She saw immediately that you have magical powers – and although you are handicapped by being a Goodwitch, she felt threatened because she recognised that your powers are at least equal to her own. But she, of course, cheats – you don't. And don't forget, Morgan has plans for Brython as great as Arthur's own, but in a totally different direction. She was afraid that if you stayed in Camelot, you might have more influence on Arthur and Gwenhwyfar than she has. And as I mentioned, you, of course, are a Goodwitch.'

'I could make an exception in her case,' I muttered.

'No, you couldn't. You're you.' Gwydion gave me a hug with his good arm. 'But I think you're right, Merlin. She will turn up to see what she's done – but I bet she'll make sure she has witnesses with her.'

'Witnesses? What for?'

'Because I think the snake was programmed to bite Merlin and me, and you would have survived.'

'Me? Why just me?'

'Two reasons. One, leaving you alive with me dead would cause you the greatest unhappiness of all. And two, what better way of landing you in the thick, thick, mucky-soup than discovering you alive – when your two companions are dead, presumably poisoned? You don't think a magical snake leaves fang marks, do you? We'd have been all swollen up and bloated with poison – and not a mark on us anywhere. And of course, who brought the food? Lancelot. He brought it, you poisoned it – two birds with one stone.'

I hadn't thought of that. 'And then Morgan turns up with witnesses, points the finger at me, says that I've just proved I'm a witch, and an evil one at that, because I've just poisoned Gwydion and Merlin –'

The room became thick with silence. How many narrow escapes were we going to have, Gwydion and I? Would we ever settle down and lead a normal life?

Outside, voices.

There was a loud rap on the door. I stood up, preparing to go and answer it, but Merlin held up a hand.

'No. Stay quiet, both of you,' he whispered. 'Don't open the door. Just wait . . .'

And so we sat silent and still, and waited. The rap came again, and again. And then the huge latch slowly began to lift. The door creaked open, gradually at first, and then it opened wider.

In the doorway stood Morgan with Arthur and Gwenhwyfar behind her. It was really gratifying to see the way her mouth fell open when she saw the three of us, alive and kicking, sitting there, smiling sweetly. We leapt to our feet to bow and curtsey.

'Your Grace?' Merlin said, a note of enquiry in his voice. 'Was there something?'

'Merlin. Our sister Morgan wishes to apologise to the Dragonking – and before witnesses – for her son's behaviour. We hope you will accept her gesture as it is intended.'

218

Yeah. Right.

'Oh, we will, we will,' Gwydion said, ever-so-sweetly.

Morgan opened and closed her mouth.

'Morgan?' Arthur said sharply. 'You have something to say, I believe?'

Morgan looked as if she'd rather be poked in the eye with a pitchfork than apologise, but she managed to squeeze out a grudging one.

'And you should, I think, also apologise to the Lady of Ynys Haf.'

This apology was positively strangled at birth, but Arthur seemed satisfied. Maybe he knew that was as good as it got with his sister!

'There,' Arthur said, 'this business is finished. The trial by combat was conclusive. Your champion won, Lady of Ynys Haf. You are innocent of my sister's accusation. Your character is unstained, and Medrawd is banished from court.'

I dropped a curtsey. 'Thank you, Your Grace.'

If looks could kill, Morgan's would have annihilated me, embalmed me and buried me six feet under. And planted a rose bush on top. One with lots of thorns.

Roll on going home time!

27

We thought it would probably be a good idea to stay out of everybody's way for the rest of the day. Out of sight, out of mind, has a lot going for it!

Merlin disappeared, leaving us alone while he put himself about a bit, probably doing the sort of interfering in people's lives that he's so very good at. At Camelot, lucky man, he had an entire court to mess with – even though he'd at last accepted that he couldn't change the legend. He stuck his head into the room around lunchtime to say goodbye.

'I'm not intending to come back immediately,' he explained. 'I still have things to do. Now that I know this Lancelot and Gwenhwyfar business is inevitable, I thought I'd better see if I can manage some damage limitation. It will be hard, but if I put my mind to it –'

'Just as long as it doesn't interfere with the legend, Merlin,' Gwydion said, with a straight face. 'Sometimes your sort of damage limitation has the opposite effect to what's intended.'

'You know perfectly well that it's impossible to interfere with legends,' he snapped. 'Haven't I always told you – oh, never mind. You never listen anyway. You didn't when you were a small boy – and a perfectly appalling child you were, disobedient and always up to mischief – and you certainly don't now!'

And he left.

'Did you hear what he said?' I spluttered.

'I heard. I'm ignoring his personal comments – after all, I've had about twenty-odd years' experience of doing it! Anyway, as long as he remembers that legends can't be changed no matter who you are, Camelot will come to no harm. And we'll be back in Ynys Haf before bedtime. Looking forward to it, Tanz?'

'Weeell . . .'

'Oh, no. What now? What have I done this time?'

'Don't look so panic-stricken, Gwyd! We will go back soon. But d'you remember you asked me a question?'

'Did I? What was that?'

I thumped him in the ribs, hard.

'Ow! You're beating up a wounded man! I nearly bled to death – and I was defending your honour!'

I raised my fist and shook it under his nose.

'Oh, all right. That question. What about it?'

'Well, when I got sort of diverted here, I was actually intending to go home to Mam.'

'Oh, isn't that typical! First little upset and off you go, home to Mother.'

'I really hope you're joking, Gwydion, or I shall be forced to pull out all the hairs on your legs, one by one, and then punch you on your bad arm.'

He relented. 'OK. What about it?'

'Well, if it's all right with you, I'd still like to go. And anyway, you've got to ask my dad, haven't you?'

He looked mystified. 'Ask him what?'

'If you can – you know.'

'No. What?'

'If you can-have-my-hand-in-marriage,' I babbled. 'I think you ought to do it properly. My dad's old-fashioned like that. Even if you are Dragonking.'

'I suppose you want an engagement ring, too?'

'Is it customary in Ynys Haf?'

'Not really.'

'Don't know why I even asked, because I want one anyway.'

'And I've got to ask your dad if I can have your hand in marriage, have I?'

'Yes. Otherwise he'll feel left out. And I don't want my dad upset.'

'Do I just get your hand, or does the rest of you come with it?'

'Oh, ha ha. Very funny. Not.'

Gwydion put on a meek expression that was totally false. 'Whatever you say, dear.'

'So we'll divert to see Mam and Dad, shall we? And then Ynys Haf, after?'

'No. Ynys Haf first. I don't trust this Time Door to get us anywhere other than there. We'll take a shuttle on to your Time from there. We'll use a more modern Door. And concentrate this time, all right? Both of us?'

I stuck out my tongue at him. 'I can concentrate – when I'm not thoroughly upset.'

Merlin put his head in again a little while later. 'Wait until it's twilight before you leave,' he said. 'If the moon is out, your powers will be stronger, Tanith, and if it's still half-light as well, that will be the best time for the Door. They never work quite as well, those old models, in sunshine, or in full dark, don't ask me why.'

So we waited, and when the moon was risen, Gwydion and I climbed up the stairs to the little door concealed in the wall.

'I'll go through first, because it's narrow,' Gwydion suggested. 'And then if there are any stray dragons, wild boars, ravening wolves or sabre-tooth hamsters out there, I can chase them away before you come through.'

'Ha!' I said. 'More likely I'll follow you through and have to rescue you. That's what usually happens.'

We slipped round the circumference of the tower, and to our relief the Time Door was fully visible, a blue light illuminating the square outline.

'Looks like it's fully charged,' Gwydion said with satisfaction. 'No problems this time, Tanz! See you in a minute.' And he slipped through, his shape blurring instantly. It was always so quick in this direction. No powerful wind, no long tunnel, just like blinking an eye, one step and we would be back in Ynys Haf.

The Door still glowed strongly, and I paused and turned, moving away from the Door to the battlements for one last look at the legendary Camelot glittering in the moonlight. After all, I'd never see it again, would I? Well, with any luck! It was wonderful meeting the real people of the legend but when one of those real people was Morgan le Fay, I shouldn't miss it too much!

Far below, the servants were lighting the torches, filling the inner ward with flickering light. Foreshortened figures moved slowly around in the warm dusk, and pennants fluttered in the breeze.

I sighed, and turned to follow Gwydion through to Ynys Haf.

There was a faint, unpleasant smell of burning, the air blurred, and Morgan le Fay was there – between me and the Door. She was smiling, and it wasn't a nice smile. It was a Gotcha sort of smile.

Oh, rats.

'Going somewhere, Witch?' she enquired. 'I heard you think of me just then, such a mistake on your part, my dear girl. All I had to do was follow your thought. And just look where you are! So close to what Merlin thinks is his secret way in and out of Camelot that you're in danger of falling through it! And your champion has already gone, I see! No-one to fight for you now, Witch. I do believe I have you! And this time, you won't escape me.'

There was that smile again. She tilted up her chin and looked down her nose at me. I could tell that any minute now she was going to zap me with some horrible spell or other.

Now there are times when I use magic absolutely unthinkingly. It comes naturally to me. It is like talking, or breathing, and all the rest of it. And there are other times when I remember that before I knew I was a witch, I was just an ordinary, rather small human girl.

An ordinary small, human, normal girl with an extremely annoying older sister . . .

I didn't even think of magic, I'm afraid. I hauled back, and let fly. I shoved Morgan le Fay so hard that she staggered backward and fell on her behind. 'Oh, get out of my way, you daft old bat,' I said. 'Get a life, why don't you?'

Then I shot through the Time Door so fast that I barely heard her scream of fury. I burst out and cannoned into Gwydion.

'What kept you?' he gasped, rubbing his injured arm where I'd walloped it.

'Morgan turned up. Tried to stop me following you. She may be coming through after me.'

'Why? What did you do to her? Zap her?'

'In a manner of speaking,' I said.

'How "in a manner of speaking", Tanz?'

'I gave her a good, hard shove. She landed on her bum. Most undignified.'

'Now that wasn't very witchlike, was it? Or even very ladylike.'

'I never said I was a lady, Gwyd. I may be the Lady, but I ain't a lady when it comes to people like Morgan le Fay. Her fault – she got in my way.' I giggled. 'I called her a daft old bat, too.'

'Daft old bat, eh? She may forgive you sometime for the daft and the bat, Tanz, but the old? Never!'

We knew there was a good Time Door right outside the village below Castell Du. It was a well-behaved one – Gwydion had used it a lot when he was a small boy. We shifted into – what else? – love birds and twittered like a Disney cartoon through the woods, then shifted back and went through the Door, arriving this time on top of the bare hill in the middle of Brechfa forest, just outside Carmarthen. It was a warm summer evening in this Time, the sun just beginning to go down in the west, and we walked down the hill and into the trees hand in hand, Gwydion holding aside the occasional bramble for me to walk through.

When we reached the road, Gwydion made sure nothing was coming in either direction, and then magicked up a car. It was rather a nice, bright blue sports job, with a roof that folded back so that we could drive along in the warm evening air, watching the bats zooming around overhead.

It didn't take long to get to my parents' house – and it was almost a shock to see how small the terraced house appeared when we drew up outside it. I'd forgotten about that. From inside the house came a shriek of 'They're here!' and the front door flew open. They were obviously expecting us.

I was out of the car and in my mam's arms like greased lightning. Even though I could talk to her any time I wanted – and we scried each other and talked as often as we could – I missed her like mad. Sometimes when things go wrong, only a mam will do. Dad was following behind, and he shook hands with Gwydion, beaming with delight at seeing us.

Then we were inside the house, straight into the kitchen, where the kettle was on and the Welsh cakes sitting on a plate ready. And Gwydion was into them, straight away. As Mam says, he's a pleasure to feed!

'You eat, cariad,' Mam urged. 'I don't expect this one ever cooks for you properly, does she?'

'Never, Mrs Williams,' Gwydion said pathetically, making his eyes round and big. 'All I ever get is what the castle cook produces. And her Welsh cakes aren't a patch on yours, I can tell you. Sometimes I dream of your Welsh cakes!'

'Plenty more where those came from,' Mam said, pleased. 'I'll pack some up for you to take back with you.'

That's my mam. If it moves, feed it. If it doesn't move, feed it quicker next time. Especially if its name is Gwydion.

After we'd eaten, Dad took Gwydion down the pub for a pint. Gwydion gave me a mock-anguished look as he closed the door behind them. Mam got on the phone to Heledd and Sion to tell them we were here, and they said they'd be right over. I felt sort of scared and excited, both at the same time. I couldn't wait for Gwydion and Dad to come back so I could see my mam in full wedding-preparation mode . . .

Heledd and Sion and my niece Cariad arrived a couple of minutes later. They only live down the road. I used to fight with Hel when we were little, but we get on quite well now we don't share a house!

I hadn't seen Cariad for ages – she's thirteen now, (thirteen going on thirty, as Mam puts it) and if I was like that at her age, I'm amazed Mam let me survive. Apparently she's turning into a teenager every bit as troublesome as Heledd was, although I found that hard to believe. Heledd had been hell-on-wheels. In fact, her nickname had been 'Hell' – the words 'spoiled brat' didn't come close to describing her. Still, Cariad stopped pouting when she saw me, and gave me a hug and was soon chattering away nineteen to the dozen.

All the time I was watching the door, waiting for Gwydion and Dad. I didn't have that long to wait. Although it seemed like hours, it was actually less than an hour and they were back. In the meantime Mam and Heledd and I caught up with family news. When the door opened, I looked up anxiously. Gwydion grinned at me, and my father was beaming so widely the top of his head was in danger of dropping off.

'They're getting married, love,' Dad said. 'Duw, isn't that good to hear? Thought it would never happen!'

I looked at Mam, waiting for her reaction. And then I saw her face. She'd known all along. Dad hadn't, but she had.

Of course she had. It was in the legend, wasn't it?

And legends can't be fiddled with!

28

Heledd, Sion and Cariad went home after we'd opened a bottle of champagne Mam 'just happened' to have in the fridge. Cariad didn't mind being bridesmaid, but – 'No way am I wearing pink, Aunt Tanz. I don't do pink, OK? Or frills!' Which was fine by me. I'm not a pink person either. Then Mam and I spent ages drawing up a list of wedding guests – which was difficult. So many people just had to be invited, and Mam kept remembering ancient cousins and second-cousins and people she'd known for ages, and there was the problem of getting them to Ynys Haf, so we had to whittle it down to those we thought we could manage to transport magically.

Heledd and Sion don't have a clue about the magical gene in the family – and although Cariad has inherited it, she doesn't, either – yet. They'd come to Ynys Haf for the wedding, we'd sort of selectively wipe their memory banks afterwards – they'd remember the wedding, but not where it had been . . . We'd plant the idea of a place in their heads, and that would be sort of superimposed on Ynys Haf so that it would still be real and they could remember it. And the amazing thing was that any people with cameras that used film would find the mechanism had jammed or the film was over-exposed, and those with digital cameras would find the memory card infuriatingly wiped after they passed through the Time Door – which they wouldn't remember either, of course!

I rang my best friend T.A. to ask her if she'd be another bridesmaid, and she was still shrieking with excitement when I rang off.

'I don't suppose there's anyone you want to invite from this Time, is there, Gwyd?' I asked. 'That'll be all our side, I expect.'

He thought about it and then grinned. 'I was about to say no, there's no-one – but actually there are some people – if that's all right? I met them when I was much younger. I came through the Time Door twice, before I was officially allowed – back when I was Merlin's apprentice – and they sort of helped me a lot. They helped me more the third time, mind. When Merlin sent me on a Quest. They live near Port Talbot. Blaengwynfi. I can probably find their addresses in the phone book, if you've got it handy, Mrs Williams.'

'Mam,' she said. 'No more Mrs Williams, lovely boy. Have another Welsh cake.'

He did.

'Who?' I asked, curiously.

'Betsan Price and her best friend, Maldwyn Bowen. You'll like them. Betsan's a bit like you. Adventurous, inquisitive, cocky – and a bit accident prone.'

'Thanks a bunch, Gwyd.'

'Maldwyn Bowen?' Dad said, frowning slightly. 'That wouldn't be the Maldwyn Bowen who plays full back for Wales, would it? Can't be two Mal Bowens coming from Blaengwynfi, surely?'

Gwydion grinned. 'Shouldn't be a bit surprised. Playing for Wales was all he ever wanted to do when he was a kid.'

'Well!' Dad said, delighted. 'Fancy having a Welsh international at your wedding, Tanith! There's an honour!'

Not to mention a Dragonking for a son-in-law. But then, Dad didn't know that.

'If that's everybody, then,' Mam said, putting her

pencil behind her ear and tucking her notebook behind the clock on the mantelpiece. 'I'm off to bed. All this excitement isn't good for me. I'm getting old.'

'Rubbish,' Gwydion said, 'you don't look old enough to have a daughter, let alone a granddaughter.'

'Creep,' I muttered.

'Flatterer,' Mam said. 'I made up your beds this morning, so they're nice and aired.'

Dad gazed at her in admiration. 'I don't know how you knew they were coming, love. I swear you must be psychic, sometimes. Do you know, Tanith, she woke up this morning and she said, "Tanith and Gwydion will be here by tonight." And lo and behold, you were.'

'Amazing,' I said, 'but that's my mam!'

Gwydion grinned.

In the morning we said our goodbyes and drove the blue car back to Brechfa. Gwydion amused me by locking it before he disappeared it – it was hardly likely to get stolen! A step through the Door and we were back in Ynys Haf, a brief shift into sparrows and we were fluttering down into the courtyard of Castell Du.

Where there was a reception committee waiting for us, waving flags and hankies and wearing great big grins. Nest, Iestyn, Flissy, Branwen, Rhiannon – they were all there, even Siôn ap Siôn, trying to look as if he didn't approve, although a smile kept breaking through his moustache. O'Liam of the Green Boots was there, and his wife Siobhan, and Wee Brendan, their little boy, who was hopping with excitement.

'Congratulations!' they chorused, and Gwydion put his arm round me.

That's the trouble with being part of a magical

230

community. You can't surprise anyone! Especially – as Merlin would say (often) – when it's in the legend!

We relented in the end and decided to get married in June so that Merlin could be there. He's a difficult, crabby, illogical, temperamental, infuriating, bloody-minded old so-and-so – but he's part of our lives like it or not (and sometimes we definitely DON'T) so he had to be there on our happy day, didn't he? Mam popped back and forth through the Door to consult with Nest and Flissy, and Rhiannon and Siobhan stitched hour after hour at my wedding dress in one of the tower rooms.

Gwydion went about his everyday business as if nothing was happening, but the rest of the castle's population got hopelessly caught up in wedding fever. Two nights after we got home, after one of our special once-a-month suppers-for-everyone in the Great Hall, he surprised me by going down on one knee in front of the entire gathering of castle inmates and village inhabitants and proposing properly. He even had an emerald and diamond engagement ring for me – I didn't even have to remind him. Diamonds for my sparkling eyes, he said, and emeralds to remind me of the Spellorium. As if I could forget. Everyone clapped and cheered, and I went bright pink when Gwydion kissed me in front of them.

And then, a day or two before the Big Day, the guests started to arrive. T.A. and her fiancé, Glyn, first, then my young cousins Owain and Dafydd. Mam took them aside and Warned them to behave – they have the family magic gene, but neither has learned to control it, and the thought of them loose in Ynys Haf, where the magic they have would automatically be multiplied, didn't bear thinking about.

They pretended to be seriously offended. 'We're far too busy . . .' Owain said.

'Drinking and carousing and wenching. Do you know, Aunt Gwen, we both went out –'

'– with the same girl for three weeks before she found out!'

Poor girl. They were so alike even their mam got confused occasionally.

Elffin, heir to the lost land of Cantre'r Gwaelod, arrived with his new bride, and he and T.A. were able to have a nice little private chat about old times – which meant they could be friends again. They'd had a brief 'thing' a while ago, and then Elffin had gone off after someone else. But that's another story.

Gwydion's friends Maldwyn and Betsan arrived, and to Gwydion's delight announced that they, too, were getting married. I loved them both immediately – I felt I'd known Betsan for ages after about five minutes in her company – she's funny and kind – and Maldwyn endeared himself to the castle kids by setting up immediate coaching sessions to help them play the Ynys Haf national game – bugsy. Bugsy is like rugby in that it has the same shape ball and two teams, but that's where all similarity ends . . . Gwydion brought back the general idea of the game from his visits to Blaengwynfi – but hadn't been there long enough to learn any of the rules, so he sort of made them up as he went along.

And then – it arrived. Our wedding day.

The sun shone from early morning when my eyes first opened, and carried on doing it as hard as it could all day.

The chapel was filled with flowers – they should probably have been roses – but we are a magical family,

232

and Welsh, and so instead the brilliant yellow of wild Tenby daffodils glowed in the gloom, outdoing even the stained glass in the windows. My bridesmaids – Cariad, Branwen, T.A. and O'Liam's wife, Siobhan, all dressed in blue, clustered in the doorway waiting for me when I arrived on my dad's arm. Dad was beaming with pride, and when we walked into the cool chapel, bright with colour and happy faces, all I could see was Gwydion's face smiling at me.

There were Best Men – rather than a Best Man – because it had been impossible to choose between them: Iestyn, Flissy's lovely husband, and O'Liam, bursting with pride in brand new Green Boots. Merlin, of course, kept an eye on the Archbishop of Ynys Haf to make sure he did it right. He prompted him once or twice, which wasn't necessary, and only subsided when the Archbishop turned and gave him a Hard Stare.

And Gwydion said 'I will' and 'I do' and so did I. And we lit a candle each at the beginning of the ceremony, and then lighted a single one from the two candles, together. Then we both blew out the first two, to signify the fact that we would be together from that moment on. Just us. And my mam cried, and Dad had to pat her and lend her his hanky. And when the service was over, Gwydion gave me a hug and a kiss and grinned at me and I grinned back, and nothing else mattered at all.

Afterwards, we went from the chapel to the Great Hall, which was decorated with greenery and more daffodils, and once we'd greeted everyone, one by one, Merlin did a typical Merlin flourish to get everyone's attention. He'd appointed himself master of ceremonies for the day, and was wearing black velvet with tasteful touches of silver lace. He is such a show-off!

He waved his hand and a silver trumpet appeared in mid-air, blew a long fanfare, and then disappeared again. The gathering became silent.

'My Lords,' Merlin said, 'Ladies and Gentlemen, please be upstanding for the Dragonking and Dragonqueen of Ynys Haf.'

And everybody stood up in their places and clapped, and smiled, and Gwydion and I came in hand in hand to the Great Hall and took our places at the table on the dais.

When we had all eaten, there were speeches. Dad did his speech, which naturally included some Very Embarrassing Anecdotes from my childhood and lots of compliments to Gwydion, which made him smirk unbearably. Then Dad sat down, glad that his part was finished, and Iestyn took over. He thanked everybody, and then did it again in case he'd forgotten anyone, and was about to do it yet again when Flissy tugged his sleeve and made him stop. So he kissed all the bridesmaids and sat down with a sigh of relief. Gwydion thanked everyone for coming, and referred several times to 'my beautiful wife', which was me, believe it or not, and gave the bridesmaids and the best men their presents.

Then it was O'Liam's turn. He stood up – on his chair, so that everyone could see and hear him. 'I'm not about to speechify,' he said, and there was a cheer. 'We have many sayings about weddings, so we do, in the Land Beneath and in the Emerald Isle in general, and so, Dragonking and Dragonqueen, I'll give you instead a wee traditional Irish blessing –

Sunshine through your windows
And in your hearts

234

Bread, always on your table
Sweet water in your well
Crops safe in your barn.
Happiness like wine
Overflowing your cups
Children to bear your name
May you be shelter and haven
Strength and sweetness
And may you always be as beautiful to each other
And as happy with each other
As you are today.
May He who cares keep you safe

– which finished the speeches off beautifully, because Mam cried, and I cried, and Cariad said, 'Oh, good grief. How mushy can you get?' and pulled a face.

Afterwards, Siobhan did some Irish dancing, and did that wiggly thing with her ankles, while O'Liam played the pipes. Then we all had a go, and then, we did some Welsh dancing, and a bit of disco dancing for Owain and Dafydd and Cariad. Then, when everyone was puffed out, we sat around while Owain and Dafydd (who just happened to have brought their guitars) played familiar Welsh songs and we all sang.

And neither Gwydion nor I stopped smiling the entire time.

At last, when our feet ached and our throats were hoarse from singing, people began to drift away to their homes in village and castle, and we said our goodnights, and our thank-you-for-comings until everyone was gone.

And at last Gwydion and I were alone together.

He gave me a kiss.

'Tanith,' he said. 'My darling Dragonqueen. My lovely new wife.'

'Mmhm?' I answered, thinking, he's going to say something SO ROMANTIC I shall remember it for my whole life. At last, at last! I should have known better.

'Tanz, I'm starving!'

I sighed. So much for romance. 'Come on, then.' So we crept down to the kitchens and raided the larder for some cold chicken and a loaf of bread, and took it back to our room and had a long-past-midnight feast.

When he wasn't hungry any more, he burped politely behind his hand.

'What was the best bit of the day?' he asked.

'Oh, I don't know. All of it. I wouldn't change a minute of it. What about you?'

'Well, I quite liked the bit where your dad said what a fine bloke I am.'

'Yes. But then he went on to say how honoured he was to have Maldwyn Bowen, Welsh International Rugby Player, there at the wedding! Poor Maldwyn didn't know where to put himself.'

Gwydion sighed. 'Do you realise that you're stuck with me now? Forever? It's too late to change your mind?'

'Yup!' I said, and grinned. I thumped him in the ribs and gave him a hug. 'And?'

'Feels pretty good, doesn't it?'

There. Romance at last.

Here ends The Book of Tanith and Gwydion

AUTHOR'S ENDNOTE

O'Liam's 'Traditional Irish Blessing' (p.234) is nothing of the kind. It was written in honour of the wedding of my two daughters, Stephanie to Conall in June 2005, and Tanith to Darren in September 2005.

Coming soon . . .

The Cariad Chronicles

What Part of No Don't You Understand?

and

Tree of Light